ADRIANA ALTER

By the Pricking of My Paws

An Edgar Beagle Mystery

Contents

Chapter One

It was a damp, gray, unseasonably chilly afternoon in early June. All over London, the lamps were being lit, and the air was thick with the rumble and clatter of carriage wheels. "I hope there will not be a storm," Mr. Edgar Beagle mused, as he methodically descended the staircase of his house in Duke of York Street on his way out for his daily walk. He paused for a moment to adjust his cravat and tighten his grip on his umbrella. It had been quite a tedious week—no, Edgar told himself, as he resumed his progression downstairs; not a tedious week, but a reassuringly, even calmingly, predictable one. Really, he was getting to be as bad as Chase! There was nothing of which he could complain; he had risen and breakfasted at his usual hour, brushed his ears until they shone sleekly, read the newspaper with the same keen attention he always accorded it, penned a long letter to his sister Lavinia, finished composing his latest monograph on the discovery of infusoria, and re-folded all of his handkerchiefs three times. And yet, throughout, or despite, these comforting routines, he had felt as if he was expecting something momentous to happen. But not every day, as he had sternly reminded Chase a thousand times, could bring excitement—and thank goodness for that! Besides, Edgar did not hold with premonitions. The unusual weather; the howling wind (which he could hear plainly as he neared the front door); even, no doubt, the peculiar and irresistible urge which had spurred him to take his walk a full quarter of an hour earlier than usual—it could all be explained perfectly soundly and rationally. Edgar gave a decisive little nod, which set his ears flapping, fastened the top button of his overcoat, pushed the door open—and nearly fell headlong over a large, furry form which was wriggling and bouncing on the top step.

"My dear Inspector Chase!" Edgar exclaimed. "I thought you were safely in Liverpool by now. What on earth has happened?"

"I came back," Chase informed him. He was not wearing an overcoat, his jacket was buttoned wrong, and his ears were so unkempt as to make him look like he had fought his way through a hurricane.

"I can see that," Edgar said blankly. "I hope, Inspector, that I have not yet sunk to hallucinating you. May I inquire as to *why* you have, as it were, materialized on my doorstep?" He took Chase's arm and tried to draw him inside, but Chase took no notice. Passers-by were beginning to stare; Edgar only hoped that no one would recognize the Detective Chief Inspector of the Metropolitan Police in his current state of undignified disarray.

"I needed to see you," Chase said, distractedly tugging at the bottom of his jacket. Perhaps he was beginning to notice that the buttons were off by two.

"Yes, I had inferred *that* much for myself," Edgar said. "Your presence immediately in front of my house seemed rather unlikely to be coincidental." It was becoming evident that bringing Chase inside was a lost cause. Edgar locked the door, and began trying to bodily maneuver Chase down the steps instead. "I see I shall have to adopt a more specific line of questioning. Why, in the midst of the preparations for your sister's wedding, did you find it necessary to come galloping all the way back to London? I flatter myself that you hold me in high esteem, Inspector, but I can hardly suppose that you were overtaken by a sudden, all-consuming longing for my company."

"No, no," Chase said at once, perhaps a shade too vehemently to be strictly complimentary. They had attracted quite a few onlookers by now. Edgar fixed his eyes straight ahead, and forcibly drew Chase down the street and out onto St. James's Square. "Which is not to say, of course, that I have not missed you a great deal. You mustn't be insulted. It is simply that I have had things of grave importance on my mind. I say," he added suddenly, as they rounded the north-west corner of the square, "aren't we going the wrong way?"

"The wrong way for what?"

"For Euston Station, of course. Didn't I mention? You are coming back with me."

Edgar stopped dead. "I beg your pardon, Inspector?"

"Well, don't stand there like a waxwork. I shall explain everything on the train."

"My dear Inspector Chase!" Edgar protested. "I cannot simply go gallivanting off to Liverpool on an instant's notice. You know I am very busy. And besides—"

"You are not busy," Chase interrupted. "What are your plans for tomorrow?"

"I shall rise at seven-thirty, as is my custom; wash my face and brush my ears; and then take my breakfast from seven-forty-five until eight-fifteen. At eight-twenty, I shall sit down

3

before that new typing-machine which you somehow coerced me into purchasing, and shall commence copying over my monograph on infusoria for submission to my publisher. I anticipate finishing this task at approximately ten thirty-five, at which point I shall—"

"You are not busy," Chase repeated. "All of that can wait. Heaven knows, it will do you some good to get away from your ridiculous routines."

Edgar knew from long experience that debating this last point would not be worth the effort. "What about luggage?" he asked instead. "Surely, Inspector, you cannot expect me to go visiting without a tailcoat, at the very least; how shall I be able to dress for dinner? Besides, for how long do you propose to abduct me? I will, you understand, eventually require a fresh shirt—"

"You can borrow my things," Chase said impatiently. His gaze fell on Edgar's expression, and he made a sweeping, dismissive gesture with his free paw. "Yes, yes, I daresay they are not as pressed and starched as you might like, but I haven't got fleas, so you may as well close your mouth before a bird flies in. Besides, we are going to my parents' house, not to Buckingham Palace; you'd look an awful fool in all your Savile Row togs. Anyhow, help me look for a cab! I can't remember what time the next train leaves; 3:00, maybe—"

"3:02," Edgar interjected.

"Yes, fine—but at any rate, that's the last one today, and we have no time to lose."

"Inspector Chase!" Edgar said. "Perhaps my inductive faculties are operating at a deficit today, but I am afraid I have yet to grasp the finer details of the situation. If you expect me to abandon my plans, whisk off to Liverpool, and"—here he gave a slight and entirely involuntary shudder—"wear your clothing, I think I am not altogether unreasonable in requesting that you supply me with a cogent explanation."

"Well, I'll tell you all about it on the train. Come *on*, we're going to be late. You hate being late."

"I have no intention of boarding any trains until you tell me what on earth is going on," Edgar said, rather more sternly than he had intended.

"Alright, alright!" Chase assumed an unaccustomed expression of solemnity, and took a deep breath. "Here goes. I appeal to you on the strength of our friendship—in memory of all our visits to the Tail & Whiskers—in memory, that is, of all the cases we have solved together—"

"Kindly set aside your flair for the melodramatic, Inspector," Edgar interrupted. "If you have a point, this would be an excellent time to make it. I sincerely hope it does not have to do with squirrels."

"Very well," Chase sniffed, sounding slightly wounded. "I suppose you will laugh at me—I have never understood why you do not trust my intuition!—but I cannot help that. Some things are worth hazarding ridicule." He paused dramatically, panting at Edgar and blinking his wide, amber eyes. "Mr. Beagle, immediately upon meeting my sister's fiancé—the gentleman to whom, in three short days, she intends to yoke herself for the rest of her natural life—I realized that I was standing in an atmosphere of the most profound evil."

"For goodness' sake, Inspector!" Edgar said impatiently. "Is that all? I imagined you were going to recount some nefarious crime, but instead, I find that you have deserted your relations—without a word to them, I expect!—and attempted to abstract me from London simply because you are having one of your presentiments again. Really, I think you grow more fanciful every day."

"This is what you do anyway, though," Chase informed him.

"Undertake impromptu journeys with no luggage and no information? I am afraid you have mistaken me for some other beagle of your acquaintance."

"Oh, don't be difficult! You know what I mean. You solve crimes. You solve crimes *all the time*. Even when no one has asked you to. Even when I would much sooner be at the Tail & Whiskers. You are always rattling on about how justice never sleeps. Do you mean to tell me that this is the one exception, simply because it involves *me*? If I were a paying client, I don't suppose you would turn me away."

"I most certainly would," Edgar retorted, with great dignity, "and I hope, Inspector, that you did not intend to insinuate that I pursue justice for pecuniary motives. If a stranger were to turn up on my doorstep, demand that I board the next train, and rant about an atmosphere of evil, I would assume he was quite mad, and the condition of his purse would have no power to persuade me otherwise. Besides, as you may have inferred from my continued participation in this ridiculous conversation, I have not in fact turned you away—although the prospect is becoming increasingly appealing."

"I don't see what's so ridiculous. Solving crimes is practically a sport to you—which is just as well, since you haven't any other forms of recreation. Well, here is a crime. Solve it."

"My dear Inspector," Edgar said, selecting his words with extreme precision, "perhaps, these many years, you have been under a grave misapprehension as to the nature of my vocation. The pursuit of justice is the highest end in this life, and the moral obligation of every dog or cat who is fit to undertake it.

It is not a sport, a recreation, or a game—and it is certainly not to be harnessed for personal gain. To any dog with my view of the world, your suggestion is in the nature of a heresy."

"Justice is not the only thing you care about."

"Indeed?" Edgar said politely.

"You care about me."

"*Touché*, Inspector, but I hardly see how my irrational partiality towards you is relevant. It is not as if this were a question of protecting you. Unless you have omitted a number of salient details, it is not even as if this were a question of a crime having been committed. You are a police dog yourself; surely you realize that sensing an atmosphere of evil does not actually constitute evidence. I understand that you are a dog of a vivid imagination and a rather charming, if frequently exasperating, regard for what you term your intuition; I understand, moreover, that you are readily swayed by strong emotions, such that what I believe is now termed the psychological effect induced by the combination of returning to your puppyhood environs and contemplating your sister's marriage—"

"We haven't got time for you to stand here tallying up my shortcomings or practicing to be an alienist, Mr. Beagle," Chase snapped. "I tell you, my sister is in danger. Perhaps I don't have any timetables or scientific diagrams or whatever it takes to convince you—but I had hoped you would recall a day nearly ten years ago, when the entire Metropolitan Police Force refused to believe you, and only I sprang to your aid!"

"Because you wanted an adventure—"

"That is quite irrelevant!"

"—and because," Edgar continued, as if there had been no interruption, "if you will forgive me for saying so, my story

7

was rather more plausible than yours is. At the very least, a crime had actually been committed."

"That is not the point, Mr. Beagle, and you know it," Chase said, his voice bristling with outraged dignity and his hackles beginning to rise. "I trusted you, with no proof beside your word, and I was prepared to gamble my entire career for your sake. I am only asking you to give up three days' worth of unimportant plans, you know. Perhaps four days'. A week, at the outside." He cocked his ears plaintively, and panted a little.

Edgar let out a protracted sigh and resisted the temptation to reach out and re-button Chase's jacket. "If you or anyone you hold dear is genuinely in any sort of peril," he said, very carefully, "then you know perfectly well that I will spring to your assistance irrespective of the cost or inconvenience to myself. But you must understand that you are asking me to take rather a lot on faith."

"Well, don't you trust me?" Chase blinked at him, the breeze ruffling the triangular tips of his ears.

"Might you, perhaps," Edgar said, disregarding this question, "two hours from now, undergo one of your infamous changes of heart, announce that the whole thing has been merely a figment of your ever-active imagination, and go tearing off after a squirrel?"

"Of course I shan't! What do you think of me?"

"Are you quite, quite certain?" Edgar persevered.

Set against the windy gray sky, Chase looked rather gallant and pathetic. "You have my word of honor, Mr. Beagle," he said.

"Well, in that case," Edgar said with another sigh, stepping around him and reaching out to hail a brougham cab, "I suppose there is nothing more to be said. Come along,

Inspector."

As they sped towards Euston Station, Edgar awaited some sensible conversation, with such patience as he could muster. But Chase was turned away from him, head lolling out the window of the cab. Either he was surreptitiously blinking back tears, or else he had already turned his flighty attentions towards sniffing the air for squirrels. Or perhaps it was laughter he was hiding; perhaps this whole maneuver was an elaborate prank, which had grown like a weed in Chase's over-fertile brain during bouts of dull chitchat with his puppyhood acquaintances back in Liverpool, and which was intended as a trial of the strength of Edgar's friendship. That seemed an eminently plausible explanation for Chase's refusal to provide any coherent information; it would be just like him to come up with the broad outlines of such an obnoxious, preposterous scheme, and then neglect the details altogether! In any event, Chase's unaccustomed silence was rather disquieting. If he was strapped for things to say, Edgar reflected, with the faintest touch of resentment, then perhaps he might begin with a word or two of thanks.

The cab paused by the Museum of Zoology, where Edgar had spent several unilluminating afternoons with Chase dragging him around by the sleeve and pointing at display cases at random as he bounded past them. But not even the proximity to a favorite locale roused Chase from his reverie. Edgar cleared his throat, rather artificially. It had absolutely no effect.

"Inspector Chase?" he ventured.

Chase flinched very slightly, and then turned towards him. Unless his acting skills had improved tremendously, Edgar reflected, scanning his face, this was not a prank after all.

"What is it, Mr. Beagle?"

"I was just wondering, now that you have secured my services, whether you intend to acquaint me with the finer details of the case at any point."

"Of course I am." Chase gave a vague wave of his paw. "I told you, I shall tell you all about it as soon as we are on the train."

"By which I suppose you mean," Edgar remarked, as pleasantly as he could manage, "that you want me to be irredeemably *en route* to Liverpool before you confirm my suspicions that we are merely, as they say in the classic tale of the Spanish Greyhound, tilting at windmills. Well, I suppose I have let myself in for it."

"I am neither foolish nor mad, Mr. Beagle."

"I am delighted to hear it."

"I am investigating a crime, and I need my team by my side. Barks is already in Liverpool; only you were missing."

"Why in the world is Constable Barks in Liverpool? I sincerely hope that his presence is due to some astonishing coincidence; the alternative—to wit, that you have drastically misjudged his suitability for the rôle of wedding guest, and have forced him on your family's hospitality—is both baffling and distressing to imagine."

"Of course I brought Barks. What would he do by himself in London all weekend?

"In that case," Edgar said, half-closing his eyes with a shudder of dread, "what have you done with him?"

"How do you mean?"

"Well, I assume he has not accompanied you back to London; I cannot help but notice that there is no one currently gnawing at my trouser leg or licking the polish off my shoe. I hope you have not simply abandoned him at the station, like a parcel."

"Of course not, Mr. Beagle!" Chase said, contriving to look simultaneously shocked and self-important. "I have left him with my sister, as protection."

Edgar extracted his handkerchief from his pocket just in time to go off into a fit of coughing. "My dear Inspector Chase!" he exclaimed, once he had recovered. "Far be it from me to question your judgment—but, if you will pardon the question, protection against *what*? I freely confess that I am no expert on the correct procedures for defense against—how did you phrase it?—an atmosphere of evil, but I should imagine that continual barking would not be of very much use."

"I had to act quickly and decisively, Mr. Beagle," Chase said, rather shortly. "I know that *you* prefer to make every little decision by spending seventeen hours poring over ledgers and lists—but sometimes one must simply take action."

"If taking action results in recruiting an outsize and inordinately slobbery Airedale as a bodyguard, Inspector, then I am afraid I must continue in my wonted skepticism of it."

"I can't think what you mean," Chase said haughtily, thrusting his head back out the window. "I am sure that Barks is proving very useful. He will guard my sister from bodily harm, stave off loneliness, *and* provide comfort; what else could anyone possibly ask for?"

Edgar briefly considered providing an honest answer to this question, along the lines of "more brains and less slobber." "That is an excellent and entirely accurate point, Inspector Chase," he said instead, even though he was nearly certain that Chase was not listening. Chase, his head still out the window and his ears twitching in the breeze, sniffed loudly, but made no other reply.

Euston Station, when they arrived, was bustling with dogs and cats—all, Edgar noted, chattering over their guidebooks in pleasurable anticipation of a weekend holiday in Blackpool or Llandudno, not girding themselves to chance the hospitality of a pack of herding dogs who were not even expecting them! Edgar was unsurprised to learn that Chase, who had attached himself once again to Edgar's sleeve, had neglected to purchase a return ticket for himself, and had already spent all his money in the new restaurant car on his way back to London earlier that day; it appeared he had ordered everything on the menu for the sake of novelty, taken a few bites of each item, and then lost interest. "I suppose I didn't think about it," he said, when Edgar pointed out that this had not been a judicious course of action. "After all, Mr. Beagle, I was coming to see *you*, and you always have plenty of money." Edgar shook him off and joined the ticket queue. Really, he thought, tapping his foot against the tiled floor and absently watching the large, beribboned Rottweiler in front of him fumble through her reticule, this whole situation was too absurd! He had anticipated a quiet, pleasant weekend, free from Constable Barks' vociferations and Chase's squirrel-laden chatter…and instead, here he was preparing to board a train to Liverpool, where he would, no doubt, be coerced into exchanging pleasantries with Chase's entire snuffling, yelping family. And that Edgar should have to pay Chase's train fare! He did not mind in the least about the money itself, but it was, he thought, rather representative of Chase's entire view of life: it was perfectly acceptable to work oneself into a senseless, overemotional lather, to neglect even the most basic of preparations, to divorce oneself utterly from practicalities and responsibilities—because, at the end of the day, one could always hurl the whole mess into Mr.

Beagle's lap and, without a particle of consideration for his schedule or his opinions on the matter, blithely presume that he would take care of everything! There was not the least doubt, of course, that Chase's overactive imagination had engendered the whole thing. Probably an irrational response to watching his puppy sister prepare to give her paw in marriage; perhaps Chase was feeling protective, or perhaps he had discovered a sore spot regarding his own bachelorhood. As Edgar neared the front of the line, he permitted himself to wonder, very briefly, what Chase's relatives, who had spent their lives laboring with their paws and who had probably never ventured outside Liverpool, would think of him. He put the thought firmly aside, stepped up to the window, and made a special point of asking for a one-way ticket for Chase and a return ticket for himself.

They boarded the train with only a few moments to spare. Edgar hurried ahead and secured an untenanted compartment; Chase's story, no doubt, was going to prove singularly unfit for strangers' ears. He settled himself as comfortably as his whirling mind and the none-too-pristine condition of the seat would permit him. "Now, Inspector," he said, "would you care to give me a full explanation?"

"In time—in time," Chase said absently, drumming his paw against the windowsill.

"I am sure you think yourself very subtle," Edgar remarked, "but I am perfectly aware that you are merely stalling until the train gets underway, lest hearing your story impel me to change my mind and disembark."

Chase stopped drumming at once, and turned to him with an expression of astonishment. "Well, well, Mr. Beagle!" he said. "I say, sometimes I wish you did not know me so well.

At any rate, I suppose it is safe; it is already 3:00."

"3:01. Really, how many times must I remind you that your pocket-watch is fifty-seven-and-a-half seconds slow? You really ought to take it to—"

"And I can hear them going round and shutting the doors. Alright, Mr. Beagle, I will begin. You may as well take off your shoes and curl up on the seat; I certainly intend to. I shall tell you everything."

Chapter Two

"As you know," Chase began, in needlessly ponderous tones, "my sister Emily is six years my junior; in my mind, she is barely out of puppyhood. It seems only yesterday that I was watching her gallop through flocks of ducks and tear rawhide bones to shreds. She has a quick wit and a lively manner, and a very refined way of speaking nowadays, but you mustn't think she's stuck-up; she's bettering herself so she can go off and be a governess or a lady's companion, not live out by the docks in Liverpool all her life—or at least she was, before this whole wretched engagement business began! Anyway, her face is half black and half white, she has dark eyes and long, moderately curly fur, and the tips of her ears flop over. You have a sister yourself, Mr. Beagle; you must understand that I would sooner give up squirrel-tracking than see any harm come to her." He paused and cocked his head expectantly.

"Enchanting though your sentimental reminiscences may be, Inspector," Edgar said with a touch of impatience, privately thinking that Chase would see the whole world come to ruin before he would abandon squirrel-tracking, "I rather hoped you would enlighten me as to considerably more recent events. And I shall be able to satisfy myself as to the details of her physical appearance only too soon. If you would confine yourself to the facts, and tell me exactly what happened upon your arrival in Liverpool last night, I would be most appreciative."

"Very well," Chase said, sounding put out. "I had forgotten your utter lack of literary flair or appreciation for skillful storytelling. I will try to stick to your dull, telegraphic style. Here you are, then: as I told you when they became engaged, but you showed every sign of not listening, which is how you usually respond when I share details of my personal life—I daresay you were thinking about your little squiggly microscope things—so I had better repeat it, Emily met a Mr. Herder in March. He is a foreigner, from Australia. I had only ever heard of them having convicts and dingoes there, but apparently they have cattle ranches as well, because Mr. Herder inherited one and is tremendously wealthy. He asked for Emily's paw in marriage only two months after meeting her, because they were desperately fond of each other and did not want to wait, but it seems rather hasty to me."

"This from the dog who was prepared to marry Miss Scott upon twenty-four hours' acquaintance," Edgar commented, to the ceiling.

"At any rate," Chase said, ignoring this, "the match was made and the date set. They had it in the papers and all, only he wouldn't have his picture put in, Emily said—and I'll tell you what: now that I've seen what he looks like, I understand why."

"If we might proceed *without* gratuitously editorializing on the gentleman's personal qualities—"

"Alright, alright! But if you yelp when you see him, don't say I didn't warn you, is all. Anyway, the wedding breakfast is to be at the new Adelphi Hotel, where Mr. Herder has been living ever since he got to England. He insisted on paying, but it isn't anything improper; it's only, my father is a steady, respectable working dog, not a gadabout foreign millionaire, and he wouldn't fling his money about on such nonsense even if he had it. But my parents are hosting a little supper party at home tonight." He reached over, yanked Edgar's pocket watch out by the chain, and attempted to read it upside down. "We'll be just in time."

Edgar had a sudden vision of a dim, cramped little house in Liverpool overflowing with carousing herding dogs, all with Chase's exuberant mannerisms and boundless energy. He shuddered violently as he tucked his pocket watch away.

"Are you cold, Mr. Beagle? It is a little drafty in here. I think this window does not shut properly; the smell of squirrel is reaching me quite distinctly from outdoors. No? Anyway, this is the part of the story where I come in. I left London yesterday afternoon, by this very train—and I daresay you were relieved to be rid of me for a whole five days." He paused expectantly.

"Not at all, my dear Inspector," Edgar said at once. "I am always delighted to set aside my work to listen to you recount your latest squirrel-related escapade in granular detail, particularly when you have taken it upon yourself to invite Constable Barks to my house. Why, what would my life be without the constant stimulation of serially rescuing each of my personal possessions from his slobbery jaws?"

Chase did not seem altogether reassured, but he went on nonetheless. "I arrived at the house late last night. It is not, of course, the home of my puppyhood; three years ago, my father was promoted to piermaster, and that is the sort of job that comes with its own house, and with a pension if he can stick it out for long enough. It is a strange sensation, going to Liverpool, but not to the house where I grew up. But this is a very nice house, for all that. It is much bigger than our old house, so I have my own bedroom that no one else ever uses, with a secret tin of biscuits under the mattress, instead of having to stay in the spare room when I visit. And part of the downstairs is for storing the things that go in and out on the ships, so there is always something interesting to sniff. Usually it turns out to just be spices or perfume, but sometimes you can tell that one of the crates has had a rat living in it, which is nearly as good as a squirrel. Squirrels are just rats with fancy tails, when you really stop and think about it."

"If you might confine yourself to your narrative, Inspector—"

"At any rate, when I got there, Emily seemed to be nervous and on edge, but I thought perhaps that sort of thing was normal in girls; she has never been high-strung or flighty before, but I supposed that being engaged might have changed her. She said that Mr. Herder had invited the whole family—me and Mum and Dad and my brother Joseph and his wife—to breakfast the next morning, in the restaurant at the Adelphi. I confess I did not expect to be much taken with Mr. Herder. I rather imagined him having a blocky head and a dull personality; one of those terribly earnest, drab dogs who practically never speak, and then when they do, nine times out of ten it is about livestock."

"Setting aside your imaginings, Inspector—"

"But when I met him this morning," Chase continued, over Edgar, "he turned out to be—well, quite different. Oh, outwardly he was ordinary enough—much as I had pictured him, in fact. Rather prone to dropping breakable things and

18

tripping over his back paws; you know the type. And yet...
Well, you laughed at me when I first said this, Mr. Beagle—yes,
you did, though of course you were too polite to show it—and
I daresay you will laugh at me again now, but I cannot help it:
the only way to describe my sensation upon meeting him was
that I suddenly felt as if the air around me had turned to pure
evil. It was just as the three Coupari sisters say in the tragedy
of the Scottish Terrier:"—here, he threw back his head and
struck an exaggerated pose to declaim—"*By the pricking of my
paws, something wicked this way claws.*"

"Do you have any specific evidence of this?" Edgar inquired,
keeping his face and voice carefully neutral.

Chase resumed his normal posture, somewhat sulkily; Edgar
rather fancied he had been hoping for applause. "You mean,
did I take a sample of the air to go under your microscope?
No, Mr. Beagle, I cannot say that I did."

"You misunderstand me. Can you point to anything specific
that he said or did to awaken your suspicions?"

"No. He does not say or do anything. I told you, he is very
dull. Anyway, noticing that sort of thing is *your* job."

Edgar surreptitiously glanced out the window. The train
was well underway; it was definitely too late. It crossed his
mind once again that this whole thing might be a practical
joke, or maybe just an elaborate scheme born of Chase's
desire to prove to his family that he really was friends
with a *bona fide* London gentleman. Or perhaps Chase had
been overexerting himself at work—although that seemed
singularly implausible—and this was the first symptom of
some exotic variety of brain fever. "Has it occurred to you,
Inspector," he said, "that, because you feel protective towards
your sister, you are automatically disposed to dislike anyone

who courts her? Why, I have quite a vivid recollection of the first time I considered Dr. Spaniel as a candidate for my own sister's paw. I thought him dull and eccentric, in both manner and speech, and certainly not worthy of Lavinia—but now, as you know, I am very nearly fond of him."

"Well, Dr. Spaniel *is* dull and eccentric," Chase said at once. "Besides, it's not that at all. There are dozens of fellows I would be pleased and proud to see Emily marry."

"Name one."

"You, if you had a heart. Mr. Tenterfield, who is to be Mr. Herder's best man. My old playfellow Hugh Shetland. Paddy Wolfhound, the grocer's nephew. Why, at this point, I would sooner see her with a *cat* than with Mr. Herder." He turned away, presumably for dramatic effect, and drummed his paw against the window with exaggerated moodiness.

"So, what did you do upon meeting Mr. Herder?" Edgar asked, leaning forward and lightly placing his paw on Chase's wrist to halt the drumming. "Does he know that you suspect him?"

"Honestly, Mr. Beagle, what do you take me for?" Chase jerked his paw away and folded his arms across his chest. "It is as if you think I have absolutely no self-control. I assure you, I was extremely subtle."

"Indeed?"

"You need not 'indeed' me in that icy tone," Chase huffed. "I know perfectly well what you are thinking. But I promise you, he has no idea that I have seen through him. I may have wanted to run screaming from the room, but I shook paws with him quite cordially. I suppose it would have been manners to say it was a pleasure to meet him, but it was *not* a pleasure, and I could not bring myself to lie. It would not have been the action of a gentleman."

"Did you, by any chance, say something about squirrels instead?"

Chase looked astonished. "Really, Mr. Beagle, sometimes I think you have the power to read minds! I shall never understand how you do it. At any rate, yes, I told him that I was going to go and look for squirrels. And then I walked right out of the hotel and straight to the train station, and…well, you know the rest."

"So," Edgar summarized, "you shook paws with him, abruptly made an irrelevant remark about squirrels, fled the premises, and have not been seen or heard from since. Although I cannot make any statements with certainty, being unacquainted with the gentleman and not having been present during the incident, I think I can safely advance the theory that this may not have struck him as entirely conventional behavior. And why on earth did you take the train all the way back to London instead of sending me a telegram? You realize, do you not, that you are currently on this train for the third time in twenty-four hours? Liverpool is a port city; I imagine it has no shortage of telegraph offices. There is probably one inside the train station, in fact. But I suppose that never even crossed your mind; you went charging straight onto the train without pausing to consider whether it was the best course of action."

"Well, it *was* the best course of action," Chase said cheerfully, rather than denying this, "because now you are on your way to Liverpool. If I had just telegraphed, you never would have come."

Edgar bit back any number of disagreeable retorts indicating that he wished he had not.

"You shan't regret this," Chase said, in tones which suggested that he had guessed what Edgar was thinking. "I am giving you an opportunity to help rid the world of evil; consider it an early birthday present."

"My birthday is not for three months and nine days."

"I know; that's why it's early. Anyway, you will have a splendid time at the party tonight."

"I highly doubt that."

"Oh, it won't be half so bad as you think. Dad's family is still in Scotland, and Mum's family stopped coming round after Joseph's teeth came in, so it won't be a mob of border collies herding you from one end of the house to the next, if that's what you're picturing. There are loads of hounds and terriers and things on our street. Anyway, you will have the chance to see Liverpool, which, by all accounts, is a very enjoyable place unless you happen to live there."

"What explanation for my presence do you propose to give your family?" Edgar asked carefully. "I imagine I shall hardly fit in with them or be able to speak to them in a manner they will find natural."

Chase threw him a look of utter scorn. "They are not foxes or barbarians, you know," he said. "I suppose, just because it is Liverpool, you are picturing the slums. But I think you will find that everyone in the house is able to hold a conversation without resorting to growls or infecting you with ringworm, even though they were not at Cambridge with you. Anyway, Mr. Beagle, I am going to sleep. This train ride was not very exciting the first or second time, let alone now; there are very few pastures of sheep along this route. You ought to rest too. I see you are planning to communicate with my family by means of grunts and gestures, so I expect you will find them very tiring." He took off his jacket, balled it up into a makeshift pillow, and, ignoring Edgar's wince, curled up with his head on it and began snoring within seconds.

Long before the train pulled in at Liverpool Station, Edgar was thoroughly repenting the journey. His limbs were cramped, and the train was unpleasantly drafty. He regarded Chase's lolling head and drool-soaked shirtfront with exasperation and mild distaste. The rational course, he moralized, would have been to invite Chase in, force a cup of calming, restorative tea down his throat, and then induce him to face the facts. It must be very trying to see one's puppy sister wed to a taciturn stranger. But there was certainly no call for theatrics—there was never any call for theatrics such as Chase's! Such histrionic goings-on, all over a perfectly normal fact of life: one's friends and relations *would* go on seeking out romantic entanglements, much as one might wish they would behave sensibly instead, and sometimes one was bound to disapprove. Edgar called to mind a few of Chase's lady friends past. Perhaps it would be good for Chase to see the situation from the other side; perhaps now there would be no more simpering little milliners' assistants with artificially fluffed-up ears, and no more flat-faced shop-girls with grating, snuffly voices; yes, Edgar thought, picturing the immured Miss Scott, perhaps Chase would even listen to Edgar's admonitions the next time he went mixing himself up with the criminal element, no matter how alluring their tawdry charms! At least some good would come of all this nonsense. For it was clearly nonsense. Utter and complete balderdash.

But if it was nonsense, yipped the part of Edgar's brain that he usually took care to keep well under control, then why did he feel as if something was terribly wrong?

23

The train stopped with a jerk. Chase snuffled a few times, sat straight up, and opened his mouth. "No, there are no squirrels," Edgar said, before he had a chance to speak.

"I say, Mr. Beagle, do you imagine that is all I ever think of? I was not going to ask about squirrels. I was merely wondering how you have managed to remain so dry, when there has clearly been a water leak." He gestured vaguely towards the ceiling, and then towards his drool-drenched shirt. "But I suppose *you* travel prepared, and have been sitting here under an umbrella or some such. You might have held a newspaper over my head, you know."

"Come along, Inspector," Edgar said wearily. "For my part, I should be delighted to dally here until the train turns around and takes us straight back to London—but I expect you would prefer to progress towards your parents' house instead."

There *was*, Edgar noticed with a touch of annoyance, a telegraph office inside the station. Outside, the platform was slick with rain, and a dull, leaden mist hung in the air. Edgar surveyed the city as best he could in the half-light. Across the street, there was a large building in the Neoclassical style; Edgar regarded its straight, symmetrical lines with relieved approbation. To the south, there was a mansion with invitingly glowing windows, which Edgar took to be the Adelphi Hotel. Perhaps he had misjudged Liverpool; the vistas before him seemed perfectly civilized. "The house is the other way," Chase said, grabbing at Edgar's sleeve and bodily turning him one hundred and eighty degrees. "All the way over." He gestured broadly for emphasis. Edgar noticed that his accent, which had dwindled almost to nothing over the years in London, was suddenly returning full force.

"I suppose the walk will do us good after our journey," Edgar said bravely, peering into the gloom. He rather fancied he could see sinister little glimmers here and there, suggestive of streetlights glancing off the upturned eyes of alley cats.

"Why should we walk? Unless that was all your money, back at Euston Station."

"Are there cabs here?"

Chase glanced in his direction with some disgust. "For goodness' sake, Mr. Beagle! Just look around, will you? This is a perfectly civilized city. You need not go on implying that I was raised in a kennel."

The ride took very little time—sixteen and a half minutes, by Edgar's calculation—but it felt much longer. The cab was rickety and uncomfortable, with slightly damp seats that smelled faintly of mackerel, and a driver who kept stopping to cough hairballs out the window. The texture of the city changed as they traveled west—gradually, at first, and then with a suddenness that made Edgar irrationally uneasy. The genteel holiday-makers who had trickled out of the train alongside Edgar and Chase had vanished; probably, Edgar thought with a touch of bitterness, they were comfortably ensconced in one of the clean, respectable concert halls or hotels near the station. Instead, in the windier, wilder approach to the river, a few narrow, bewhiskered faces loomed into view at intervals, around the corners of squat brick buildings, or just ahead, masked by the heavy fog. They peered curiously, and not altogether benevolently, at Edgar in his three-piece suit and pressed cravat. There were bargemen and carters, pickpockets and beggars. Edgar had little attention to spare them, because closer at paw, there was Chase: tugging on Edgar's sleeve, bouncing on the creaking seat, yipping in excited and increasingly wearisome tones about what Edgar surmised were meant to sound like pleasant memories from his puppyhood. "Look, Mr. Beagle, there is the trash heap where I used to dig holes with the Muddypaws brothers, before —Look, Mr. Beagle, our old house is just down that street, the one with all the pot-holes—Look, Mr. Beagle, I slipped out to meet Nora Roughcoat in that alley once; the sweetest girl in the world, I thought, but—Look, Mr. Beagle, do you see that very high hill? Squirrel Point, we called it. Do you want to know why? No? Well, it was because, on windy days, you can climb straight up to the top and then stand there and sniff for squirrels."

Edgar waved off these fond reminiscences with a furrowed brow and an abstracted motion of the paw. Unpleasant though the journey had been, he was dreading the arrival even more. He understood perfectly well how to comport himself when questioning witnesses, or making conversation with the nobility, or ordering from tradesmen. Even an invitation to tea at Buckingham Palace would not have discomfited him. One simply followed the appointed script—"good morning" or "good afternoon" or what have you, because one's interlocutor expected it, even if it was *not* a particularly good morning or afternoon—and then proceeded to the object of the conversation, whether that was to obtain half a pound of butter at the grocer's, or to secure the friendly acquaintanceship of some frivolous lordling by feigning admiration over his latest escapade at the casino. But what did one do in a house such as Chase's was sure to be—a loud, tumultuous house, where everyone was over-friendly and under-educated, and where there was no clearcut goal to any interaction? Edgar did not know the script. Possibly, Chase's family would not know the script either. Possibly—

here, he shuddered a little, causing Chase to grip his arm in concern—there was no script at all. He had heard before—mainly, admittedly, from his sister Lavinia, whose own ideas of social conduct were very peculiar and who was therefore not necessarily a credible source of information anyway—that he was liable to come across as cold, or aloof, or dull. Ordinarily, that did not matter to him. But he was really very fond of Chase, when all was said and done. He should not like for Chase's family to think badly of him.

"I say, Mr. Beagle," Chase said, breaking into his thoughts by means of an even firmer grip on his arm, and staring up into his face in wide-eyed, panting consternation, "you look as though you were going to be sick. The smell from the river is not so unpleasant, once you get used to it. But anyway, you needn't worry—the house is just up ahead."

The cab ground to a halt. There was absolutely nothing to indicate that there might be a house anywhere nearby, just a lot of hulking brick buildings on one side and an expanse of murky, ship-laden river on the other. Edgar was far too weary to point this out. He paid the driver and swung himself down onto the damp cobblestones. Chase, as he might have predicted, was already several feet ahead, vanishing into the mist and shadows. Edgar hurried after him, shoes clattering ominously into the murky stillness all along the narrow quay. He could not shake the feeling that there were innumerable pairs of bright eyes fixed on him from around every corner.

The house turned out to be around the next bend. At least from the outside, it was substantially better than Edgar had expected. He had been half-consciously imagining a ramshackle clapboard affair, with one story and a hole in the roof—perhaps, he thought with a note of compunction, there was something to Chase's surmise that he was picturing the slums!—but it was moderately large and appealingly square, with a perfectly respectable brick facade, two chimneys, and three rows of windows. The little front garden badly needed weeding, but it would have been surprising if any property occupied by Chase's blood relations had been kept in perfect order. As he and Chase approached, Edgar could discern the unmistakable and dismaying strains of an enthusiastic group conversation in the back garden, but these were almost immediately drowned out by a tremendous barking. There was the thundering of heavy paws, and then a screeching, hackle-raising noise of nails against brick—Edgar forced down the urge to cover his ears—and then a large furry mass came careening around the corner and down the path.

"Constable Barks!" Chase cried joyously.

"I see he has scanted his duty as sentinel at your sister's door," Edgar said, shying away from Constable Barks' exuberant salutations.

"Well, he is young and full of high spirits," Chase said. "And besides—oh. Oh dear." He froze midway through tugging his trouser leg out of Constable Barks' mouth. Another figure had appeared: a bulky, blowzy border collie wearing a bright purple Polonaise basque over an aggressively bustled tartan skirt. She had brown and white fur, and enormous pale blue eyes. Her ears were fluffed up—owing more to art than to nature, Edgar thought—and tied with incongruously puppyish ribbons.

"Gabriel!" she shrieked. "Where on earth have you been? Disappearing without a word to anyone! I couldn't think what to tell the neighbors. I was just saying to your father, if Gabriel isn't back before dark, I go straight to the police."

"I *am* the police, Mum," Chase said.

Chase's mother continued undeterred, peering hard at Edgar. "And who have you turned up with now? Do you call this polite, bringing a stranger to your poor sister's party? What if there hadn't been enough food to go round?"

"He's my best friend, Mum," Chase said. "Mr. Edgar Beagle."

"*This?* Really? My word, he doesn't look a thing like I expected, after all your yapping on about him. Awfully ordinary sort of prissy, stuck-up fellow, isn't he?"

"It is a pleasure to make your acquaintance, madam," Edgar said, bowing slightly. Chase's mother simply peered at him in unfriendly silence. Perhaps, Edgar decided, a slight falsehood might be permissible. "Inspector Chase has often mentioned you, with warm affection and regard."

Chase's mother sniffed disapprovingly. "He's just plain Gabriel Chase while he's under this roof," she said. "Gives himself enough airs in London. He's forgotten where he came from, that's what."

"Be that as it may," Edgar said, uncomfortably aware that Chase's hackles were rising in his peripheral vision, "Inspector Chase has risen with impressive speed through the ranks of the Metropolitan Police Force—"

"Well, I never looked for any of my puppies to go rising anywhere. Hard workers and plain dealers—that was good enough for me! But he was just a scatter-brained puppy, always sniffing for squirrels. I said to him—I said, why don't you go and round up some nice sheep, like a proper border collie should? Take a normal, healthy interest in herding, like your brother, and then make up your mind to work in the dockyard, like your father and all of your friends? But no, it was always squirrels with him, nothing but squirrels, all day

29

and all night. Forever running in a circle like a fool, barking after squirrels—and barking at the moon—and barking at the sun—and barking at the clouds—always just barking—"

"*Mum*," Chase said, between his teeth.

"Then he ran off to London to give himself fancy titles and make friends above his station—and Joseph is…well, we cannot all be clever—and now our poor Emily all set to ruin this fine match, like as not, if she keeps sulking up in her room—"

"Isn't she at the party?" Chase demanded.

Chase's mother shook her head, making her ears flap violently. "That she is not—and what I'm supposed to tell the neighbors, I'm sure I don't know. Moaning all the afternoon, she's been, and never lifting a paw to help with the cooking. He's changed, she says. He's not the dog she met. Well, I told her straight out—I said, you listen, my girl, there's many a fellow is not what he seems, and if you hadn't found it out now, you would have found it out after the wedding, so what difference does it make? Warned her, I did, the minute she met him. You stick to your own class, I said. You've no business forgetting your place, and no good can ever come of it. Much better marrying that nice Tommy Muddypaws, if he'll still have you, and settling down among your own kind. But she was like this from a puppy, that sister of yours—always had to have her own way, and then didn't like it once she had gotten it! Well, I said, you've gone and made your bed now. Made the neighbors think you fancy yourself a cut above them. You go throwing your fine gentleman over, and you'll never get another chance. You're twenty-three already; wait much longer, and you'll wake up one morning and see a spinster in the looking-glass, and then where will you be? No, you wanted him, and now you've got to stick to him. He doesn't drink, and he doesn't gamble, and he has all the money in the world, so why should you care if he's a little peculiar in his manner?"

Edgar thought privately that a few minutes in Mrs. Chase's company might render anyone's manner peculiar. Very possibly, Emily's fiancé was not to blame. He wondered whether there might be a tactful way to relay this to Chase.

"Come on, let's go see Emily," Chase said to Edgar, in tones that suggested he had listened to very little of this.

"No you don't," Mrs. Chase said. "Not without saying how-do-you-do to our guests. I can't have them thinking that *two* of my puppies are too stuck-up to talk to them."

"Fine," Chase said impatiently, tugging Edgar around the corner. "But only for a minute. Come *on*, Mr. Beagle."

Edgar decided that this was as formal an invitation as he was likely to get. There were some circumstances, he supposed, under which it was better not to stand on ceremony.

Chapter Three

The back garden was decorated, Edgar thought, with rather more enthusiasm than taste. Streamers and little paper lanterns hung from the trees—Edgar made a mental note of the fire hazard—and there were ribbons in festive, cheaply dyed colors wound about the broken-backed chairs. Everything was festooned with nosegays and tureens and sheaves of flowers: armloads of homegrown daisies and forget-me-nots and marigolds, and a few lonely and slightly wilted bunches of roses and heliotropes that must have come from a flower shop, presumably via Mr. Herder. Edgar, who preferred wax flowers, resisted the impulse to sneeze. There was no denying that the table, groaning under its floral burdens, took up an inconvenient amount of space; the garden was not quite wide enough for supper parties. Edgar noted that it was very silly to go to all the trouble of bringing a table outdoors and then eating all crammed in together, when there was probably a perfectly serviceable dining room inside. He supposed it must be something to do with aesthetics.

Beyond the table, at the far end of the garden, there was a smattering of guests, all talking at once. Edgar registered a large Irish Wolfhound in a checked waistcoat; an elderly, emphatically bewhiskered Schnauzer vigorously scratching his ears; a family of bulldog-like creatures of uncertain pedigree; a gray and white sheepdog whose drink sloshed out of his cup as he gesticulated exuberantly; and an elderly tabby with spectacles. And border collies; more border collies than Edgar had ever seen, or wanted to see, in one place. Chase, who was still gripping Edgar's arm; and his mother, who had plastered on what was clearly her company smile; and a border collie in an ill-fitting sack suit, moving closer with disheartening alacrity; and a border collie in a flower-laden straw bonnet; and a stocky, muscular border collie earnestly telling a story that, from his gestures, seemed to consist mostly of pummeling and digging.

"Return of the prodigal, eh?" the border collie in the sack suit remarked mildly, as he reached Edgar and Chase. "Where've you been gadding all day, then, Gabriel? And what's this you've brought home with you? A new guest? Splendid!" He extracted a pair of spectacles from his voluminous pockets, and jammed them onto his nose. "Goodness me, a beagle! Why, that's grand—we hadn't any beagles. No scent hounds in the slightest. Well, I suppose there's no need to ask who *you* are: you're the fancy city gentleman who Gabriel is forever blathering about. We always thought he was making you up."

"Indeed, sir, I am Mr. Edgar Horatio Beagle, private investig—"

"Well, you seem real enough." He seized Edgar's paw and wrung it with startling enthusiasm. "Welcome to my house, Mr. Beagle."

"It is a pleasure to make your acquaintance, Mr. Chase."

"It's awfully nice to finally know you exist," Chase's father said genially. "Just fancy—a real London gentleman taking an

33

interest in our little lad! Unless—now then, Gabriel, tell the truth: did you hire an actor to call himself Mr. Beagle and pretend to be your friend?"

Edgar hastened to assure Chase's father that he was not an actor.

Chase's father was plainly unconvinced. "Well, you don't look a thing like the fellows who catch criminals are supposed to," he said. "I don't reckon you're half big enough for tackling highway-cats and vampires and cannibals and all."

"That's only in stories, Dad," Chase said.

"'Twould be just like Gabriel to hire an actor," Mr. Chase countered. He addressed himself to his wife, with sudden enthusiasm. "Do you remember, Tessa, when the circus was in town and he brought a monkey home? This might be just the same. Oi, you,"—here, he turned once again to Edgar, with disconcerting rapidity—"did you go to Eton?"

"I attended Merchant Taylors, sir."

"Well," said Chase's father, glancing at his wife with the air of a dog who has scored a direct and satisfying hit, "I've never heard of it."

Edgar mentally debated the potential merits of attempting to explain his academic credentials. Chase caught his eye, and shook his head very firmly. In any event, the stocky border collie had trundled across the garden and was staring saucer-eyed and lolling-tongued at Edgar, rather too close and too unblinking for manners. "Ah," Mr. Chase said, looking uncomfortably from the newcomer, who had dropped food all down his front, to Edgar in his pristine frock coat and decorous silk cravat. "My second son. Joseph. He lives just down the street."

"Hullo," Joseph said, continuing to stare at Edgar.

34

"It is a pleasure to renew our acquaintanceship, sir," Edgar said courteously, holding out his paw. "I trust you have been well?"

"Joseph," Chase prompted, "you remember meeting Mr. Beagle, when you visited me in London in '74."

"Do I?" Joseph asked, regarding Edgar's proffered paw blankly and without marked interest.

"Of course you do," Chase said. "When we had such a time getting you out of the Thames, and I took his umbrella to hold out to you. I say, Mr. Beagle, did I ever give you back that umbrella, after Joseph finished biting it? Surely I must have. No? Well, I am frightfully sorry. You must remind me tomorrow, and I'll take you out and buy you one straightaway. There's a very good second-paw shop not far from here—old Mr. Schnauzer's, unless he's dead."

"Not dead," Joseph interposed. "Eating biscuits." He gestured vaguely towards the Schnauzer, who was holding a heaping plate of biscuits in one front paw and still scratching himself with the other.

"Sometimes you have to darn the things, of course," Chase went on, ignoring this, "and it takes a little while for the smell of camphor to fade, but on the whole, he has very nice goods, at quite reasonable prices. Do you remember my green cravat, with the dragons?"

"It is seared into my memory, Inspector."

"Well, that's where I got it from. When was that—two Christmases ago? Yes, I believe it was; I remember it was just before I got that very bad bout of fleas. I say, Mr. Beagle, you don't suppose—? Well, never mind. It's a smashing cravat. Anyway, Joseph, of course you remember Mr. Beagle. We took you out for that walk by Covent Garden, where you kept nipping off to buy oranges and things, and we had to go wandering in circles and shouting your name."

"Oh, that was you?" Joseph said, blinking at Edgar with astonishment. "I remembered it being someone else—someone quite stodgy and dull. One of those by-the-book chaps, don't you know?" He peered even harder at Edgar. "No, I say, that *was* you!"

"You must be mixing Mr. Beagle up with someone quite different," a female voice interposed pointedly. The border collie in the straw bonnet had arrived on the scene. She was somewhat shorter than Joseph, with brown markings and a slight tendency toward embonpoint. Her dress was a sensible dark blue and was freshly pressed, and a matching ribbon passed around her neck and culminated in a neat, symmetrical bow at the base of her throat. Edgar regarded her with approval. "How do you do, Mr. Beagle?" she said. "I am Mrs. Wilhelmina Chase, Joseph's wife."

"No, I'm sure he was you," Joseph persisted, with a mulish tenacity that was not altogether unreminiscent of Chase. "He talked funny, and he didn't smile. Oi, Gabriel, what are you poking me for?"

"I must apologize," Edgar said, to fill the awkward silence that followed, "for my attire. It is to my great shame that I am wearing a frock coat on this festive occasion. I was not expecting to attend a supper party, you see, and so I have not my tailcoat with me."

The tension abruptly broke. Chase's father let out an explosive guffaw, and Joseph, after glancing uncertainly around to ascertain that something humorous had occurred, emitted a few doubtful chuckles. Chase's mother gave Edgar a jocular nudge, evidently indicating that she now considered them to be on terms of intimacy.

"Well, anyway," she said, "you're not stuck up, for all your fancy talk."

"Just fancy wearing a tailcoat in our little house!" Chase's father wheezed, dabbing his eyes with his front paw instead of with a handkerchief. "Very witty, Mr. Beagle—upon my word, very witty! And he says it so serious-like—for all the world as if he meant it! A tailcoat!"

Edgar racked his brains in perplexity, trying to imagine what Chase's family could possibly find so entertaining. He came up utterly blank. Perhaps groups of border collies just behaved like this sometimes. He tried to catch Chase's eye, but Chase had already turned away.

"Come and meet the neighbors," Chase's father said, in an expansive, jovial tone. He lay a warm, heavy paw on Edgar's shoulder. Edgar struggled to remain perfectly still. "Isn't it wonderful we have this garden now? We never would have been able to have so many friends to supper at our old house. Don't you think life is very exciting, Mr. Beagle? You never know what wonderful thing may happen. Just see our little lass—she never had any notion of being rich, and now look! Walking along the piers one day, and said how-do-you-do to a fellow, and now she'll get to live like a princess for the rest of her days!"

"Not if she keeps crying upstairs," Mrs. Chase interjected.

"Anyway," Mr. Chase said, over her, "it's a grand turnout—all for our Emily! And everyone so happy to be here! I do like to see folks enjoying themselves, don't you, Mr. Beagle? See, Mr. Schnauzer looks pleased as anything, and you can hear old Mrs. Mouser purring all the way from here."

"And you needn't go craning your head around looking

around for Nora Roughcoat," Mrs. Chase informed her son, not troubling to keep her voice down, "because she and her parents have been laid up with kennel cough all week."

"I never was!"

"And besides," Mrs. Chase continued placidly, still at the top of her voice, "she's been walking out with the Mastiffs' eldest, and he's as big as ten of you. He gives her the loveliest presents, they say. Necklaces and tail-rings and things. A waste of money, I call it—but there, he's simply silly about her, just like you always were. Do you know, old Captain Mastiff came round here and asked me the most ridiculous questions about you and Nora? Near as I can tell, they won't let Roddy propose to her until they've decided she's good enough. Yammering on about their pedigree, as if anyone cared. Well, that family always was stuck up. And I'll tell you what, Nora's no better nowadays. Swanning around in her brazen silk dresses—her father was with the East India Company, Mr. Beagle—clutching at Roddy's arm and expecting everyone to envy her." She sniffed loudly. "Well, I wouldn't trade places with her for all the world. I wish her joy of her mastiff, and I hope the fancy presents from him are worth it. If a mastiff gave *me* something, I'd take it straight to the scullery and scrub it down with lye. Oh, perhaps they can't help all the drooling, what with the shape of their jowls—but it isn't very nice, is it?" She paused expectantly for a moment, and then, to Edgar's relief, swept on without waiting for him to reply. "I hope the Mastiffs won't be too insulted that we didn't ask them here tonight, but I had such a job washing everything after the last time. Mr. Dewlaps is just the same. I had to invite him, we've known him so long—he lives just down the street from our old house, Mr. Beagle—but I breathed such a sigh of relief when he said he couldn't get away from work tonight. He's the concierge at the Adelphi Hotel, you know. Doing awfully well for himself, and I'm sure he deserves it, if ever any dog did. He used to come round and romp with our boys when they were little, and he never even minded when Joseph would nip at his ears. But I don't like to think what his desk at the Adelphi must look like. Soaking wet all the time, I shouldn't be surprised. Gabriel, what are you staring off in the distance with that funny glazed look in your eyes for? Don't tell me you're standing here thinking about squirrels. I don't know why I bother talking to you; I don't believe you've heard a single word." She reached out and jostled his arm. "I've been saying, there's really something rather horrid about dogs who drool all the time, isn't there?"

"Tommy Muddypaws is drooling *right now*," Chase said, coming back to himself with a start and pointing accusatorially towards the family of bulldogs. "You never call *him* horrid."

"Yes, yes, the Muddypaws are here!" Chase's father said jubilantly. Edgar got the distinct impression that he had not been listening either. "They were our neighbors before we moved house, Mr. Beagle, and I'm sure they couldn't help it about all the snuffling. Dear me, Ollie has dug a hole again, and now he's eating grass. Go and stop him, Tessa, before he's sick under the table—there's a love."

"No one can stop that creature from doing anything," Mrs. Chase said darkly. "I can't think how such a nice family turned out that mongrel. There's his brother Tommy, you see, Mr. Beagle—that's our Emily's old beau. Look what elegant posture he has. I do like a fellow who can stand up straight and have a sensible conversation, instead of running back and forth and yelping all the time."

"He's just slipped the big silver ladle into his jacket, Mum," Chase said wearily. "He's only standing like that so it won't fall out."

"Oh, nonsense, Gabriel. I absolutely forbid you to make a scene about Tommy Muddypaws and spoil your sister's party. You've always said the unkindest things about him, ever since he started walking out with Emily."

"Well, he's not half good enough for her," Chase blazed. "Nasty, common little urchin."

Edgar mentally filed this away. Perhaps Chase was simply predisposed to suspect criminal activity in anyone who harbored romantic sentiments towards his sister.

"I hate Tommy," Joseph offered. "He bit me on the ear when we were puppies."

"Yes, dear," Wilhelmina said, "but you bit him first. You've bitten everyone here."

"*Anyway*," Mr. Chase said, a little too heartily, renewing his grip on Edgar's shoulder, "there's Mr. Nipper—oh dear, he's spilled his drink again—and there's Mr. Wolfhound, and I'm sure they'll all be perfectly tickled to meet a real gentleman from London. Come on, then."

"Half a minute!" said a new voice—an urbane, polished voice with a decided foreign lilt to it. "Aren't you going to introduce us too?"

Edgar turned. Three more dogs had come up behind him; they must, he supposed, have been lurking around the far side of the house. The foremost one—who, as Edgar took it, had spoken—was a slim, dapper, sharp-muzzled terrier, impeccably attired in a brocade waistcoat and a silk top hat. He regarded Edgar with his head slightly cocked, and with an expression of genteel, almost detached, amusement playing across his glossy brown and black face. His posture and bearing managed to convey a self-deprecating, but unapologetic, awareness that his extravagant dress and gentlemanly bearing placed him in a wholly different sphere from that of any of the other guests. It was as if he had been bodily lifted from an entirely different party miles away and gently set down in the Chases' garden through no act of his own, and was now, without the least tinge of hauteur, making a show of accepting his fate with exaggerated equanimity. Behind him, there shuffled an unprepossessing cattle dog with blotchy fur, and an enormous, heavily grizzled creature of uncertain pedigree, with sawtoothed ears and a slavering mouth.

"Mr. Herder!" Edgar said, extending his paw to the terrier. "I am delighted to make your acquaintance."

The terrier's air of amusement grew. There was something distinctly appealing about his manner: so perfectly correct as to be almost ironic, with the suggestion of a quick mind and a well-developed sense of humor sparkling just beneath the surface. Perhaps a little too flamboyant to wholly endear himself to the Chases, Edgar supposed. Perhaps just the slightest bit too self-congratulatory. But by no means an objectionable match. And certainly not a criminal type. It was only too plain that, yet again, Chase's imagination had run away with him.

But the terrier was shaking his head. "I am afraid you are mistaken," he said in his languid Australian drawl. "Alas! I have not the fortune to marry the exquisite Miss Chase. I am only Mr. Tenterfield, Mr. Herder's best man. This is our puppyhood friend Mr. Mongrel. And *this* is the happy bridegroom." He indicated the blotchy-furred dog, who

41

promptly let out a gruff, discomfited yelp of alarm and tripped over his own back paws.

"You see?" Chase muttered darkly into Edgar's ear, slightly too close and too loud to be strictly comfortable.

"I beg your pardon, Mr. Herder," Edgar said at once. He held out his paw again. Mr. Herder, staring blankly off into the distance, displayed no awareness that he was expected to step forward and take it, much less any desire to do so. Edgar assessed him covertly. Black and gray fur with unremarkable tan and white patches; clothing slightly bedraggled, though of visibly superb quality; ears a trifle matted; a fine, soft, satin cravat, frayed around the edges as if he had been nervously chewing on it; and expensive shoes in desperate need of polish. Flimsy, cheap cufflinks, at odds with the quality of the rest of his ensemble; an engagement present from his less-affluent fiancée, Edgar imagined. Extraordinary eyes: one amber, and one icy blue. Sinister, perhaps, if one were a very small and rather silly puppy—or, apparently, if one were Chase!—but Edgar was full-grown and not a border collie, and he had read Dr. Snuffles' monograph on heterochromia twice over. An expression that seemed to have flirted with diffidence before hurtling straight to what Edgar took for self-loathing, so marked as to suggest that Mr. Herder was anxiously waiting for the garden path to open up beneath him so that he could plummet into its receiving jaws. Much to his own annoyance, Edgar found himself diligently checking, although he knew perfectly well that it was ridiculous, for the atmosphere of evil that Chase had described. Predictably, of course, there was absolutely nothing. Merely a herding dog who was probably unimpeachably respectable, albeit not gifted with savoir-faire—Edgar had seen the type a thousand times; and a groomsman who was, unfortunately, more appealing than the groom; and their other friend, that rough-hewn Mr. Mongrel, still skulking in the shadows and saying nothing. Constable Barks, whose physique was markedly unsuited to slinking, slunk nonetheless between Edgar's legs, peered up at Mr. Mongrel, and let out a long, low, growl. Mr. Mongrel gave no indication of having noticed. He was turned the other way, evidently fascinated by something on the supper table. From the angle of his head, Edgar could not quite determine whether it was the roast or the carving knife. Perhaps, Edgar thought, Chase had simply picked up on Mr. Mongrel's undeniable air of malice and somehow managed to misattribute it to Mr. Herder. Just the sort of thing, really, that Chase *would* do.

"Why isn't Emily here?" Chase demanded of Mr. Herder.

"I don't know," Mr. Herder said. His tone revealed absolutely nothing.

Chase threw him a single, unmistakable look of disgust, and then turned pointedly away and attached himself to Edgar's sleeve. "Come on," he said, "let's go in and fetch her." He tugged at Edgar's sleeve with such vehemency that Edgar could feel a few threads snap. Edgar idly wondered whether this was Chase's idea of a clever ploy for forcing him to get straight to borrowing clothes more suited to the environment.

"Yes, yes," Mrs. Chase said, her voice wavering. "You remind her that all the neighbors are here, waiting to have dinner with her and her fine gentleman bridegroom." She glanced with unconcealed trepidation towards Mr. Herder and his friends, and maneuvered her face into a ludicrously unconvincing smile; Edgar noted, parenthetically, that this was probably where Chase had gotten his acting abilities.

At that moment, there were a few hurried, pattering steps,

and then the click of the back door being unlatched—and then a girl stood poised in the doorway, regarding the assembled company.

Edgar's first impression was that she was very young, and very unhappy, and—although beauty could not, of course, be meaningfully assessed or defined by any objective metric—unusually well-constructed, according to conventional aesthetic standards. Delicately molded features, and clearly defined markings, and immense, velvety eyes, and expressive ears covered in dainty little curls of silken fur. A sizable diamond ring glimmered up from her left paw. Edgar became very aware that Chase was staring at him expectantly—waiting, no doubt, for Edgar to decide that Emily was the loveliest girl he had ever seen, and that she was worth helping no matter how annoyed one might be with her relatives or what the details of one's profession might entail! But Edgar was a private investigator, not a matchmaker or a patcher-up of lovers' quarrels—and so the silly, protective impulse that was unfurling itself within his brain was utterly *de trop*. Perhaps, he thought, there was a scientific explanation for it; it might easily be an evolutionary quirk: an impulse left over from his fiercely loyal lupine ancestors. Perhaps, therefore, the underlying machinery of his brain left him no choice but to automatically register this girl, who shared Chase's blood, as a pack-mate; as defenseless; as desperate for rescue. Perhaps he was *not* being willfully sentimental.

Emily's eyes met Edgar's, and his gaze slid reflexively away. It occurred to him that he was probably going to have to make conversation with her all evening. Never mind about protective impulses. A common girl, really. A girl whose fiancé, Edgar thought irritably, probably had nothing whatsoever the matter with him apart from cold paws; a girl who had absolutely no need of a private investigator's services; a girl who would have gotten along quite nicely if he had not been dragged up from London and practically commanded to perform magic tricks!

But all the same, he thought, as she looked away, a frightened girl; a young, unhappy girl; a girl whose limpid eyes shone in mute appeal and whose ears drooped pathetically. After all, Chase was right; Edgar would not have liked to see his own sister approaching marital disaster.

A girl who, backlit by the swirling yellow lamplight, with her simple white dress and dark, luminous eyes, looked altogether out of place in this tawdry, workaday setting. A girl who could have been a princess in exile, from the fairy stories that well-meaning relatives had tenaciously endeavored to press on Lavinia in her puppyhood; or a marble statue; or a young priestess in a painting at the National Gallery.

When all was said and done, a beautiful girl.

Then, she spoke, and the spell was broken. A pleasant-mannered girl with regular features, Edgar told himself sternly—nothing more.

"Oh!" she said. "Are you Mr. Beagle? When Gabriel ran off, I thought he might be going to fetch you, but I didn't suppose you would come." She spoke very simply and prettily, but Edgar could detect faint traces of a Liverpool accent and an unrefined cadence, which it was apparent she had taken great pains to suppress.

"My daughter," Chase's mother said, unnecessarily. "Miss Emily Chase. Going to be Mrs. Herder in three days, though—aren't you, Emily?"

Edgar ventured a glance at Mr. Herder. He seemed to be

pretending that Emily was not there, and Edgar dared not hazard the merest guess as to what the cold, closed expression on his mottled face might signify. Behind the blank mask of his features, was he frozen by some unspeakable source of terror or misery? Merely devoid of personality—and, perhaps, intelligence? Or mentally occupied with constructing some secret plot, and adept, from long and not necessarily benign practice, at being deliberately unreadable—but *that*, no doubt, was only Chase's nonsense! Mr. Herder was not, when one really stopped to consider him, doing anything that might be considered remotely suspicious. His apparent lack of interest in his fiancée spoke rather poorly of his character—but what, precisely, did Chase imagine that Edgar could do about it? Being an inattentive suitor was not synonymous with being evil. Just another one of Chase's flights of fancy. There was absolutely no reason to feel uneasy. The uncertain wavering sensation in Edgar's stomach was to be expected; after all, he probably should have found his way to the restaurant car at teatime. Everything was perfectly alright.

The assembled dogs and cats settled themselves around the table. The light was fading, and moths were beginning to materialize around the paper lanterns. Mrs. Chase, plainly in the end stages of desolation behind her brittle, would-be jubilant smile, pressed food on the guests and stared around the garden with manic eyes.

As a rule, Edgar was not overfond of parties. He could recall, with an aching discomfort that the passing years had no power to fade, every miserable little school picnic and birthday luncheon and Christmas festivity he had ever been forced to attend as a puppy: his sister Lavinia, heedless of the weather and her attire, running wild in the back garden and scorning every would-be playfellow; meanwhile, himself, very stiff in his starched collar and buttoned boots, keeping to himself in a little corner while the other boys his age cheerfully kicked the table legs and discussed cricket and toy soldiers and the fire brigade with a level of animation utterly foreign to him. Edgar knew quite a lot of things relevant to the fire brigade, as it happened—all about the first force-pump back in ancient Alexandria, right down to Captain Manby's potassium carbonate extinguisher, from just before Father had been born—besides plenty of information on *really* interesting subjects, like trains and microscopes. Yet, somehow, he could never work out the right way to enter the conversation until long after the moment had passed. Occasionally, a well-meaning mother would nudge her offspring and issue whispered instructions not to leave Edgar out. The resulting resentful condescension, from some grubby-pawed boy who was not even clever but merely *loud*, was rather worse than being ignored had been. One of the nicest things about being an adult, Edgar had discovered, was that nobody could compel one to go to parties.

And yet, Edgar now reflected, glancing across the table at Emily's drooping ears and red-rimmed eyes, even with so many unpleasant memories to choose from, this was by far the worst party he had ever attended. It turned out that frequent silences at a party, which he had often fancied would be pleasantly restful, were instead a source of agonizing strain— like the drawn-out, paralytic moment in a nightmare just before the monster appears. Edgar had never imagined that Chase was even capable of being this quiet; something about it was profoundly unsettling. Mrs. Chase flung out a few pieces of desultory gossip—Edgar found himself markedly unedified to learn that the Pouncers had managed to sell their house even though it reeked of catnip, that Roddy Mastiff was performing admirably at his job as Mr. Schnauzer's shop assistant, and that somebody with the unprepossessing name of Beatrice Biter now had more puppies than she knew what to do with—but eventually gave up. Joseph, eating steadily and with gusto, blurted out disjointed observations at intervals, invariably showering the table with bits of semi-masticated food. Edgar briefly attempted to make stiff conversation with Mrs. Mouser, the elderly lady seated to his left, but gave up when he discovered that, being hard of hearing, she would reply to whatever remark he made with nothing but a volley of querulous, interrogative meows. At the far end of the table, Mr. Mongrel shoveled meat into his mouth—surely it was not quite normal to have so many teeth, and all of them so sharp?—and growled to himself between gulps of beer. Closer to Edgar, Mr. Herder stared downwards in despondent silence. The one time Mrs. Chase addressed him directly, he started violently, overturned the gravy, and then mumbled into his plate as if communicating some dismal secret to his potatoes. Emily, seated next to him, sat up perfectly straight, so that no part of her body might brush against his. She stared straight ahead and moved the food around her plate with desultory little nudges. Even Constable Barks, who could generally be counted on to generate a more-or-less continuous stream of noise, spent a few moments snuffling under the table for scraps, then settled heavily on top of Edgar's feet and went to sleep.

"What happened to that other girl?" Chase abruptly asked his parents at one point, as a small, nervous-looking tabby in a wrinkled apron scampered around the table refilling wineglasses. "The daily maid you had last time?"

"Gone to stay with her ailing aunt in the country," Mrs. Chase said.

"A likely story," Chase said to Edgar, too quietly for manners and too loudly for subtlety. "Anyone can have an ailing aunt. I suppose she took one look at Mr. Herder and sprinted away with an earsplitting yowl."

"You cannot lay all the evils of the world at Mr. Herder's paws," Edgar told him.

"Perhaps not," Chase rejoined, glaring at Mr. Herder with undisguised loathing, "but I cannot find any good in him either." After that, he relapsed into a moody reverie, and Edgar's end of the table was utterly silent once more.

The only thing averting even greater catastrophe was the eventual intervention of Mr. Tenterfield. He was witty; he was debonair; he paid Mrs. Chase innumerable delicate compliments on the food and decor. He spoke with joyous anticipation about the upcoming wedding, and about his eagerness to serve as Mr. Herder's best man, and he made flattering remarks about Emily's suitability for his dear old friend. Watching him, Edgar could not help but privately agree with Chase's sentiment that Mr. Tenterfield would be a preferable bridegroom. He wondered what extraordinary latent attractions could possibly have induced so charming a girl to become enamored of a wooden, laconic oaf instead— one who, moreover, kept such company as Mr. Mongrel! Edgar snuck a glance down the table. Mr. Mongrel had finished his dinner, and was now chewing on his napkin. Slaver dripped continuously from his muzzle, and he was so big that his dinner companions on either side—Wilhelmina and Mr. Tenterfield—had been obliged to eke out a modicum of elbow room by moving their chairs several inches away from him. The effect was that he appeared to be a solitary savage, perhaps pestilent or cannibalistic, marooned in the middle of the table—which, Edgar thought, was probably not far from the truth.

As soon as dinner was over, Emily excused herself from the table with a few perfunctory words, and fled indoors. Chase immediately jumped up, knocking over his chair in the process, and beckoned imperiously to Edgar.

"Gabriel," Mrs. Chase said icily, "I am sure you and your friend are not thinking of abandoning our guests so soon after dinner."

"You haven't so much as looked at the new flowerbeds!" Chase's father joined in. "The evening primroses have come up a treat."

"I can see them in the morning, Dad," Chase said impatiently.

"That you cannot, Gabriel, because they're *evening* primroses—"

"It is bad enough," Mrs. Chase said through her teeth, leaning all the way across the table, "that the bride has disappeared from her own party. I can't have her brother running off too—"

"I'm still here," Joseph said, reaching across the table and dragging the tureen of potatoes towards himself.

"—or the neighbors will think you fancy yourself too good for them, and then they'll think *she* fancies herself too good for them, and then if she goes breaking the engagement, the whole neighborhood will be against her, and all the local boys will wash their paws of her—"

"Well, she *is* too good for them," Chase interrupted, not particularly quietly. In the ensuing aggrieved silence, there was a very slight metallic clatter, as of various silver utensils coming into contact inside a jacket, from the general direction of Tommy Muddypaws.

"That's so," Chase's father said heartily. "The world is too big and too beautiful to only ever see this little corner of it. If she wants to set her sights elsewhere, then I say, well done."

"Just because *you* were born off in Scotland and went gadding around for your work, Angus—"

"And a good thing too, or else *these* are the only faces I ever would have seen—"

Wilhelmina and Mr. Tenterfield exchanged glances behind Mr. Mongrel's back, and then struck up an exceedingly loud conversation about gardening.

"Look at Mr. Herder," Chase told his mother. "If you want to worry about what the neighbors will think, then worry about what they'll think of *him*. Emily's probably off crying again, and everyone can see he hasn't the least particle of concern."

Edgar ventured a glance in Mr. Herder's direction. It yielded irritatingly little information. He had pushed his chair back from the table and hung his head, so that his ears drooped and his face was in shadow, and Edgar had absolutely no idea how much he had heard.

"What are your thoughts on calceolarias, Mrs. Muddypaws?" Wilhelmina was shouting across the table, very brightly. "I find I can never get the soil right."

"No good," Joseph said indistinctly, shoveling potatoes into his mouth. "Too bitter. And they stick in your teeth."

"I must see more of your beautiful English gardens while I am here," Mr. Tenterfield said, matching Wilhelmina's volume.

Chase swept the table with a scornful glance, and then seized

Edgar by the arm, rather too firmly for either manners or comfort. "You can all go on talking nonsense, if you want," he informed the assembled company. "I expect it is all you know how to do. My sister is upstairs breaking her heart right now, and if you care more about flowers and dirt than about her, then I think you are all heartless as well as dull, and I have never been so glad I ran away."

And, leaving the table in horrified silence, he tugged Edgar over to the back door and marched into the house.

Chapter Four

"My word, what an ordeal!" Chase exclaimed in a low voice as soon as the door had slammed behind them, releasing Edgar and vigorously mopping his own brow with a none-too-pristine pocket handkerchief. "Not one of them, except for Mr. Tenterfield, knows how to have a conversation. It's like having dinner with a bunch of waxworks out of Madame Tussaud's. I say,"—here he fixed Edgar with an accusatory glare—"a fine lot of good *you* were! Not that you're ever the life of any party, but I thought I could count on you for your society conversation or your rules of etiquette or whatnot—and I'm sure I don't know what sort of etiquette tells you to sit at dinner gaping like a stuffed frog, with never a word to anyone."

"I was making observations," Edgar said with dignity, picking his way around a pile of crates at the foot of the stairs. There were, in fact, crates everywhere. It was hard to be certain in the evening half-light, but Edgar fancied there were also piles of dust, and any number of grubby paw-prints scattered across the floor.

"Making observations about *what*? You don't like my family—that's all there is to it."

"Kindly do not be absurd," Edgar said, with some asperity.

"You dragged me—that is to say, prevailed upon me to accompany you—here to do a job, not to pay a social visit. It was paramount that I form my impressions of the various players in your little drama, such as it is."

"Well, how do you expect to form impressions if you never talk to any of them?" Chase demanded.

"I will talk to them tomorrow."

"But they were already right here tonight."

"I prefer to handle my witnesses singly."

"They are not *witnesses*. They are my immediate family and my puppyhood neighbors."

"Inspector Chase," Edgar said, coming to a stop, "it is only my great personal esteem for you that has persuaded me to take you on as a client—but, if you are to be my client, you must permit me to handle your case in keeping with my usual professional protocols."

"By which you mean," Chase sniffed under his breath, "that you haven't any idea how to make conversation with a table full of working dogs, and you don't care to learn."

He seized Edgar's arm, perhaps more firmly than was strictly necessary, and steered him up the stairs.

"May I ask where we are going, Inspector?"

"Up to Emily's bedroom, of course."

Edgar came to an abrupt stop. "My dear Inspector Chase! Surely, you must realize the impropriety—"

"Oh, here he goes," Chase muttered.

"—of the suggestion that I should plunge boldly into a young lady's boudoir! Even if you have no regard for the intrinsic unseemliness of the thing, I am sure you have a care for your sister's reputation—"

"You sound like my mother," Chase said. "Next you'll be

asking what the neighbors will think."

He pointedly turned his back on Edgar and tapped on the third door to his right.

"Come in, Gabriel," Emily's tearful voice rang out.

"You see," Chase said, with some pride, "she knows my knock."

"No," Emily said, opening the door, "I heard you quarreling all the way up the stairs and down the hall, and I do wish you wouldn't. Come in, if you're coming to see me, unless that Airedale is hiding behind you again—and Gabriel, for goodness' sake, be civil to your friend. I think he is very nice."

Edgar could not help but preen himself very slightly, despite his pervasive awareness of the indecorum of the situation. Bound as he was to Chase by friendship and long acquaintance, he found himself regarding Emily, as she drew them into her bedroom and settled herself on the brass bedstead, almost as if she were his own sister. He idly wondered how it might feel to have a sister who spoke of him so admiringly. It would certainly make for a contrast with Lavinia, who had, in their very early puppyhood, once spent an entire afternoon lugging him about to various shopkeepers and asking to exchange him for either a bag of toffees or a brother who did not memorize railway timetables, whichever they had in stock. Perhaps the key thing was to have a sister younger than oneself.

Edgar had expected any space inhabited by Chase's kindred to be hopelessly chaotic, but Emily's little bedroom was surprisingly tidy. There were sky blue ribbons wound around the bed rails, and the frame on the slightly cracked mirror above the washstand was painted with cornflowers. The blue and white rag rug by the bed grated somewhat on Edgar's own aesthetic sensibilities, but he mentally conceded that, by any objective metric, it suited the room admirably. In the midst of all this homespun finery, Emily, curled up in a disconsolate little ball in the middle of the counterpane, looked achingly pathetic. She waved her visitors towards a shabby rocking chair—Chase sprawled headlong into its depths at once—and a little vanity stool covered in only slightly threadbare velvet, upon which Edgar seated himself with his back very straight.

"I apologize, Miss Chase," he said, once he was settled, "for the impropriety of my presence in your bedroom, but your brother seemed to think the circumstances justified it."

"What is the danger, Mr. Beagle—that my gentleman friend should get the wrong impression, and become cold and aloof in his manner towards me? I am afraid it is too late to worry about that."

"Don't you worry, Emily," Chase said, in hearty, elder-brotherly tones. "Mr. Beagle is going to fix everything. He knows all about criminals."

"But James is not a criminal! He is just a very ordinary sort of herding dog, who, I suppose, has gotten cold paws at the last moment, or else is ashamed to show me to his fine gentlemen friends." Her voice broke very slightly on the last few words. "I may be miles below his station, but I am sure I love him just as well as any heiress would do. And I assure you, Mr. Beagle, when I met him, I had no idea he was a millionaire. He just seemed a nice, normal, unassuming cattle dog. He told me he lived on one of the most prosperous ranches in Australia, but I assumed he meant he worked there; it never crossed my mind that he owned it. Of course, I was awfully pleased when I found out the truth; I won't be so silly as to pretend that money means nothing at all to me. But I would have wanted to marry him even if he hadn't a penny to his name. Mr. Tenterfield has been very kind to me, but I suppose he secretly thinks that I set my sights on James because of his fortune. Perhaps you think so too."

"Not at all, Miss Chase," protested Edgar, whose mind this very suspicion had crossed at least once.

"I suppose you are wondering, then, how I could have made my mind up to marry someone like that. I hope you will believe me, Mr. Beagle, when I say that James has changed past all recognition. Well, my mother says that girls always see a different side of their husbands sooner or later, so I suppose I am lucky that I have seen this side of James before becoming his wife. Anyway, Mr. Beagle, it was kind of you to come all the way here, but I do not think there is anything you can do; you are an investigator, and there is nothing for you to investigate. I am sorry if Gabriel has been very bothersome about it. I know he can be terribly trying when he gets one of his fixed ideas."

"Miss Chase," Edgar said, before Chase could voice the inevitable protestations, "since I am already here, perhaps you might tell me how you came to meet Mr. Herder."

Emily sighed prettily, her lovely eyes melancholy. "I don't see what good it will do, Mr. Beagle. I should never dream of imposing on you to mix yourself up in my little tragedy—and besides, it is not as if there were a crime to be solved."

"Just answer his questions, Emily," Chase said authoritatively.

"Well, I like that! If you aren't the one always complaining that he asks everyone so many questions, when your intuition could just solve the whole affair!"

"I am sure I have never said any such thing," Chase said with dignity. "Mr. Beagle, does that sound the least bit like me?

Anyway," he added hurriedly, before Edgar could respond, "you'd better tell him all about it, Emily."

"There is not very much to tell, I am afraid. It was all very commonplace and quiet. I was walking out on the piers one afternoon, and he approached me—not like *that*, Gabriel; sit back down. He was very polite, and he was only asking for directions. He told me he was new here, and had lost his way. I thought perhaps he wasn't very clever, because it is not usual to lose your way on the piers; the water is on one side of you, and the city on the other. But I realized later on that he had just wanted a reason to speak to me. And then he was there again the next day and said good afternoon to me, and then I started looking out for him every day, and we got up quite a little friendship. He told me all about Australia."

"I suppose he talked to you about cows," Chase interjected scornfully.

"Not at all! He was perfectly charming. He said he had come to England to put through some point of business concerning the ranch, but had taken such a fancy to the country that, if only he had a reason to stay here—well, you know how gentlemen talk. And we saw each other more and more. Walks, and restaurants, and tea. Like something out of a dream. And then he led me one day to the spot where we first met, and got down one one knee."

"Silly, sentimental way of doing it," Chase remarked.

"At what point did Mr. Herder's manner become unusual, Miss Chase?" Edgar said, forbearing with some difficulty to point out Chase's own tendencies towards sentiment.

"Not until three days ago, when his friends arrived here. They surprised him, you know. It was a fine evening, and we had been sitting out by the river, just the two of us—*talking*; sit

58

down, Gabriel!—and he walked me back here, and came inside to say goodnight to Mum and Dad, and to tell them he had reserved the restaurant at the Adelphi for this morning and ordered the flowers for the party—and there his friends were, just sitting in the front parlor, where no one ever goes! It was very odd; the two of them were like no one I had seen before, and there they were on the settee that the mice have gotten to, with the sheet crumpled up on the floor where Mum had thrown it off in a hurry, and Mr. Tenterfield was saying lovely things about the room, although of course they weren't true, and Mr. Mongrel was just sitting there growling and drooling. But I was awfully pleased to meet them, all the same. James' parents are dead, and he hasn't any family in England anyway, so of course no one had come to call on me. You mustn't think I had minded too terribly—I would sooner have had James than all the customs and conventions in the world!—but it was still a little hard on me sometimes, hearing all my friends talk about the parties and suppers and things that their young men's families were getting up. So it was very nice that I could at least meet someone from his life."

"Awfully convenient," Chase broke in at this juncture, "that his family should all be abroad or dead! Do you realize that we know nothing of his antecedents other than what he has told you? He may not even be wealthy."

"Don't be horrid, Gabriel. I never had the least reason to think him a liar. And of course he is wealthy; he has been living in a suite in the Adelphi Hotel for months, and sending me heaps of jewels ever since we got engaged, and flowers every day."

"*Or has he?*" Chase demanded ominously. "We have only his word that he has been living at the Adelphi, or that the jewels are not stolen. My career has brought me up against jewel thieves before, you know. Very likely, he is an escaped convict. Australians usually are. And anyway, his head is a funny shape."

"Leaving aside your idiosyncratic theories on criminology and phrenology, Inspector," Edgar interposed, "perhaps you might allow Miss Chase to tell us what happened on the fateful evening of Mr. Tenterfield and Mr. Mongrel's arrival."

"Nothing happened, Mr. Beagle. That's just the thing. It was all very proper and uneventful. Mr. Tenterfield said that I was even lovelier than he had imagined, and that he wished he were half as fortunate as James; you know the silly things gentlemen always say. Mr. Mongrel kept to himself, but I thought he might just be shy in front of strangers. I supposed they were here on business, like James. But Mr. Tenterfield said they had come specially for the wedding as soon as they saw it written up in the newspaper, though the voyage took ever so long, because he couldn't let his oldest friend stand up at the altar without any groomsmen."

"What do they take the Liverpool newspaper for?" Chase interrupted. "That's the worst of rich folks; they always spend their money on the dullest things. If I were rich, I would do something *interesting*, like set off on a squirrel-tracking expedition in the Himalayas, or buy a pub and make it allow Airedales."

"Mr. Tenterfield is a business dog, like James; I expect he has to take newspapers from all over."

"But wouldn't it take ages for the newspaper to get from here all the way to Australia? By the time they got there, all the news would be three months old. Not much good for business."

"I believe, Inspector," Edgar said, "that some of the new clipper ships can make the voyage in approximately a month and two thirds. And besides—"

"That's not any better. Who cares what happened a month and two thirds ago?"

"*And besides*, I assume Mr. Tenterfield no longer resides in Australia. Even if the newspaper had traveled on the very swiftest of clippers, and if Mr. Tenterfield had boarded a similar vessel the very next day, the newspaper would have to have been published at least three months and ten days ago, i.e. in February. By your report, Inspector, Miss Chase and Mr. Herder did not even make each other's acquaintance, much less pledge and publicize their steadfast love, until March. It logically follows that Mr. Tenterfield lives significantly nearer to England. Isn't that right, Miss Chase?" He made Emily a courteous little bow.

"I shouldn't be surprised. He said something about having been parted from James when they were puppies. I suppose it must have been because Mr. Tenterfield's parents took him to live in another country. Anyway, you would think James would have been frightfully pleased to see them for the first time in so many years—I thought it was perfectly sweet of Mr. Tenterfield, myself—but his eyes went as round as saucers and he froze right up. Mr. Tenterfield made a little joke about how he hoped James would stand them supper, or else they were liable to take their revenge by telling me all his embarrassing puppyhood stories. And Mr. Mongrel stood there staring with his big mad eyes, and kept on baring his teeth and growling under his breath. And then James hurried them away without even saying goodbye to me. And every time I've seen him since then—well, you see how it is. I was terribly worried about him at first; I fancied he must be ill. But that wouldn't make him pretend I don't exist, would it? It is as if, overnight, I had become nothing to him. He will neither look at me nor speak to me. It seems I can't get him alone; his friends always turn up with him, and of course it is perfectly natural that he would want to spend time with them, not having seen them in so long—but he still ought to pay me *some* attention, oughtn't he?" She sighed, and visibly blinked back tears. "I wish he would at least tell me why he has stopped caring for me. Perhaps his friends *have* been persuading him against me, or perhaps he has heard some slanderous rumor; the neighbors do nothing but gossip all day long, and none of it is ever true. But I am sure I never gave him any reason to be so cold."

"Perhaps he is mad," Chase suggested cheerfully. "I expect he will start howling at the moon any day."

"Of course he is not mad. He is, I imagine, finally sane. The presence of his friends has recalled him to his proper station in life, and he has realized that these past months have been in the nature of a lovely dream, which he ought not to have mistaken for reality." She wiped away a tear, so swiftly and stealthily that Edgar could not be sure he had not imagined it. "Well, he has woken up. For my part, I am afraid I am dreaming still. Having imagined my future as his wife, I cannot, you see, un-imagine it now."

"We have no evidence," Edgar said, attempting a consoling modulation of his voice, "that Mr. Herder has any intention of breaking his troth. His erratic behavior may be wholly unrelated to your impending nuptials; his friends may have borne him distressing news from home, or he may be prone to bouts of all-consuming melancholy, or of debilitating illness. What we take for coldness may be merely dyspepsia. Or perhaps his puppyhood parting from Mr. Tenterfield is linked in his mind with some distressing circumstance, of which he does not like to be reminded. For all we know, the fit will pass, and the gentleman will be himself again."

"Perhaps," Emily said, looking Edgar full in the face, "the gentleman is himself already. Perhaps the last few months were merely an aberration, and he reverted to his normal behavior when his friends arrived. What do you think, Mr. Beagle: shall I call off the wedding myself, or shall I wait for him to leave me at the altar? Either way, of course, I shall never be able show my face among my neighbors again. Or shall I go ahead and marry him—if he will still have me—and hope that one day he will go back to loving me?"

Edgar wondered whether he was supposed to answer this. On the whole, he rather thought not.

"Call it off, of course," Chase said, bounding up out of his chair. "Why should you care what anybody around here says? You can't go marrying something evil for fear of what the neighbors will think."

"He isn't *evil*, Gabriel. Don't be ridiculous."

"He is, though. I could tell at once. I don't care what Mr. Beagle says—my intuition is awfully good."

"Well, it never has been before. Remember when you tried to convince everybody that Mr. Toller, at the butcher's, was secretly a fox?"

"None of you ever proved that he wasn't," Chase said, scowling. "He was a sight too interested in the poultry. Anyway, Emily, you ought to get married to someone who actually cares for you. This fellow couldn't even be bothered to look you in the face all evening. I bet he's been running a smuggling ring this whole time—that's why he was always loitering by the dock—and he needed a plausible cover for being there, so he made everyone think he was hanging about to court you—and now his associates have arrived and given him the signal to move on to the next place, so he needn't keep up the pretense any longer."

"What a beautiful imagination you have, Gabriel," Emily said, rather cuttingly. "If all that were true, then why should he have come to dinner tonight?"

"Free food?"

"Not everyone," Emily said, "is like *you*."

"Look, how should I know why a scoundrel like that does anything? Maybe he thought it would look too suspicious to slope off directly his friends arrived. I expect he'll fake his death—suicide just before the wedding, probably, so everyone thinks he couldn't go through with it and doesn't ask any more questions—and never be heard of again."

"Thank you," Emily said, in slightly clipped tones, "for making the prospect of marrying me sound so very enticing."

"You needn't take it personally," Chase said, looking very surprised. "Criminals are bound to do horrid things. Sometimes you think somebody—you know, a terrier or something—really cares for you, but then it turns out she only means to lock your friend in a pantry and take you hostage to the Inner Hebrides—"

"What on earth are you talking about?"

"It was only an example. A story I heard once. *Anyway*—" He broke off abruptly. An ominous, heavy tread had become audible from the hallway. Chase sprang across the room to open the door, with an expression of sudden jubilance. "Ah, here's Barks at last!"

"I don't want him," Emily said.

64

"He came looking for me!" Chase said defensively. "I can't very well send him back down to fend for himself amongst strangers."

"Do you think that creature cares who you leave him with? He is perfectly happy so long as he has furniture to chew on."

"He is not *that creature*; he is my esteemed colleague and personal friend—"

"Miss Chase," Edgar interjected, as Constable Barks propelled himself across the room and burrowed joyfully under the bed, "you said that Mr. Herder had not seen Mr. Tenterfield or Mr. Mongrel in years?"

"I can see perfectly well that you are trying to distract me," Emily said, "but I don't suppose it much matters now if he chews up my trousseau. Have it your own way, Gabriel. Anyway, it is just as you say, Mr. Beagle—they had not seen each other since they were puppies. Mr. Tenterfield said he was surprised at how much James had changed."

"And when Mr. Herder was telling you about growing up in Australia—did he mention his friends often?"

"I believe he spoke of Mr. Tenterfield a few times—not by name, perhaps, but he certainly said there was a terrier he had often played with. I do not recall him mentioning Mr. Mongrel. Really, Mr. Mongrel seems a very odd friend for James and Mr. Tenterfield to have had! But James has such a beautiful, selfless nature, I suppose he must have taken on Mr. Mongrel as a sort of pet, or charity case. Like you with that wretched Airedale, Gabriel."

"Constable Barks is not a charity case!" Chase cried, bouncing indignantly out of his seat. "He is an invaluable member of the Metropolitan Police Force."

Constable Barks popped his head out from under the foot

of the bed, and enthusiastically sniffed in the direction of the washstand. "Woof," he said.

"Since you brought him here," Emily said, "he has drooled all over my shoes and tried to swallow three of my hair-ribbons."

"Well, you oughtn't to leave your things lying about."

"Oh, I like that! You never tidied your bedroom a day in your life. Socks all over the floor. I don't believe you know what a chest of drawers is for. I suppose you are just the same in your fancy rooms in London—isn't he, Mr. Beagle?"

"I am a dog of action and resolve," Chase said, scowling, "and I am habitually engrossed in important police affairs. Why should I waste my life fiddling with socks and handkerchiefs and things, when there are worthier activities to occupy me?"

"Like what—going to the pub and following squirrels around?"

"That is *not* all I do. Mr. Beagle, tell her that isn't all I do."

"This concludes tonight's interview, Miss Chase," Edgar said, reaching for Chase and forcibly tugging him towards the door. "I shall call on Mr. Herder tomorrow, and endeavor to glean some information which may elucidate his erratic behavior."

"Anyway," Chase persisted at the top of his voice, just as if Edgar had not said anything, "at least *I* don't stand around thinking about cows and looking evil."

"Well, at least James doesn't say odd things about squirrels and then run off," Emily retorted.

"What's that got to do with—"

"You have been exactly no help at all; you have been abominably rude to James ever since you met him. I suppose now he and his friends think my family is mad."

"Oh, because *he's* such an expert conversationalist?"

"Come along, Inspector," Edgar said, very firmly, maneuvering Chase out into the hallway. "Goodnight, Miss Chase."

"And take your Airedale with you!" Emily called after them. "He'll knock the washstand over in a minute. Stop eating soap, Constable, and off you go." There was a series of loud barks, and then Constable Barks erupted out of the bedroom as if shot from a cannon.

"There's gratitude for you," Chase exclaimed bitterly, as soon as Emily's door was closed. "Three times in twenty-four hours I made that railway journey, Mr. Beagle, and I assure you, it was not for my health or recreation. I was doing all that I could to help her."

"We would get along faster if you did not continually interrupt her and insult her fiancé," Edgar said, a trifle severely. "It was very difficult for me to get any information."

"Never mind lecturing me," Chase snapped. "We got all the information we need. Obviously, her precious Mr. Herder is an impostor."

Edgar blinked a few times. "I beg your pardon?"

"You heard her! You remember, he did not want his picture in the papers—and now we learn that his friends had not seen him since puppyhood, and found him much changed—*much changed*, Mr. Beagle! Because he was not the same dog they had known! And he hadn't the least idea who they were. He had never spoken of them to her, because he did not know they existed. Anyone can claim to have played with a terrier. Terriers are quite common."

"Woof," said Constable Barks, reproachfully.

"It is perfectly natural that a gentleman should not weary his lady friend with the names of his puppyhood playmates," Edgar said. "And dogs often change very much when they become adults. Had I had friends as a puppy, I daresay I should not recognize them now."

"And that," Chase concluded triumphantly, as if Edgar had not spoken, "is why he is so stiff in his manner around them. He is afraid to speak, lest he reveal some detail which will lead them to realize he is not really Mr. Herder at all."

"Surely a better strategy, if he were an impostor," Edgar commented, "would be for him to appear natural and sociable, not to behave in a way which is sure to arouse remark."

"Well, he is not intelligent. He has spent his life looking at cows."

"Australia is quite civilized nowadays; it is not merely a wilderness of cows. Besides, Inspector, one might point out that you have devoted the better part of your life to fixating on squirrels."

"Woof," said Constable Barks.

"Well, squirrels are *interesting*. They scamper about. Cows only stand there looking at you and chewing. Not unlike Mr. Herder. Or, should I say"—here he paused and made a dramatic flourish with his paw—"the *pretended* Mr. Herder?"

"You should say no such thing," Edgar said. "Pray be sensible, Inspector. What possible motive could an impostor have in passing himself off as Mr. Herder? It is not as if he were angling for a wealthy society bride."

"I resent that remark very much. My sister is as worthy a gentleman's love as any fine lady in the world. Anyway, it needn't have anything to do with the wedding. Perhaps he heartlessly and nefariously killed the real Mr. Herder for his money, and took his place. One cattle dog looks much like another, you know."

"If he were the type of criminal mastermind you are describing," Edgar said wearily, "he would not fall to pieces upon the arrival of some harmless old friends of his victim's. This is all perfectly ridiculous, Inspector. You must stop reading so many stories about crime in the Strand."

"This is *not* all in my head. He is behaving very oddly. You heard Emily—and you saw him yourself. You may not know this, but it is not normal to go all evening without saying a word or looking anybody in the eye."

"I am quite aware of that," Edgar said, the barest touch of irritation suffusing his voice. "I am not disputing that Mr. Herder's demeanor is unusual, and I am quite prepared to believe Miss Chase's statement that he has undergone an abrupt transformation. It does not, however, follow that he is a criminal. More probably, he is preoccupied with some private and entirely lawful concern which does not warrant police interference. I will, as I said, call upon him tomorrow, but I am not optimistic about the outcome; he has no particular reason to confide in me, and I can scarcely hope to extract a criminal confession when there is nothing to indicate that any crime has been committed."

"He hangs around with Mr. Mongrel. That's awfully suspicious, isn't it?"

"Gentlemen occasionally form personal connections which are utterly mystifying to onlookers. Rather like yourself and Constable Barks. It is out of the ordinary, but it is not necessarily evidence of anything sinister."

"Can you believe," Chase demanded, his attention diverted, "that Emily called Barks a charity case? Why, he is worth more than half of Scotland Yard combined."

"While I appreciate that your inexplicable affection for Constable Barks may have temporarily compromised your mathematical skills—"

"Well, he is worth twenty of Jowls, at least. Why would anyone value a dreadful slobbery bloodhound when they could have a nice faithful Airedale instead?"

"You know I have no great love for Assistant Commissioner Jowls, but if one were to juxtapose his accomplishments over the course of his career with those of Constable Barks—"

"Nonsense! Don't you remember how Barks saved us from Miss La Chatte? We should be dead if not for his timely intervention." He reached down and patted Constable Barks fondly.

"A fortuitous coincidence, Inspector, derived from a mania with squirrels—"

"Woof!" said Constable Barks.

"—which I suspect to have sprung up in his mind purely through your influence, and which no one could have predicted would have been of any use—"

"You are down on the fellow, that's all," Chase said stoutly. "You always have been."

"I believe it is the duty of the employees of the Metropolitan Police to right injustices wherever they may find them, not to chew on the furniture—"

"You have some silly prejudice against terriers, no doubt."

"I grant I may have a prejudice against terriers who systematically destroy my clothing—"

"Well, perhaps if your clothing wasn't twenty years behind the times and practically crying out to be destroyed—"

"Really, my dear Inspector—"

"I'm sure I don't know why you won't buy something modern and cheerful with one of the new dyes. It is 1877, you know. There is no call to dress like an undertaker. Gentlemen's clothing will brighten up any day now; wouldn't you like to jump ahead of the trend? You could be the first one to get a lovely magenta waistcoat."

"I can assure you that I do not want a magenta waistcoat, lovely or otherwise, and I am afraid you are rather wandering from the point."

"Christmas is just around the corner—"

"Christmas is six months and seventeen days away—"

"—and I am sure I could find you a bargain in Petticoat Lane—"

"*Middlesex Street*, if you please—and how many times must I tell you not to go gadding about Whitechapel? Besides, I implore you to abstain from giving me a magenta waistcoat, either for Christmas or at any other time."

"Well, not magenta, then. But perhaps a very bright blue."

"Just because we have new dyes, Inspector, does not mean they need to be indiscriminately splattered onto every surface."

"That would be something, though, wouldn't it? Colors everywhere! The office looks so dull—all the constables in their uniforms, and everyone else wearing dreary black and gray too, even though they needn't. It's hardly *my* fault that I always fall asleep at my desk. Imagine the sensation if I went in there next week dressed all in exciting bright blues and purples and reds! Old Jowls would just about faint from envy. And then perhaps we might have him for a doorstop, and he could finally be some use."

Edgar could get no more sensible conversation out of him for the remainder of the evening.

Chapter Five

Edgar slept in what Mrs. Chase had assured him was a spare room, overlooking the garden. It in fact appeared to be a sort of repository for unwanted furniture; he supposed half the contents of the family's previous home had been wedged protestingly into it upon arrival in the new, already-furnished piermaster's house. There was a chest of drawers blocking most of the window, and he found himself obliged to edge sideways around a hulking grandfather clock and a large, rather battered credenza in order to get to the washstand. The bed, when he got into it, creaked rather ominously. The pillows were lumpy and uninviting, and the counterpane smelled distastefully musty. Despite all this, he slipped into sleep with unexpected alacrity.

He dreamed that he was sitting at a desk in a long, high-ceilinged room, wood-paneled and dim and cluttered with disorderly stacks of books. It could have been the library at a manor house somewhere, if the whole building had been picked up and vigorously shaken. Through the window, the rushing, roiling darkness might have been deep water. He was a very small puppy; his back paws did not reach the floor. On the desk in front of him, an immense, crackling-paged book lay open. He was meant to be doing his lessons, before he went away to school in the fall, but he could not even remember how to begin, and everything trembled and blurred before his eyes. He squinted hopefully at the letters on the page, turning his head this way and that, but it was no use; they were a mass of liquid squiggles, and they would not resolve themselves into any semblance of meaning. He thought he had been able to read; he remembered having been able to read! His new schoolmasters would think he was altogether useless. The scene around him melted and shifted like watercolor. He was in a schoolroom, now—not his old schoolroom from Merchant Taylors, but a big echoing box like his father's courtroom. It was very dark, and he was all alone. He had the prickling, nauseating sensation that, just out of his field of vision, something terribly important was happening, but when he tried to turn and look, he found that he had no command of his body; his head was rooted to the frozen pillar of his neck, and his gaze was ineluctably pinioned straight ahead, where the window stood open. Outside, it was daytime, and he could hear the schoolmasters passing to and fro. Such a disappointment, they were saying behind their paws, that the brilliant, sober-minded Justice Beagle had produced this foolish, floppy-eared little whelp! No good at playing fetch, or at making friends. Stiff and timid and dull, standing frozen in the corner while the other boys shouted and chattered, avoiding everyone's gaze, regarding the world with an immobile, un-puppyish expression. An obedient, non-disruptive boy—that was all that could be said of him. There had been, of course, rumors about *that* unfortunate situation, which would have made any puppy rather odd. One would be inclined to pity him, if only he were more likable. One would be inclined, even, to forgive him all his peculiarities, if only he were at least clever! Brilliant dogs could be allowed their idiosyncrasies. But, as it was—well, as it was, no wonder that even his—

Edgar woke, very suddenly, and without the least idea of what time it was. His heart was beating very hard. He glanced over at the grandfather clock, although he was dubious that it was in working order, but, in the thin, milky wash of moonlight that trickled through the curtains, he could not make out where the hands were. He lay very still, trying to remember where he had put his pocket watch. If he were at home right now, safely cocooned in his own comfortingly orderly bedroom, it would of course be sitting neatly in the little brass dish on top of the mahogany chest, flanked by his wallet and his ivory-handled brush, all spaced perfectly evenly—but he was not at home. All around him, the assorted items of furniture shaped themselves into a hostile, mountainous landscape, as if they resented their exile. His pocket watch was probably on top of his clothes, which were neatly folded on the chair by the door—unless, of course, it was still in his pocket—or hanging by its chain from the bedpost— or in the drawer in the rickety little table next to the bed. How vexing to be unable to remember—and how vexing to be awake, at whatever disreputable hour this might be, when he needed his wits about him for the coming day! He felt a stab of irritation towards his own body. Sensible, respectable adult dogs were meant to sleep through the night. His brain must be thoroughly awash in Chase's lurid imaginings; he must be fretting, without even knowing it, over the supposed villainy of Mr. Herder. How intolerably ridiculous that Chase's nonsensical perturbations should dictate Edgar's sleep! Or perhaps something had happened to wake him—yes, on the whole, that seemed more likely. Inured as he was, however, to the constant, liminal symphony of the London streets, he doubted that some unaccustomed Liverpudlian sound had managed to break into his slumber. Indeed, the night seemed unnaturally quiet. Perhaps a noise from within the house, then; possibly Chase, slipping downstairs to raid the larder, or Constable Barks on heavy-pawed patrol through the corridors. There was certainly *something*, if he strained his ears—unless being in a house full of herding dogs was proving contagious, and he was letting his own flights of fancy overwhelm him! He had been having a dream, he rather thought, although he could not quite remember it. Probably something to do with Mr. Herder. Perhaps he had dreamed the sound. No, there it was again—a faint crunching noise—but surely that *was* coming from outside the house. Edgar rose from the bed, his borrowed nightshirt tangling uncomfortably around his legs, and maneuvered himself around the furniture and to the window with some difficulty. He pulled the curtain aside. It was a cloudy, dismal night. As he peered into the darkness, trying to resolve all the unfamiliar silhouettes into fenceposts and shrubs, the noise drifted up to him again. There must be something directly under his window, although he had no reason to think it was not merely some specimen of the local wildlife.

Then, past all mistaking, a mass of shadows hurtled towards the house. There were more crunching noises, and then a long, low growl, and the sounds of a vicious scuffle. Edgar froze where he stood. It was probably nothing, he told himself; this was probably how the neighborhood adolescents disported themselves. He raked the room with his eyes, trying to work out how to get to his clothing with a minimum of falling over the furniture, as a plan slotted itself neatly into his half-awake brain: he would go find Chase, and possibly Chase's father, and the three of them would slip downstairs—ideally without rousing Barks, whose typical investigative methods did not lend themselves to stealth operations—and creep into the garden…and, he thought bitterly, probably find nothing more sinister than an outsize fox gnawing noisily at a late-night snack! He could practically hear Chase's triumphant barking already: "you see, Mr. Beagle? You can feel the atmosphere of evil too!" And Chase's family—what would they think of him? Was he doomed to become a byword all through Liverpool: the pampered, sheltered London gentleman, so accustomed to living on a quiet, genteel side street that visiting a working-class neighborhood automatically afflicted him with unreasoning paranoia; the unwanted and painfully out-of-place guest who had forced himself on the family's hospitality and then raised the whole house in the middle of the night for nothing?

He was being ridiculous, he told himself sternly. If there was even the slightest chance that any sort of crime was currently in progress, then he had an obvious duty to fulfill. He had set himself up as a champion of justice; if he did not take action, then who would? The opinion of Chase's family should be of absolutely no consequence to him; it would be selfish and irrational beyond all measure to let such trivial personal concerns outweigh his principles and responsibilities. And, even though he could still see nothing under the window, he was *not* imagining the noises—he was sure he was not. Indeed, they were growing louder: violent thudding and crashing, punctuated by that low, sinister growl again, and then by a

76

single, high-pitched yelp. There was no time to get dressed. Edgar caught up his shoes and hurried to the door, colliding painfully with the furniture as he went, and slipped out into the impenetrable darkness of the hallway. He had no idea where Chase's bedroom might be. He closed his eyes and stood very still, letting the house build itself up in his mind, brick by brick and room by room: Emily's bedroom had overlooked the east side of the house, and there had been two other doors beside it, and two, he thought, across from it—

Edgar's eyes flew open. There had been another noise— not outside, but close at paw, practically on top of him. For the barest of seconds, his heart juddered under his borrowed nightshirt, and lurid visions flashed across his mind: armed burglars, perhaps, or ragged-clawed alley cats, or some homicidal mongrel with a knife; who knew what stalked the streets of Liverpool by night? But it was only Chase, emerging from a room just around the corner. He was clutching a guttering candle that illuminated the front of his exuberantly colorful dressing gown and cast jagged, disquieting fragments of shadow all along the wall.

"Inspector Chase!" Edgar breathed, edging towards him. "You heard it too?"

Chase started so violently that he nearly dropped the candle. "Mr. Beagle!" he exclaimed, rather too loudly for the hour. "What in the world are you doing out of bed? It is nearly half past three; it is a time for sleeping, not for roaming about."

"*You* are out of bed," Edgar pointed out.

"I am going to the pantry to hunt up the rest of the cake from last night, obviously. But I thought you never got up in the night. Doesn't Dr. Snuffles or anyone tell you to sleep straight through till morning?"

77

"Actually, in Dr. Snuffles' monograph on biphasic sleep, he hypothesizes that there may be some benefits—"

"I say, do you fancy some cake? There's plenty to go round."

"I require your assistance, Inspector Chase."

"Getting at the cake, you mean? Well, come along, then. This candle won't last forever."

"No, no—something else. Come outside with me. I do not wish to alarm you, but I am afraid I heard quite a vicious struggle under my window just now."

Chase cast him a look of mild exasperation. "Probably a couple of local boys roughhousing in the street," he said. "I realize *you* may not be accustomed to such goings-on, but—"

"You don't understand. There was yelping. Someone may be injured."

"Well, some of these youngsters have flick-knives," Chase said, rather carelessly. "You are not in Duke of York Street anymore, Mr. Beagle."

"Don't you think there's the slightest chance this is worth investigating? You are a police dog, you know."

"I am on holiday."

"Inspector Chase," Edgar said, more severely than he had intended, "if some dog or cat is currently bleeding to death in your parents' garden, do you really think that being *on holiday* gives you license to turn a blind eye?"

Chase gave a gusty sigh, perilously close to the candle. "Must you be so dramatic, Mr. Beagle?"

"*I,* dramatic? May I remind you, Inspector Chase—"

"Oh, now what? I was right! You can see perfectly well that something is wrong here."

"A lovers' quarrel, however mysterious in origin, does not qualify as an atmosphere of evil, Inspector. In any event, given that I accompanied you all the way to Liverpool despite firmly believing the whole thing to be a mare's nest, I think I am not unreasonable in requesting that you merely step out of doors with me for a moment—"

"Alright, alright!" Chase said, sounding very put out. "But then you must come down to the kitchen and have cake with me afterwards. Fair is fair."

The two dogs descended through the murky shadows of the back staircase. Outside, a chilly breeze ruffled the trees. Chase shielded his candle with his paw, and shivered over-dramatically. The garden seemed smaller than it had the night before. Without the table in the way, Edgar could see that there was a row of flowerbeds nestled against the back of the house, and a little gravel path—which, he supposed, explained all the crunching noises—wrapping around the other three sides of the garden. There was certainly no feckless stranger bleeding to death in the dim starlight. There was, in fact, absolutely nothing out of the ordinary, aside from the trampled remains of some party decorations, a few overturned chairs that had not been put away, and the ragged-edged hole that Ollie Muddypaws had dug. Edgar braced himself for Chase's scorn. He had made quite the fool of himself, he thought bitterly. Firing himself up with melodramatic visions—preparing to raise the whole house in the name of duty! The whole thing was too absurd. "Inspector Chase," he began, rather shyly, "I am afraid I owe you an apology—"

"Look, these must be Dad's evening primroses," Chase said, plainly not listening. He had wandered down to the far end of the garden and was peering at one of the flowerbeds. "It's a wonder Joseph hasn't tried to eat them. Oh—I say!" He stooped suddenly. "Come over here, will you?"

Edgar hurried to his side. In the flickering light from Chase's candle, he could just make out a surprisingly tidy heap of small rocks. Several of them were slightly jagged. Beside them, the front half of a shoe print was nestled into the soft flowerbed, pointing towards the house.

"You were right, as usual, Mr. Beagle," Chase said, in hushed, awestruck tones. "There *was* somebody here. I beg your pardon for having doubted you."

Edgar bent and examined the print. It yielded irritatingly little information; evidently, the shoe's wearer had paws of average size, and was not partial to any outré fashions involving toe shape.

"Who was it, Mr. Beagle?" Chase demanded.

"An unknown gentleman," Edgar said, straightening up. "Or perhaps an unknown lady, although I deem that less probable."

"But who?" Chase pressed.

"I am afraid, Inspector, that I am neither a seer nor a magician; I cannot reconstruct an entire dog or cat from half a shoe."

"They always do in stories."

"If we were in a story," Edgar said, smiling slightly, "then our mystery intruder would have worn shoes of a shape unique to a single shoemaker in Torquay, and sold exclusively to circus performers. Real life is seldom so obliging. All I can tell you, Inspector, is that we may have a very suspicious circumstance, involving someone who ought not to have been here, and that I shall have to collect some more data before I can form a theory."

"*May* have a suspicious circumstance? What else do you call someone jumping around in the flowerbeds at half past three?"

"There was, after all, a party here last night. It is perhaps somewhat improbable, but by no means inconceivable, that one of the guests should have stepped here while attempting to pull out a chair."

"Nonsense," Chase said. "That would be two prints, pointing the other way; nobody pulls out a chair by turning their back to it and standing on one foot. My parents' neighbors are shopkeepers and shipwrights and things, not acrobats. Besides, that doesn't explain all those rocks. You were right the first time; someone was here just now. I'll bet it was Herder."

"What business do you envision Mr. Herder having had in your back garden in the dead of night?"

"Maybe he wanted to dognap Emily," Chase said, scowling. "No, no—listen! He could see that she was reconsidering getting married to him, so he brought along a ladder and a bottle of chloroform, and meant to pull her right out her window."

"Her window does not overlook the garden; her bedroom is at the side of the house, not the back."

"Well, Herder might not know that."

"Surely he has been shown all over the house."

"He is not clever. Maybe he forgot. Or maybe he fancied that the rooms at the back would be empty, and he meant to creep all through the sleeping house until he reached her—"

"You forget that, of late, Mr. Herder has not evinced even the expected level of enthusiasm over marrying Miss Chase, let alone a criminal level of desperation to do so. Besides, if he wishes the wedding to proceed, then it seems like rather less effort to come round in the morning and apologize for his erratic behavior."

"He is *evil*," Chase said, prodding moodily at the flowerbed with the toe of his slipper. "Perhaps he likes to do things in perverse ways."

"Or perhaps," Edgar said, "he has been blamelessly in his bed at the Adelphi all night, and this print was made by someone else."

"Don't be silly, Mr. Beagle. Who else could it possibly have been?"

"The possibility of criminals does suggest itself."

"Just because we are in Liverpool—"

"No, Inspector Chase," Edgar said, his voice betraying the faintest hint of exasperation. "Regarding late-night trespassers with suspicion is not location-specific."

"I still say it was Herder," Chase said sulkily.

"You forget that there was more than one intruder. I told you, I heard a struggle."

Chase muttered something in which the words "probably your imagination" were just discernible.

"I assure you, Inspector," Edgar said, more hotly than he had intended, "that I am not plagued with violent auditory hallucinations."

"Well, you wouldn't know if you were, would you?"

"In any event," Edgar said, ignoring this, "I shall investigate further tomorrow. I will need to amass more data."

"And in the meantime," Chase said, with sudden jubilation, "it is finally time for cake. Come along."

* * *

"Fools, the pair of you," Chase's mother said over breakfast, in between tutting over a long, ragged scratch on the dining room table.

"Are not," Chase said blearily. He was still wearing his dressing gown. Several cake crumbs clung to the sleeves.

"That you are. Housebreakers! I never heard of such goings-on, in our little corner of the world. 'Tis perfectly plain what has happened."

She flung back her head irritably, turned away, and paused, apparently for dramatic effect. In the sudden silence, Edgar tapped Chase on the arm and pointed out the cake crumbs. "Yes, Mrs. Chase?" he prompted.

"'Twas Tommy Muddypaws, of course, making one last push to win her. He saw how unhappy she was at the party last night, so he came dashing right over—holding a nice big bunch of flowers, I shouldn't wonder. Gabriel, why in the world are you licking your sleeves?"

"If it was Tommy Muddypaws," Chase said, scowling and folding his arms, "then he was looking for more things to nick, not visiting Emily."

"How do you account for the second intruder?" Edgar asked.

"Ah, that will have been Mr. Herder himself, come to make poor Tommy clear out."

"Or else the local constable," Chase said, "finally taking Tommy where he belongs. Mum, didn't you *notice* that the silver ladle went missing last night?"

"'Tis not against the law to court a girl," Mrs. Chase said placidly, "and, ten to one, your brother has buried the ladle in the garden again. 'Twas Mr. Herder, I tell you."

"I can scarcely envision Mr. Herder laying violent paws upon a rival suitor," Edgar said, furrowing his brow.

"Love makes us all do funny things. I married Angus, didn't I? And him only a dockpaw, back then."

"Moreover," Edgar persisted, "how would Mr. Herder have

known that Mr. Muddypaws was here?"

"Never you mind," Mrs. Chase said, suddenly irritable. "These rich gentlemen have their ways. Having poor Tommy followed night and day, I'll warrant."

"Although I can by no means be certain," Edgar said, "I rather think that the second dog was somewhat larger than Mr. Herder."

"Well, gentlemen look bigger when their hackles are raised."

"I don't know what you are talking about," Emily said, stepping unexpectedly into the room, "but the idea of James getting into a fight is perfectly ridiculous. He utterly deplores violence at any price."

"Good morning, Miss Chase!" Edgar said, rising from the table at once.

"I am afraid it is not a good morning," Emily said. She looked very small and wan in her pink morning dress. From her hollow eyes and drooping ears, it was altogether possible that she had sat up all night. "I am meant to be married in forty-eight hours, you see, and I have not the least idea of what to do. But, for the sake of social niceties, good morning to you too, Mr. Beagle. I hope you slept well."

"Will you look at this!" Mrs. Chase interjected, forcibly drawing Emily's attention to the scratch on the table. "Right where that Mr. Mongrel was sitting! I think the creature never pares his claws. A surprising sort of friend for your fine Mr. Herder to have, Emily!"

"Many things about Mr. Herder have been surprising lately," Emily said, expressionlessly. Mrs. Chase, rubbing at the claw mark with her sleeve, gave a loud sniff, but made no other reply.

"Perhaps," Edgar said to Chase, by way of breaking the

uncomfortable silence that had settled over the table, "you will accompany me today, Inspector, as I continue to gather data."

To Edgar's vast surprise, Chase shook his head. "I'm afraid I must run an important errand," he said, rather grandly.

"You don't mean to go pestering Nora Roughcoat again, do you?" Mrs. Chase broke in, glowering.

"What? No!" Chase said hotly. "I haven't thought of Nora Roughcoat in years."

"Well, all I know is, you were dead gone on her—"

"When I was *seventeen*, Mum!"

"—always sneaking off to go and howl under her window—"

"I never did! Anyway, that was ages ago."

"Has he got a girl in London?" Mrs. Chase demanded of Edgar.

"It is hardly seemly, madam, for me to disclose Inspector Chase's personal affairs."

"That means lots of girls," Mrs. Chase said with grim satisfaction, "or else none at all."

"That doesn't mean I've been pining after Nora!" Chase said at the top of his voice.

Emily took the opportunity to lean closer to Edgar. "What were you talking about when I came in?" she asked him in an undertone.

Edgar briefly recounted the night's events.

"James, sneak about in the back garden to see me?" Emily repeated wonderingly. "If he wanted to talk to me, goodness knows he could have done it yesterday."

"Perhaps your mother's hypothesis, then: that Mr. Muddypaws—"

Emily hastily muffled her laughter, with a sidelong look at

Mrs. Chase. "I know—she thinks Tommy is still stuck on me, after all these years. I assure you, I am not one of those fascinating creatures who inspire lifelong devotion in every spurned suitor. And there was never anything in it anyway."

"Your brother, meanwhile," Edgar said cautiously, "theorized that Mr. Muddypaws might have entered the premises for less innocent and more acquisitive reasons."

"What, to burgle the house, you mean? Of course he didn't."

"You are not, then, in accordance with Inspector Chase's assessment of Mr. Muddypaws' character?"

"Oh, Tommy is a thief, alright," Emily said, very calmly. "That's why I broke it off with him; I found out that all the pretty flowers he brought me had been dug up from his neighbor's garden. But I shouldn't think he was making a career out of it. There's a long way between nicking silver spoons at parties, and housebreaking in the dead of night. Besides, he lives two streets away; he could come and burgle us any time he liked. Why should he do it on the one night when two police dogs and a private investigator are in the house?"

"I entirely take your point, Miss Chase. However, I have very little data upon which to base even the most preliminary of conjectures. Only two dogs have been advanced to my attention as possible suspects: Mr. Herder and Mr. Muddypaws. It is, I realize, entirely possible, and eminently likely, that the true culprit is a third, as-yet-unknown individual. However, if only for the sake of adhering to proper methodology, I deem it most prudent to begin by definitively ruling out—"

"Come on, Mr. Beagle," Chase said, very suddenly and very loudly, jumping up and grabbing Edgar by the arm. His hackles were raised very slightly, and his ears were even more disheveled than usual. "I must get dressed and then go and attend to *important police matters*."

* * *

The morning air was heavy with the smell of the river, and the sky was a bright, uniform white. Chase scowled and glowered by Edgar's side, and occasionally directed half-hearted kicks at pebbles in the road. Edgar gave him a suitable interval—precisely three minutes—to compose himself, and, once this had proved futile, ventured to speak.

"Before I call on Mr. Herder," he said, "I should like to spend some time with Mr. Muddypaws."

"What, on purpose?" Chase asked, without looking up. "Well, better mind your shiny pocket watch, is all I can say. I expect he'll take you in too, and then you and my mother can form the Tommy Muddypaws Appreciation Society."

"I am not in the habit of appreciating thieves, Inspector Chase. I merely wish to ask him about his movements last night. Will you do me the favor of accompanying me?"

To Edgar's surprise, Chase shook his head. "I *said*, I have police matters to attend to," he informed Edgar, a trifle snappishly.

"I heard you, Inspector, but I rather supposed—"

"You supposed what? That I couldn't possibly have any? Well, everyone else around here seems to have forgotten that I am Detective Chief Inspector at the Metropolitan Police, so I suppose it was only a matter of time before you did too."

"You mistake me entirely—"

"Anyway, you could talk circles round Tommy with your eyes closed and one paw tied behind your back, don't you worry. You don't need me there. The house is two streets east; you'll know it by all the holes in the garden next door. I'll see later, Mr. Beagle. You wait and see—I've had a clever idea."

And, with a sudden grin, he turned and strode briskly away.

Chapter Six

As Edgar approached the Muddypaws' house, a volley of protesting barks assaulted his ears. Ollie, it transpired, was keeping a ferocious lookout from the window. Edgar pointedly fixed his gaze straight ahead, strode up the front path, and rapped on the door.

"No one's home," Ollie growled from inside.

Edgar rapped again, and waited. He painstakingly turned up his collar against the wind. It occurred to him that there was a significant chance that Chase—and Emily, who was, after all, related to Chase—had been wildly wrong about Tommy. It seemed, he thought, to be rather the theme of the weekend. He had probably been coerced to Liverpool to investigate one perfectly innocent dog whom Chase happened to dislike, and he was quite possibly about to confront another one. And, once again, he reflected bitterly, there was no clearcut script for the impending interaction! He was nearly certain that there was not a Tommy Muddypaws-shaped hole in his mental library of conversational templates; no one, surely, would have known how to initiate a conversation whose précis was on the order of "I have absolutely no reason to suspect you, apart from the fantastical theorizing of my historically unreliable associate and the word of his sister, the general accuracy of whose statements I have had no opportunity of assessing; your nocturnal activities, accordingly, are almost certainly none of my concern; and it is therefore overwhelmingly probable and entirely justifiable that my questions will, at best, utterly perplex you, and, at worst, mortally offend you; but, all the same, would you mind telling me whether you happen to have been stalking your former *inamorata*, or possibly attempting burglary, and also building an odd little cairn out of garden rocks at some uncertain hour in the obscurest watches of the night?" On balance, he thought, this was not likely to go well.

He tapped his foot against the step. Perhaps he was deliberately being made to wait. Perhaps it was for the best; perhaps he should take the opportunity to abandon all of this nonsense and go straight to the train station—or, at the very least, to go explain to Chase, in carefully enunciated words of one syllable, that there were innumerable reasons why he ought not to have been dragged into any of this in the first place.

But then, there were footsteps, stumping towards the door with no great air of alacrity. The door swung slowly open, revealing not a servant, to whom Edgar would have known what to say, but rather the wobbling, slobbering bulk of Tommy Muddypaws himself.

"It's too early for a visit," he informed Edgar.

"I apologize for the unusual hour," Edgar said, "but, you see, this is a professional visit, and therefore not bound by the same temporal conventions that would typically dictate the circumstances of a social call."

"And what profession would that be?" Tommy inquired, with a smirk playing around his mouth. "You sound like you make your living swallowing dictionaries. Not selling anything, are you?"

"Certainly not!" Edgar said, drawing himself up. He was fleetingly, self-consciously aware of the contrast between his own slight build and Tommy's robust physique. "I am a private investigator. As you may recall, we met last night."

"Oh, *right*—you're Gabriel's little friend, aren't you? From all those silly letters. Mr. Bayer or Mr. Floppy-ears or something."

"Mr. Beagle."

"Well, what are you doing here, Mr. Beagle? If it's about my brother, then you needn't bother. He isn't a criminal; he only barks and digs a lot."

Edgar took a deep breath. He was intensely, viscerally aware of Tommy's cold, deep-set eyes, fixed steadily on his face. "Might I come in?" he ventured. "I have matters of a complicated and not readily categorizable nature to discuss."

Tommy looked very amused. "Alright," he said. "If you're determined to be a bore, you might as well do it indoors."

Edgar followed him into a cramped, low-ceilinged passageway, and thence into a rather dismal sitting room. Once Tommy had spent a few moments neglecting—pointedly, he rather thought—to offer him a seat, he settled himself onto a lumpy settee.

"Well then," Tommy said, perching himself on the edge of the table opposite and favoring Edgar with a mocking little smile. "What do you want?"

Edgar cleared his throat. "It may surprise you to learn," he said expressionlessly, "that there was a disturbance at the Chases' home last night, after the party."

"Emily invited a gentleman friend over at some scandalous hour, you mean? No, that doesn't surprise me in the slightest."

"Certainly not!" Edgar said, suddenly and unhappily aware that this particular hypothesis had not even crossed his mind.

"Are you sure, Mr. Beagle? I guess you haven't much experience with girls. They're awfully sly."

"I should have spoken more precisely," Edgar said, lifting his chin and looking Tommy directly in the eye. "I have reason to suspect that there was an attempted burglary last night. I thought perhaps you might know something about it."

Tommy merely laughed a little. "I see you've swallowed Gabriel's tall tales about me. I promise you, I am decidedly *not* a burglar. Gabriel doesn't like me, Mr. Beagle—it's as plain as that. He's been spreading insulting rumors since the moment I started walking out with Emily."

"Ah yes, you were once a friend of Miss Chase's! Perhaps," Edgar said lightly, "you still have a lingering fondness for her."

Tommy's expression darkened at once. "Why should I? She's a very ordinary sort of girl, for all she gives herself airs."

"Oh, I meant no offense, Mr. Muddypaws; the young lady is very charming, and I only wondered—"

"Well, you needn't wonder anymore. I'll tell you quite plainly, I don't care two pins for her. I could get twenty better girls any day of the week."

"By giving them flowers, perhaps?" Edgar inquired delicately.

Tommy's hostile, stolid gaze barely flickered. "Well, why not? Girls like flowers. Are you here just to talk about girls, Mr. Beagle? It's not that I mind giving advice to fellows who need it, but I do have some things to be getting on with."

"You mistake me, sir," Edgar said, with his most level gaze. "What I would actually like to know is this: where were you last night?"

He scrutinized Tommy's drooping face for any sign of chagrin, but Tommy merely snorted. "Well, I'll tell you this much: I wasn't loitering around the Chases' house. I was keeping company with a pretty friend of mine—and," he said, holding up a paw when Edgar's ears twitched—"you needn't ask me about her, either. I know better, I hope, than to bandy a girl's name about."

"How very convenient."

"Is it so unbelievable that I should know some girls, or that I should know when to keep my mouth shut about them? I'm a decent fellow, really, Mr. Beagle. You've got no reason to suspect me, besides Gabriel's say-so. I hope you haven't gone making up to Emily; the minute he begins to suspect that you don't mean to love her for all eternity, he'll decide *you* belong in prison too." He smiled engagingly. "Look, I've already told you, I'm not a burglar. After the party, I went and visited my friend. There's nothing for you to concern yourself with."

"After calling on your friend, did you come home?" Edgar asked.

Tommy looked very surprised. "Well, I certainly didn't dig a burrow like a fox."

"I shall take that as a yes. What time did you return?"

"Round about ten or eleven, I should think. I'm afraid I didn't write it down; I didn't know you were planning to interrogate me."

"And did you go out again afterwards?" Edgar persisted.

"No, of course not. I went to sleep. Next you'll want to know what color my dressing gown is."

"Can anyone corroborate that?"

"No; everyone else went to sleep too. It was nighttime. I don't know what you expect me to say."

"There is, once again, no need to take offense, Mr. Muddy-paws. I want only to establish a coherent timeline that can help me elucidate the incident—"

"Are you the police?" Tommy interrupted.

"No; as I mentioned earlier, I am a private investigator. I often consult with the police in an unofficial capacity, but—"

"In that case," Tommy said, "it doesn't really matter what you want, does it? Good day, Mr. Beagle."

And, flashing Edgar a sudden, slobber-laden smile, he waddled straight out of the room.

Edgar waited for a few moments, on the off-chance that Tommy might decide to return and grace him with any further communications, and then decided it was time to show himself out. In the front hall, he found his path blocked by the hulking, intensely brachycephalic form of Mr. Ollie Muddypaws, glowering at him and snuffling menacingly.

"Who are *you*?" Ollie demanded.

"Good morning, sir!" Edgar said, very brightly. "We met at the Chases' supper party last night. My name is Mr. Beagle."

Ollie snorted up at him. "What do you want here? I don't like strangers in my house."

"I had rather inferred that," Edgar said, "from the remarkable clamor with which you heralded my arrival earlier. I am very sorry to have caused you distress."

"Get out, then."

"Presently, I assure you. But first, I should like to offer you an opportunity to range yourself on the side of truth and justice, and promote the rule of law."

Ollie squinted at him, drooling slightly. "See here," he said, "you can't fool me. Gabriel Chase brought you here, didn't he? I know what you are: you're a *spy*."

"I beg your pardon?"

"Well, you hang about with the police, but you aren't a police dog yourself. The police wouldn't hire anyone like *you*." He eyed his own stocky, muscled limbs with some satisfaction.

"I give you my word, sir, that I am not a spy."

"That's what all spies say. Are you here to spy on Tommy?"

"Your brother," Edgar said, smiling very slightly, "wondered whether I might be here to investigate *you*."

"I haven't bitten any neighbors in *years*," Ollie said, his furrowed face turning sulky at once. "Well, months, anyway. And drooling on other folks' lawns is *not* against the law, if you do it over the fence; I asked a constable. So you needn't go spying on *me*."

"I am sure you are utterly blameless in every regard," Edgar said courteously.

"And you'll never pin anything on Tommy," Ollie continued, adopting a wide, truculent stance and squaring his blocky shoulders. "You can try, but nobody will believe you. Everyone thinks Tommy's *perfect*."

"How wonderful that your brother is so highly regarded among his neighbors," Edgar said, with a pleasant smile. "He must, I suppose, have many friends."

"That's right. Everyone likes Tommy. Except for Gabriel Chase, but he doesn't count."

"As a matter of fact," Edgar persevered, "I understand that your brother's robust social calendar included an additional excursion after the party last night."

Ollie blinked balefully up at him. "Nothing wrong with that."

"Oh, nothing whatsoever! No doubt he was disporting himself in some harmless and entirely lawful fashion. I only wondered whether you might tell me what time he came home."

"How should I know? I was sleeping."

"In that case, might you at least happen to know where he was?"

"Of course I know *that*," Ollie said at once, glaring as if Edgar had insulted him. "Do you think I'm stupid? He always tells me where he's going. He was off with that Flossie Yapper again."

"Ah, no doubt some specially charming young lady of his acquaintance."

"No, just another one of Tommy's girls. I don't know how he gets so many girls. It's because he brings them flowers, I reckon. Maybe I should start digging up flowers too."

Edgar considered advising an alternate course of action, involving judicious modifications to Ollie's personal hygiene and style of conversation, but decided to forbear; that sort of thing, he had learned, was often received in the wrong spirit, no matter how helpfully it was intended. "Where might I be likely to find Miss Yapper?" he said instead.

"She's a chambermaid at that big hotel by the station."

"The Adelphi?"

"That's the one. Where the rich folks stay. That's why he likes Flossie; she's dead useful, like all his girls. Tommy's no fool."

"I beg your pardon? *Useful?*"

"Of course. He always comes home with a load of cufflinks and earrings and things after he sees her. Last night, he got a shiny silver heart on a chain, with some fancy letters written on the back—an E and an R. And it *isn't* stealing, because she gives him the things as a present. And then he can go to the pawn shop. Tommy likes going to the pawn shop. I nicked the heart out of his pocket before he woke up today," he added happily, "so now I can go to the pawn shop too."

"How very nice for you."

"Well, I might as well get something," Ollie said, scowling. "Tommy shouldn't always get *everything* good, should he? Everybody likes Tommy. They don't like me. Everybody is *so cross* when I sneak into the garden and dig *one little hole,* but nobody minds when Tommy goes tearing up Mrs. Mouser's flowerbeds next door. Tommy's too clever. Tommy doesn't let them see. Just blames me all the time. And besides, Tommy always gets all of the girls—lady's maids and governesses and silk merchants' daughters and the girl from the jewelry counter at Lewis's Department Store—and I never get any of the girls, and—"

"I have heard," Edgar hastily interposed, before Ollie could re-enlarge upon this theme, "that your brother cared at one time for Miss Emily Chase."

"What? Oh, that was only a bit of fun. He used to laugh over how cross it made Gabriel."

"You would not say, then, that he might harbor any lingering fondness for her?

Ollie gulped and stared. "For *Emily*? No, why should he? She never gave him anything to pawn. Tommy's got no use for a selfish girl like that."

And that, Edgar thought grimly, as he buttoned up his coat and stepped out into the street, was that. So much for Mrs. Chase's wistful theorizing. Chase, for a wonder, had been absolutely right about Tommy's predilection for petty theft. What a relief it would be, Edgar thought, in an unguarded corner of his brain—what a glorious, magnificent relief—if

Chase should turn out to have been right about Mr. Herder also! Emily, no doubt, would be terribly disappointed should her fiancé turn out to be inherently evil, but she was young and possessed of symmetrical features and a figure that suited the current fashions; she would attract another beau soon enough. It was perfectly plain that the wedding was not going to proceed. Better, surely, for the problem to be a preexisting, irreparable defect in Mr. Herder's character. That seemed infinitely less distressing for Emily than the only other likely explanation: that Mr. Herder's affections had been so flimsy all along that his friends had, in the blink of an eye, dissuaded him from marrying below his station. And Chase, who had turned trusting amber eyes on Edgar and practically implored him to manifest a last-minute miracle— Chase, whose faith in Edgar had never once wavered—would at least have the satisfaction of having been right. Perhaps it would distract him from the revelation that Edgar was not in fact a master magician capable of unfreezing hearts and unraveling mysterious quarrels. Edgar would have to endure decades, of course, of Chase preening himself over his own perspicacity, but it would be well worth the minor aggravation. It was not *fair*, Edgar thought passionately, before he could stop himself, that Chase ever should have thought him capable of fixing this absurd situation! A knack for ratiocination only went so far. It was one thing to solve crimes, by methodically slotting all the little pieces together, but it did not logically follow that he should be able to miraculously divine what was happening behind Mr. Herder's dull, unhappy eyes, much less to preserve Emily's marital hopes. How ridiculous for Chase to have tumbled this whole mess into Edgar's lap, merely because Edgar had demonstrated a talent for solving an entirely different type of problem! Was Chase really such a fool as to imagine that all unexplained happenings fell conveniently into the same class? And how unjust that, even though Edgar had never once touted himself as a patcher-up of lovers' spats, Chase had made the unilateral decision to rely on him, and was sure to be horribly, melodramatically devastated—as only Chase could be!—by his inevitable failure!

Perhaps, Edgar thought, rounding the corner and setting his teeth against the wind and wrenching all emotion out of the cold, clear prism of his mind, there was really something to this business of the nighttime intruders. Perhaps a crime had been committed; perhaps there existed a situation of the type that he actually knew how to handle. Perhaps, as a matter of fact, he had very little choice but to go ahead and handle it; perhaps the one justification he could possibly offer Chase for failing to magically salvage Emily's betrothal—that of being a private investigator and nothing else—would fall rather flat if he bungled the investigation that was right under his nose!

But if Tommy Muddypaws had not been involved, then who could possibly have been prowling the Chases' garden by moonlight? Edgar set very little store by Chase's hypotheses about Mr. Herder's involvement. Even if Mr. Herder were the epitome of all evil, he could have no conceivable motive for lurking under windows like a pantomime villain. And who could the second dog have been; why should anyone care to stalk Mr. Herder through the nighttime streets? No, the thing was utterly senseless. There must be some other explanation, but, try as he might, Edgar could not force it to take shape in his imagination. On the one paw, he theorized, one of the guests from the party must be involved in some capacity. It was too much of a coincidence, surely, for there to have been a completely unrelated disturbance on the same night. On the other paw, perhaps he should rule out the guests, since they definitely knew that Chase was in the house; what fool would knowingly undertake a crime right under the cold wet nose of a high-ranking police dog? And besides—on the third paw—who among the guests could possibly have taken on the rôle of nighttime intruder anyway? The geriatric, yowling cat? The flea-ridden shopkeeper? The tippling sheepdog? They all passed through Edgar's mind in a lurid procession, outlandishly costumed in burglars' masks and dark cloaks. The whole thing was simply too ridiculous to be entertained.

Very well, Edgar conceded, folding his arms across his chest as the wind snaked chilly tendrils down his collar, perhaps this was not a burglary either. Not a burglary—and not anything to do with Tommy Muddypaws—and not anything to do with Mr. Herder. There was only one remotely plausible option remaining: perhaps someone intended violence to the Chase family. Stranger things had happened amongst groups of neighbors before. Perhaps someone was angling for Mr. Chase's job, or envious of Emily's prowess at attracting suitors, or, not altogether inconceivably, exasperated to the point of homicide by protracted exposure to Mrs. Chase's personality. The mysterious heap of jagged-edged rocks had, no doubt, been some psychopathic low-life's idea of a clever impromptu arsenal.

The trouble was, just as it would have been unwise for a burglar to have made an assay on the house while Chase was in town, it would be absolute madness for a would-be assailant or murderer to have done so. Perhaps, then, it was someone who did not know he was there. But surely, out of all the nights in the year, for the intruder to have coincidentally and

100

inadvertently chanced upon one of the pawful of nights when Chase was in the house—well, it was far too improbable to be entertained.

And, really, that left only one possibility.

Edgar fought down a sudden wave of nausea. The smell of the river, he supposed, must be affecting him more than he had realized.

A resentful puppyhood acquaintance, perhaps. A neighbor mortally offended by Chase's little outburst at dinner. A hardened criminal whose time-sensitive machinations were in danger of being derailed by Chase's presence. Or perhaps Mr. Herder himself, turning out to be evil after all. Perhaps he was on a mission to assassinate the Detective Chief Inspector of the Yard. Perhaps he had only courted Emily to get close to Chase in the first place—but *that*, Edgar told himself, was supremely ridiculous! No, someone else—some desperate dog or cat—had loitered outside the house in the dead of night, with a rock in his paw and murder in his heart, until he had been interrupted—by whom? A vigilant passer-by? A wiser associate, come to point out the idiocy of scaling the wall and bludgeoning Chase under his family's noses?

Chase had *said* he sensed an atmosphere of evil. Perhaps he had simply been wrong about its source. Perhaps, all these years, Edgar had given Chase's intuition far too little credit.

Well, Edgar thought grimly, he had come to this wretched city for Chase's sake—and for Chase's sake, he would put an end to this, or any, danger. He would hurry back to the house, and he would stick by Chase's side all day and all night, until they were safely back in London.

But Chase, he realized, with a suddenness that stopped him in his tracks, was not at the house. Chase, being Chase, had rushed off on some mysterious errand, without telling anyone where he was going. Chase was reckless and naïve and maddeningly difficult to keep out of trouble.

If anything were to have happened to Chase, whilst Edgar had been sniffing his way along a false trail—

Well, if anything were to have happened to Chase, anything at all—

Telling Chase's family—that would devolve, no doubt, on Edgar. Explaining, or failing to explain, that Chase had fallen prey to criminals, even though Edgar had been right there in the same city. Watching Mr. Chase's face crumple and his ears droop, as his view of the universe's fundamental beneficence imploded. Listening to Mrs. Chase's piercing lamentations. Desperately, fruitlessly casting about for a way to console Emily, as she wept and wept and wept over the double loss of her brother and her fiancé.

Edgar would write the elegy, of course. Chase, after all, had written one for him once. Chase was much better at that sort of thing. All the words that Edgar could marshal sounded stiff and unnatural. There was no combination of syllables that could convey Chase's foolhardy courage and careless bravado and puppyish loyalty.

And afterwards—afterwards! Days and weeks and months and years of sitting alone at his desk, writing little scientific monographs that nobody would read, missing Chase's unnecessarily exuberant step on the stair—missing, that was to say, the opportunity to advance the course of the law by helping Chase solve crimes. That would, obviously, be the primary drawback to Chase's untimely demise. Edgar folded his arms more tightly. There was absolutely nothing to be gained by being sentimental—and friendship, he had learned at an early age, was for the rest of the world, not for him. He had been to school, and seen it blossoming everywhere, while he sheltered in quiet corners with his books. Friendship was the birthright of dogs who were capable of inspiring positive sentiments in their peers. Well, he had logic and reason and a first-rate education, and most other dogs did not. It was *not* as if the world were unfair. And personal ties, after all, were merely a liability. It was really for the best that he had nothing to distract him from the straightforward pursuit of justice.

"Mr. Beagle?"

Edgar stumbled and nearly fell. The Chases' house was looming up in front of him. He was not sure at what point he had begun walking again.

"Mr. Beagle!" Emily said again, stepping directly into his path. "Are you alright? You look as if you were about to faint."

"I never faint," Edgar said. "Miss Chase, do you have any notion where your brother might be?"

"I expect he has gone back to London to get another investigator," Emily said, with a completely straight face. "Did you need him for anything in particular?"

Edgar mentally weighed the *faux pas* of needlessly alarming a lady against the possibility that Emily might be able to help him track Chase down. Surely, he decided, Emily would be more distressed if she missed her chance to help her brother. Besides, lying to her would be very improper too. He settled for a half-truth. "In light of the disturbance outside your house last night," he said, "I deemed it wise to see him as soon as possible."

"You already saw him at breakfast this morning," Emily said, "and you look as if something were dreadfully wrong." She peered up into his face for a moment. "You don't think that business last night was anything to do with *him*, do you?"

"I very much fear that it may have been," Edgar said, endeavoring to keep his voice steady.

"You had better sit down on that bench before you topple right over. No? Are you sure? Well anyway, Mr. Beagle, I know Gabriel doesn't always show it, but he can take care of himself alright."

"Your optimism is admirable, Miss Chase, and I have no wish to disillusion you, but—"

"He is a high-ranking police dog, not a lost little puppy. I daresay you are much cleverer than he is, but that doesn't oblige you to look after him all the time. Anyway, what makes you think he is in trouble? Whoever was here last night, they were under *your* window; perhaps you ought to watch out for yourself instead of worrying about him."

"It is quite absurd," Edgar said, "to think that I would have enemies in Liverpool. I have only arrived yesterday. Inspector Chase is a more logical target."

"Why weren't the intruders under *his* window, then?"

"They were under the spare room window. An assailant who is not on intimate terms with the family would not necessarily know that there is a bedroom reserved for Inspector Chase's personal use, and would very reasonably assume that he was sleeping in the spare room."

"But how would anyone know where the spare room is, unless they knew us well enough to have been shown around the house? Anyway, you needn't look so frantic; nobody is going to ambush Gabriel in public at ten in the morning. If a gang of desperate criminals is after him—which I very much doubt; I shouldn't think attacking him would be worth the trouble—then they're much more likely to come back tonight.

You can station yourself in the garden with a bread knife if you like. In the meantime, if it makes you feel any better, he isn't wandering about alone. He came back after you left, and got that awful Airedale."

"I am afraid that does not altogether set my mind at ease. I have limited faith in Constable Barks' pugilistic abilities."

"I don't suppose he would be much good in a fight," Emily conceded, "but he would certainly kick up a ruckus and bring the whole street running. Anyway, it's just as well they aren't back yet, Mr. Beagle. I want to tell you something, and it will be easier without them here. You see, I got a letter while you were out."

Edgar forced his attention back to his immediate surroundings, and looked at her carefully. The diamond ring, he realized, had vanished from her paw. She was clutching a crumpled sheet of paper, and her eyes were very faintly rimmed in red. "If you will forgive the indelicacy of the question," he began tentatively, "I cannot help but wonder whether—"

"Yes, yes, I've been crying," Emily said impatiently. "I don't care who knows it." She held out the piece of paper to Edgar. "You may as well read this for yourself."

"A lady's private correspondence! Really, Miss Chase, I should hardly like to meddle—"

"Oh, why stand on ceremony, Mr. Beagle? There's no such thing as privacy around here; I expect the whole street will know all the details by teatime." She took a deep breath, and gave Edgar a sad little smile. "The fact of the matter is," she said, very calmly, "Mr. Herder has jilted me."

Then, she sat down on the bench, and burst abruptly into tears.

Chapter Seven

E dgar had never been quite sure what gentlemen were supposed to do when a lady was crying. His primary experience of ladies involved his sister Lavinia—who, on the rare occasions when she had given way to tears as a puppy, had ordered Edgar out of the room in no uncertain terms, and glared murderously at him had he dared to ask her any questions afterwards. But Lavinia, he was fairly certain, was atypical in any number of ways. Emily would probably find it insulting or insensitive if he were to walk away right now. He had read, more than once, that smelling salts were to be administered in the event of hysteria, but he was uncertain as to whether Emily's current behavior constituted hysteria. On the whole, he thought not. And anyway, he did not have any smelling salts. Perhaps he ought to have made a habit of carrying them for such occasions. He considered what else a lady might find comforting. According to Tommy Muddypaws, who undoubtedly knew more about this sort of thing than Edgar did, girls liked flowers. But there might be some impropriety associated with offering flowers, even if he had some, to a lady to whom he had no romantic or familial connection. And every moment he stayed by Emily's side, aching with wholly uncommunicable sympathy and almost certainly failing to offer any meaningful form of comfort, was another moment of wondering what had become of Chase! He settled for hovering just in front of the bench, with a posture designed to indicate that he could not tarry indefinitely, and an expression that he hoped conveyed a suitable measure of compassionate distress.

"If you are going to be sick," Emily said unexpectedly, ceasing to cry and looking him full in the face, "kindly step backwards so you don't do it into my lap. All my dressmaking money for the year has already gone into my wretched trousseau. Go on and read the letter, and then tell me what on earth I am to do, for I am sure I haven't any idea."

She thrust the letter firmly into his paw. Edgar un-crumpled it and painstakingly smoothed it out. It was scrawled, in very round letters, on writing paper emblazoned with the name of the Adelphi Hotel. Towards the bottom, there was a sudden spray of ink, as if the writer had hurriedly flung down his pen.

"My very dearest Emily," Edgar read to himself, "There is only one honorable course of action open to me: I must sunder all connection between us and return to Australia at once. I would be unforgivably selfish to marry you, knowing that our connection would, sooner or later, undo you utterly. I freely admit that I am a cad of the lowest order—but, I assure you, I did not trifle with your affections. In a better world than this, I would have made you the truest and most devoted husband who ever lived. Please tell your neighbors that it was your decision to terminate our engagement; devise whatever plausible fiction will leave your reputation unstained; I shall not challenge anything you may choose to say about me. I will not beg your pardon, for I know my behavior has been unpardonable—but my every prayer is that, one day, you will think of me softly, if only for a moment. In the meantime, you may console yourself with the certain knowledge that I am not worth mourning; your tears are too precious to be spent on me. I hope that you marry and find happiness someday. I know I never shall. Yours faithfully, and with all regret, James Herder."

Edgar endeavored, very hard and very unsuccessfully, to square the letter with his mental image of the graceless, unbecomingly taciturn dog who had blighted the dinner table last night—let alone with the embodiment of evil that Chase had described. "Do you know this to be his writing?" he asked Emily.

"I have never seen his writing; he is hardly the type of dog to court a girl by penning sonnets. But it sounds exactly like him, Mr. Beagle."

"I should hardly say it was in accordance with my observations of him."

"I *said* he had changed."

"To what is he referring when he writes that your connection would undo you?"

"I haven't the faintest idea."

"You know of no—er—unfortunate incidents from his past?" Edgar coughed delicately.

"You're every bit as bad as my brother. James—Mr. Herder, I mean—is not a heartless seducer or a vicious murderer or whatever it is you are picturing. Anyway, you needn't go looking for elaborate solutions. It's quite plain what has happened: he has simply gone off me."

"Such a conclusion does not logically follow from this letter, Miss Chase. Mr. Herder has made it quite clear that he holds you in the highest esteem, and that this estrangement is not due to any misapprehensions on his part concerning your conduct. I will be bold to conjecture that your pride may be wounded or your feelings bruised, or that you may be experiencing some other outpouring of negative sentiment, but you must remember that it is not necessarily justified. Very possibly, there is a perfectly cogent explanation for Mr. Herder's strange behavior."

"Certainly there is. Mr. Herder, having wearied of me or having been persuaded against me by his friends, has hit upon a clever way of ending our engagement without purchasing himself a reputation for faithlessness. Perhaps he has already set his sights on some other girl—a rich one this time, I expect. He imagines me to be so soft-hearted and credulous that, by playing on my emotions with all this melodramatic drivel, he can stop me from turning up and ruining his chances with a story of my ill-usage."

"You speak out of your injury," Edgar said, rather gently. "I have only the most glancing of acquaintanceships with Mr. Herder, but I can scarcely imagine him to be so calculating. Besides, it seems most implausible that his friends would have, or indeed could have, persuaded him against you. Mr. Mongrel does not strike me as being overly eloquent. And Mr. Tenterfield appears to be a gentleman through and through; it seems most unlikely that he should have gone about to deliberately part a lady from her fiancé."

"He would have if he thought he was protecting his friend," Emily said. "No doubt he supposes that I am a false-hearted fortune-hunter unworthy of Mr. Herder and his millions."

"And do you imagine that Mr. Herder, who has been aware of your financial situation ever since he met you, would be so weak-willed as to believe that?"

"I shouldn't have thought so. But I shouldn't have thought he would jilt me either, so I suppose my opinion of him means very little."

"Perhaps," Edgar said very delicately, glancing around and lowering his voice, "Mr. Tenterfield carried a different sort of story to Mr. Herder. Miss Chase, if there is any little indiscretion from your past that has come to Mr. Tenterfield's ear and compelled him to influence his friend against you, I strongly advise you to tell me about it. Without knowing all the facts of the case, I can be of very little use to you."

Emily laughed, a little wildly. "Of course there isn't, Mr. Beagle," she said. "I suppose this is the moment when your society clients tearfully confess their shocking misdeeds—but I assure you, I have nothing at all by way of dark secrets." She gave another little laugh, and ended by blinking back more tears.

"We must return, then," Edgar said, "to Mr. Herder's own history. We may be doing him an injustice by refusing to take his words at face value; given what little I have observed of his character, it seems rather more likely that he is telling the truth than that he has concocted an outlandish lie. There may really be some detail of his history too terrible to come to light, which his friends have prevailed upon him for his honor's sake to acquaint you with."

"Mr. Herder has no history. He buys and sells cows, and reads dull books, and plays the pianoforte rather badly."

"You have known him for only a few months," Edgar said. "There may be aspects of his life with which you are wholly unacquainted—and which, without further information from the gentleman himself, we cannot hope to unveil. It is not inconceivable that Mr. Herder might be persuaded to reveal the mystery to you. If I were to accompany you to the Adelphi and draw his friends out of the way—"

"I don't know, and I don't care either; I haven't the faintest desire to see him. And why should he tell me his secrets anyway? I am not, after all, his fiancée."

"In that case, perhaps we ought to instead turn our attention to locating Inspector Chase."

"Are you worrying about him *again*?"

"Certainly not!" Edgar said hastily. "I only meant that, in his professional capacity as a high-ranking police dog, he might be able to help us determine a course of action."

"Yes, perhaps I could exact revenge by herding a dozen squirrels through James' window. Honestly, Mr. Beagle, Gabriel knows Liverpool like the back of his paw, and he can handle himself in a fight. There's absolutely no cause for concern. I'm sure he'll come bounding up any moment. In any event, there *is* no course of action to be determined. I have been jilted, that is all there is to it, and now I suppose shall have to endure months of gossip from the neighbors. Half of them will pity me, and the other half will think I've gotten what I deserve for trying to rise above my station."

From just around the bend, there came a tremendous panting noise, and a percussive din suggestive of four heavy paws hitting the pavement with unnecessary force.

"I expect that's Gabriel and that Airedale now," Emily said. "There—you see? I told you he was perfectly alright. Don't tell him about me and James, will you?"

Indeed, Chase was careening down the path towards them at a breakneck pace, with Constable Barks galloping alongside him. He skidded to a stop just in front of them. Constable Barks sat down just behind him, heavily and precipitously,

111

and began drooling onto the path.

"Inspector Chase!" Edgar exclaimed, hurrying forward. "I must express my deepest sentiments of relief—that is to say, I am very pleased to see that you are unharmed."

The look Chase cast Edgar was puzzled, but not displeased. "Why in the world shouldn't I be unharmed, Mr. Beagle? All that happened to me was that I met Mrs. Mouser in the street and had to listen to her yowling on about her grand-kittens for ten minutes. But that doesn't cause harm; she didn't get her claws into me or anything, only meowed my ear off."

"I formed a conjecture, based on last night's events—"

"Never mind about last night just now. I have something extremely important to tell you." He struck a dramatic pose, and the very tips of his ears quivered gently with excitement. "By carefully designing and executing rather an inspired stratagem—with, I may say, considerable stealth and finesse—I have—"

"What have you done this time, Gabriel?" Emily inquired wearily.

"I have, at length," Chase continued, ignoring the interruption, "learned everything." He elaborately glanced around, then positioned himself even more dramatically, teetering slightly—Edgar took a step forward, in case he overbalanced—and dropped his voice to a stage whisper. "Mr. Herder is a compulsive gambler!"

To Edgar's surprise, Emily burst into laughter. "Thank you," she said at length, wiping her eyes. "I have not heard anything half so humorous all week."

"It is *not* humorous!" Chase said, abruptly resuming his normal voice and posture. "He gambles, I tell you!"

"Oh, don't be absurd! He leaves the house with an umbrella

every day of his life, even if the weather is glorious. He will not walk out to the end of the pier, in case it prove unstable. And I have heard all about his business dealings; he would be twice as rich if he could bring himself to speculate."

"It is dogs such as that," Chase explained sententiously, "—dogs who adhere to tedious schedules and regulations, and who take so few risks they may as well be dead—who are often drawn to dangerous pastimes in their private lives. Why, even Mr. Beagle here has taken to fighting crime."

"My investigative work is not a pastime, Inspector, and I assure you its appeal does not lie in the danger, but rather in the satisfaction achieved in the knowledge that I have done my duty in upholding justice."

"Well, that's what you *would* say. You don't know yourself as well as you think, Mr. Beagle."

"I beg your pardon, Inspector?" Edgar inquired coldly.

"Anyway, will you listen to me? Mr. Herder has been behaving very suspiciously with his money."

"And how would you possibly know that?" Emily demanded.

"Well, I had some words with the bank—in my capacity as Detective Chief Inspector of the Metropolitan Police, you understand—I made sure to have my badge, my paw-cuffs, and my constable all in plain sight—and gave them to understand that the Yard sent me to help with an urgent investigation—"

"Oh for goodness' sake, Gabriel!" Emily cried, at the same time as Edgar remonstrated, "*Really*, Inspector Chase!"

"You needn't 'really, Inspector Chase' me. It was a clever idea, and I didn't hear *you* suggesting anything. Anyway, what's the use of being Detective Chief Inspector if I cannot protect my family? Besides, it is not as though it were a fraudulent investigation. I have believed all along that he was a criminal.

And, you see, I was quite right."

"Gambling is not illegal," Edgar pointed out.

"At any rate," Chase said, over him, "the evidence speaks for itself." He paused to arrange his limbs into an even more dramatic pose. "Mr. Herder has been making withdrawals from his account!"

"Congratulations, Gabriel," Emily said icily. "You have learned how banks work."

"No, no—*large* withdrawals! And besides,"—here he leaned forward self-importantly, stumbled backwards to steady himself, and nearly tripped over Constable Barks—"the bank clerk said that his manner was tense and unhappy!"

"It is a phenomenon we have very often observed during our investigations, Inspector," Edgar said, "that witnesses are inclined to embellish details after the fact to make themselves seem more important, or simply more observant, than they really are. In all probability, the bank clerk sees hundreds of dogs every day. It is most unlikely that he should accurately recall the exact demeanor of Mr. Herder, who is not a particularly memorable personality."

"Well, he has seemed tense and unhappy ever since I met him," Chase said sulkily. "It is unlikely he should be all sunshine and biscuits for the bank clerk, when he can barely even trouble himself to say how-do-you-do to his fiancée's brother."

"Mr. Herder is unusually wealthy," Edgar persisted.

"Or says he is," Chase interjected darkly.

"It is quite plausible that he should withdraw sums of money that seem startlingly outsized to you and me, straitened as we are by our more sensible and less extravagant way of life, but that he considers perfectly normal for his everyday expenditures."

"I am not a fool, Mr. Beagle," Chase said at once. "And you needn't try so bloody hard to be tactful; you aren't any good at it. I quite realize that Mr. Herder's expenses are higher than mine. But he has only been making these withdrawals for the past few days. Clearly, he has taken up wagering on horses. The Ascot races are coming right up; perhaps he means to nip off to them before the wedding."

"They are not for a fortnight, Inspector, and we are over two hundred miles away from Ascot."

"Well, baccarat, then. Or picquet or wombat or whatever Australians like to play."

"Your theory, then, is that Mr. Herder, who is by your own account an extremely dull dog with no discernible personality, has, conscious of his impending matrimony—a state which, I am told, typically sobers young gentlemen and awakens them to their responsibilities—gone from a perfectly normal pattern of spending to throwing about vast sums of money at the card table?"

"Some dogs cut loose right before they get married," Chase said. "Their last chance, as it were. I knew a young constable who tried to run away and live at the zoo. Disguised himself as a wolf and everything. He used to practice howling in the barracks. He was awfully good at it, but it did rather wear on the nerves after a while."

"It is all very well for you to stand here discussing the giddying effects of betrothal," Emily broke in, "but I am the only one who actually knows him. I tell you, it is as impossible that James should be a gambler as that Constable Barks should take up a position as a barrister."

"Constable Barks would make a fine barrister," Chase said,

sounding very slightly hurt. "His greatest weapon is his tongue."

"Only because he's always licking things."

"In any event, Inspector," Edgar said, over them both, "let me recapitulate the scenario you are envisioning, to be sure that I am following your reasoning correctly. Mr. Herder, as per the evidence given by Miss Chase, has never gambled—yet, in the days leading up to his marriage, he suddenly begins. Moreover, he finds himself either so ashamed of or so transformed by his newfound pastime—although is perfectly legal and quite common amongst gentlemen of his age and station—that he immediately undergoes a radical shift in personality and behavior. You must admit, it rather strains the imagination. Besides, Mr. Herder has been largely in the company of his friends; I hardly imagine he has been sneaking off in the dead of night to play cards or wager on horses."

"Maybe his friends are gamblers too," Chase said. "They might have corrupted him."

"Whatever you may think of him," Emily said, "he is not so weak-willed as all that. And Mr. Tenterfield is quite respectable, and perfectly lovely; of course he would not drag his friend off to a gambling den."

"Maybe it was Mr. Mongrel, then."

"I know, Inspector," Edgar said, "that you have always subscribed to the theory that I am detrimentally unimaginative. Perhaps that is why I experience such difficulty envisioning Mr. Mongrel comprehending the rules of whist."

"Alright—*alright*!" Chase exclaimed. "Maybe the money is for something else."

"Like what?" Emily demanded.

"Maybe your Mr. Herder is supporting ten wives, scattered

all across England!"

"All of whom he has acquired over the last few days?" Edgar inquired.

"Oh, very well, Mr. Beagle! I suppose it could not be that anyway; he is not the sort of fellow to have gotten ten girls. How he got even one is more than I can tell. Alright, then—perhaps he is a coiner. He is from Australia, you must remember."

"Although I cannot claim to have tried coining myself, Inspector, I believe the general idea is that it leaves one with *more* money than when one started, not less."

"No one ever believes my theories," Chase said sulkily.

"Well, what does that tell you about your theories?" Emily said.

"Oh, don't be so jolly clever. I don't understand why no one listens to me. No one ever listened to me about Tommy either. According to you lot, I am such a fool that I ought to be turned out to bury bones in the back garden. I *can* do my job, you know."

"That was never under debate, Inspector Chase," Edgar said graciously.

"I suppose half the city saw you marching off to the bank," Emily said soothingly. "Reports of your very dashing and impressive investigation will be all over Liverpool in an hour."

"No they shan't. I dodged everyone except for Mrs. Mouser; cats sneak up on you, you know. I went around the longest way I could. The neighbors are very dull. Why should I stand about listening to them blather on about their begonias or their coelacanths—"

"Calceolarias," Edgar said, sotto voce.

"—or whatever you grow in a garden, when I have a

dangerous coiner to investigate? I say," he added suddenly, "what were you two doing out here? It is not like you to promenade yourself by the water, Mr. Beagle. The wind might disarrange your cravat."

"Mr. Beagle was just going to tell me about his interview with Tommy," Emily said at once, giving Edgar a sharp little glance which he supposed was meant to remind him not to mention Mr. Herder's letter.

"Ah, yes!" Edgar said. "We are no closer, I am afraid, to finding last night's intruders; Mr. Muddypaws claims to have been asleep at the relevant hour—"

"Well, what did you think he was going to do—meekly confess everything the moment you asked him?"

"No, but I assume that, if he were the culprit, he would have placed more emphasis on telling me what time he came home. Instead, he took pains to provide me with an alibi, as it were, for *earlier* in the night, even though his activities immediately after the party are of no relevance to us. Unless you consider him clever enough to construct rather an elaborate double bluff—"

"That's not a double bluff; that's just him being too stupid to even cover his tracks properly. Or maybe he needs an alibi for earlier too. Maybe he came back here right after the party to lay the groundwork for burgling the house. Hiding lock picks in the shrubbery or something."

"Such a measure seems both unnecessary and foolhardy—"

"And anyway, anyone can have an alibi. Tommy is a liar and a cheat; I expect he has a dozen alibis ready at a moment's notice."

"That strikes me as entirely possible," Edgar said. "However, this particular alibi was corroborated and enlarged upon by

Mr. Ollie Muddypaws, and I am altogether inclined to believe it."

"Well, what does *he* say Tommy was doing—burgling a house on the other side of the city?"

"No, he reported that Mr. Muddypaws was in the company of a young lady of his acquaintance—a Miss Flossie Yapper, who works at the Adelphi Hotel—and—"

"And why shouldn't that be a lie?" Chase demanded. "He's probably just trying to shield Tommy. Or else Tommy fed him some ridiculous story in case anyone came asking questions."

"As it happens," Edgar said delicately, "this story is not to Mr. Muddypaws' advantage. Mr. Ollie Muddypaws further reported, you see, that Miss Yapper was passing stolen goods to Mr. Muddypaws; apparently, he brought home a monogrammed locket belonging to a hotel guest. This is, I gather, a regular occurrence."

Chase's eyes brightened maniacally. "Do you mean to say," he demanded, "that we could go and arrest Tommy right now? Why didn't you tell me at once?"

"We *cannot* arrest him on the sole basis of a chance word from his brother. Besides, in light of the intrusion onto your parents' property last night, not to mention your sister's situation, I hardly think that this is the moment to prioritize your apparent grudge against Mr. Muddypaws."

"Do my ears deceive me, Mr. Beagle? Are you—*you*, out of all the dogs in the whole world!—seriously suggesting that I should suppress my knowledge of an ongoing pattern of criminal activity—that I, a high-ranking champion of justice at the Metropolitan Police, should permit a law-breaker to walk free, simply because I am occupied with personal affairs?"

"Although I cannot fault your line of reasoning, Inspector—"

"And is it your recommendation as a private investigator or a champion of justice or a Grail Knight or whatever you think you are, that rather than tracking down this Yapper girl and either disproving the suspect's alibi or gathering further evidence to arrest him for theft, I should sit idly by?"

"Certainly not, but—"

"Just let him get on with it, Mr. Beagle," Emily interrupted. "It will distract him from this business about James. There's nothing you can do to help me anyway."

"Surely, Miss Chase, there must be some additional step I can take—"

"Yes, you can stop my situation from getting any worse, by making sure that Gabriel doesn't go scandalizing the neighbors with ridiculous rumors. I don't fancy having everyone think I was taken in by a coiner; the gossip will never die down."

"Come *on*, Mr. Beagle," Chase said, seizing Edgar by the sleeve. "Today is a day for doing things. And do you know what else? I am having one of my presentiments—don't sigh at me, Emily! I think today is the day when the world finally sees Tommy Muddypaws for what he is."

"Not ten minutes ago," Emily said crisply, "you were all for pinning fanciful crimes on Mr. Herder. Now you want to go and arrest Tommy. I realize our little corner of the world probably seems very dull to you, compared to your exciting life in London, but this is getting out of paw; you seem to have an extraordinary mania for harassing my former beaux."

"No, I have the unerring instinct of an experienced police dog—did you say 'former'?" Chase let go of Edgar's sleeve and whirled around. "Made up your mind to be rid of Herder, then?"

Emily hesitated only for a second. She looked extremely cross with herself, but her voice was perfectly steady. "Mr. Herder and I are no longer affianced," she said. "There—I hope you're pleased."

"Pleased! Emily—"

"I'm alright, Gabriel," Emily said gently. "Get on with your investigations. One of us ought to be happy."

"Here, keep Barks with you," Chase said, thrusting the leash into Emily's paw. "You need him more than I do."

He turned away, drawing Edgar with him, before Emily could protest.

"Inspector Chase," Edgar said, "while I have the utmost respect for your generous intentions, I hardly think your sister will find comfort in—"

"Has Herder jilted her?" Chase interrupted in a grim undertone, checking over his shoulder to make sure Emily was out of earshot.

"Although our long years of friendship make me loath to conceal information from you, my honor forbids that I should betray a lady's confidences—"

"I thought as much. Herding dogs are supposed to be *loyal*. Perhaps he's broken." Chase's expression brightened very slightly. "I wish I had a dueling pistol. The type with the shiny white stuff in the handle."

"Mother of pearl?"

"You tell me. You're the one who knows things."

"I am afraid my expertise does not lie in the realm of decorative weaponry."

"Oh, and a hat with a feather, like a musketeer," Chase added, plainly not listening. "Well, come *on*. Maybe we can corner him at the Adelphi when we're done talking to the girl."

"Inspector Chase, I fully understand that you wish me to accompany you. You need not belabor the point by pawing at my arm."

"Well, you walk too slowly."

"I assure you, I shall stop walking altogether if you forcibly detach my sleeve."

"Look, if you don't *want* to come—"

"You mistake me," Edgar said quickly. "As a matter of fact, if I may so bold, I deem it advisable that I remain in your company for the remainder of our time in Liverpool." He took a deep breath, and found himself pulling his coat around him more tightly. Extraordinary, that sudden chill in the air, with no wind to cause it. He supposed that something about Liverpool's topography must give rise to unexpected fluctuations in temperature. "Inspector Chase, perhaps this is the moment to broach a serious matter with you." Another breath, deeper and steadier this time. "I am afraid you may be in grave danger."

He braced himself for a theatrical gasp, or even an extravagant display of bravado, but Chase merely laughed. "Don't be ridiculous, Mr. Beagle. Who should I be in danger from?"

"I do not know from whom you should be in danger, but it is imperative that you remain on your guard while I work to find out."

"I can take care of myself, Mr. Beagle."

"There is no call for overconfidence, Inspector Chase," Edgar said, more sharply than he had intended. "You would not be the first high-ranking police dog to overestimate his indestructibility and overplay his paw."

"Mr. Beagle, it is difficult to feel anxious for my safety, when you cannot even tell me who is after me or what they want to do to me."

"The element of the unknown makes the situation *more* dangerous, not less so."

"But what makes you think I am in danger at all? I made it all the way to the bank and back this morning, without any cats leaping out at me with rapiers or slingshotting rats at me or anything."

"The incident last night! Given that it appears not to have been perpetrated by Mr. Muddypaws, then it logically follows that you were the intended victim."

"That is *not at all* how logic works, Mr. Beagle," Chase said gleefully. "There, you see? I do pay attention when you try to teach me things. Listen, we have no reason to think that there was any intended victim. Maybe it was ordinary housebreakers. Nothing to do with me."

"Although I am not versed in the finer details of housebreaking," Edgar said, "I cannot help but think that it would be rather an inexperienced burglar who would seek ingress by staring up at the window, when the back door is right there."

"For all I care," Chase said impatiently. "they meant to climb a tree and catapult themselves onto the roof and down the chimney. And anyway, they were under *your* window, not mine—but you don't see me clinging to your side like a flea and planning out your funeral in my head."

"I am not *clinging to your side*, Inspector Chase; I am attempting to protect you from a violent crime."

"What are *you* going to do if attackers turn up? Read an encyclopedia at them?"

"No," Edgar said stiffly. "I had hoped that the fact of my presence would deter your enemies."

Chase looked rather flattered. "Do you really think I have

enemies? I shouldn't have thought so at all."

"We must, I am afraid, confront the facts, however unpleasant—"

"It sounds rather splendid, doesn't it? Having enemies?"

"I should not have sought out the experience myself."

"Well, I suppose I might have expected it, being a bastion of justice and all. I stand between the world of upright dogs and cats and the criminal underworld—isn't that right, Mr. Beagle?"

"Certainly, if you really must phrase it in that manner."

"Or do you know what else it could be? Herder, having seen my noble demeanor and identified me as a champion of the law, tried to assassinate me before I could reveal his villainy."

"This fixation on your melodramatic and wholly unfounded suppositions concerning Mr. Herder," Edgar said, his tone sharper than he had intended, "is only distracting us—that is to say, distracting *you*—from a clear appraisal of—"

"Or maybe Tommy," Chase continued enthusiastically, "tired of bearing the constant weight of my hatred and scorn, sent his minions to eliminate me whilst he cavorted with his mistress."

"I very much doubt that Mr. Muddypaws has managed to acquire anything resembling minions."

"At any rate," Chase said, his voice brimming with suppressed jubilation, "if you really want to protect me, you'll have to follow me around wherever I go, so that means you're coming with me while I work on finding a reason to arrest Tommy." He gave Edgar's arm a sudden squeeze. "You're my secret weapon, Mr. Beagle. I know you'll be able to figure out a way to get him."

Edgar kept his face impassive. For goodness' sake, he thought, why should Chase have developed this irritating penchant for blithely throwing personal problems at him? Apparently, Edgar's uselessness at ameliorating the situation with Mr. Herder, which any rational dog would have taken as clear evidence that one should not expect miracles, had instead struck Chase as an opening for saddling Edgar with a new, and equally ridiculous, task. He wondered how much Chase cared whether Tommy was actually guilty. Typical, really, Chase's hatred of Tommy. Any sensible dog would long since have forgotten all about petty puppyhood enmities. Edgar had detested sundry neighbors too, but he had *not* persisted in his hatred once he grew up. The fates of Archie Dewclaws and Georgie Boxer and Bertie Bobtail and all the other boys who had eyed him with hostility and mocked his patterns of speech and his collection of timetables were of absolutely no concern to him. But Chase, apparently, was pathologically incapable of relinquishing grudges! Edgar chanced a sidelong glance at Chase, and immediately regretted it. Chase's eyes were bright with anticipation, and his tail was wagging uncontrollably. He looked for all the world like a puppy who had been given a new chew toy. The thought flashed across Edgar's mind, entirely unbidden and too quickly for him to examine it, that Chase would be absurdly, ecstatically happy if Edgar could find evidence against Tommy Muddypaws. Happy enough, perhaps, to skip over being disappointed by Edgar's utter failure to work out anything at all about Mr. Herder. Happy enough, even, for his faith in Edgar to survive the weekend unblemished.

More importantly, of course, Edgar told himself, if Tommy was actually a criminal, then bringing him to justice was, after all, an ethical imperative. It would be selfish beyond measure for Edgar to let his private opinions or personal priorities lure him away from strict adherence to the course of law.

He glanced at Chase again.

"Alright, Inspector," he said. "Lead the way to the Adelphi."

Chapter Eight

The Adelphi Hotel was a long, imposing building, sporting a generous profusion of arches and balconies. Edgar found himself wondering how Chase, with his unpressed shirt and battered hat, would fit in amongst the clientele. The smartly uniformed Manx who sprang to attention to open the door seemed to have similar doubts; his golden eyes lingered on Chase a trifle longer than was strictly polite. As they passed into the lobby—all velvet and ferns and parquet, studded with Ionic columns and dripping with chandeliers, alive with the sharp, bright ring of the concierge's bell and the murmurs of genteel travelers gossiping over tea—Edgar reached over and tried to surreptitiously smooth down Chase's collar.

"Ah, there's Mr. Dewlaps at the desk!" Chase said, shaking Edgar off and pointing towards the concierge too openly for manners. "Used to scold me for tracking squirrels too close to his house. Well, I'm the police now, so he'll have to finally be civil, won't he? Watch this." He puffed up his chest and strode over to the desk. "Good morning, my good fellow," he said, rather too loudly. "I understand that you have a Flossie Yapper working here. It is of the utmost importance that I see her right away, for reasons which are"—here, he lowered his voice mysteriously—"classified."

"Don't you go putting on airs with me, Gabriel Chase," Mr. Dewlaps said wearily. "I've known you since before your eyes were open. Flossie's in trouble with the police, is she? I always thought that girl was no good. Well, who's she bitten?"

"Miss Yapper does not stand formally accused of any crime," Edgar said hastily. "We merely require her assistance in our inquiries."

Mr. Dewlaps looked Edgar up and down. He did not appear to be impressed. "So, you're that investigator Gabriel was always going on about!" he said. "Mr. Howler, was it?"

"Mr. Beagle," Edgar said, with great dignity.

"Well, Mr. Whoever-you-are, I read the papers. I know what 'assisting the police in their inquiries' means." He leaned suddenly forward. "I suppose you couldn't wait a few weeks, before you haul her off to prison? Chambermaids don't grow on trees, you know. We'll have to put an advert in the paper. You police ought to compensate us for it."

"We only require a few moments' conversation with Miss Yapper," Edgar said, unhappily aware that more and more guests' heads were turning toward him. "There is, at this juncture, no question of hauling anyone to prison."

"Except for Tommy Muddypaws," Chase interposed.

"Still thinking of your old feud with Tommy Muddypaws?" Mr. Dewlaps demanded, chuckling a little. "I remember the two of you used to go at it hammer and tongs when you were puppies. Bark, bark, bark, all over the neighborhood. Very upset about it, your poor mother was." He leaned across the desk conspiratorially. "Look, Nora Roughcoat has been walking out with Roddy Mastiff since Christmas. He means to marry her, they say. So you needn't imagine that taking

Tommy away will get you anywhere."

"I haven't the least interest in Nora Roughcoat," Chase said shortly, "and I'm sure I don't know why you should bring her into this. She can walk out with the whole neighborhood, for all I care. It's nothing to do with me."

"Not stuck on her then anymore, eh?" Mr. Dewlaps inquired, eying him shrewdly.

"I haven't thought about her since I was seventeen! Why does everyone in Liverpool imagine I'm in love with Nora Roughcoat?"

"When I heard you had joined the police, all those years ago," Mr. Dewlaps continued, undeterred, "I knew you had only done it to try and impress her. Everyone knew it."

"That is absolutely untrue," Chase snapped. "Listen, will you fetch Flossie Yapper for us, or are you going to make me arrest you for interfering with official business?"

Mr. Dewlaps snorted and snuffled with sudden mirth. "Little Gabriel Chase? Wouldn't that be a sight."

"I beg your pardon, Detective Chief Inspector Chase, sir," Edgar broke in as Chase's paw started twitching in the direction of the paw-cuffs attached to his belt. "In keeping with your excellent plan, perhaps we might proceed up the stairs and find Miss Yapper ourselves. This worthy gentleman"—here, he made a courteous little bow in Mr. Dewlaps' direction—"no doubt has more pressing concerns than advancing the pursuit of justice by cooperating in our officially sanctioned and extremely legitimate investigation; we ought not to impose on his valuable time any longer. I am sure none of the guests will mind any disturbance we make while we search the upstairs. After all, in addition to being a distinguished and accomplished member of the

Metropolitan Police, you are an expert in tracking squirrels; no doubt the same techniques will apply." He smiled at Mr. Dewlaps brightly.

"Alright, alright! I remember your squirrel-tracking well enough, Gabriel. Don't go you barking and sniffing at my guests. There—go and wait in my office, and keep out of sight. I'll have the porter fetch her down for you."

Mr. Dewlaps' office was elegantly appointed—but, Edgar noticed with some distaste, littered with what appeared to be drool-soaked handkerchiefs. "Always did give himself airs," Chase said inconsequently and not particularly quietly, commandeering the chair behind the desk. "I expect he's secretly insecure, on account of he slobbers so much."

"Strangers are making a habit of recognizing me from your descriptions," Edgar remarked mildly. "I trust, Inspector Chase, that you have not, for the last ten years, spent all your visits to Liverpool talking about me."

"Certainly not!" Chase said at once. "It's only that it's very dull around here. The locals seize on any newcomer like a bone."

"Indeed, the concierge at this large hotel must be at a tremendous loss for newcomers."

"Well, he knows my mother," Chase said, changing tacks immediately. "I expect she used to read my letters to the whole street. I might have mentioned you once or twice. Only in passing, of course."

"Of course."

"Oh, you needn't look so pleased with yourself." Chase slouched moodily in the chair. "What else was I supposed to write home about? You can see no one has a particle of interest in my job. And they haven't any proper appreciation for squirrels. So really—"

The door was opening. Chase hurriedly broke off and sat up very straight, just as a girl with a sharp, vivacious face and dark gray fur stepped into the room. She was holding a tremendously fluffy feather duster, and a ruffled cap was pulled neatly over her pointed ears.

"Ah, this must be Miss Yapper!" Edgar said, stepping forward.

Flossie Yapper eyed him very dubiously. "I've never been mixed up with the police," she said. "I don't want any trouble, I'm sure."

"No more do we," Chase said jovially, steepling his paws with a sidelong glance at Edgar. "We only want to know a few things from you. Come in—come in, we haven't got fleas. That's right. Close the door behind you. Now then—when you were consorting with the suspect last night—"

"My esteemed colleague means," Edgar said, over him, "that we have just been calling on a Mr. Tommy Muddypaws. The gentleman is, I believe, an acquaintance of yours."

"Oh! Yes, I know Tommy well enough, sir."

"How very pleasant for you," Edgar said courteously. "I wonder if you might tell me: at what hour last night did your rendezvous with him take place?"

Flossie cocked her head and panted a little. "I'm sure I don't know what a rondy-voo is, sir," she said sternly, "unless it's another type of fancy cat from France, as if we didn't already have enough trouble trying to say 'Chartreux'—but if it's anything less than decent, then you oughtn't to mention it to a girl. Anyway, I haven't seen Tommy since Thursday."

"The day before yesterday! Are you certain, Miss Yapper?"

"Of course I am. I should know when my evening to go out

is, I suppose."

"You did not, perhaps, in a quiet interval of the night, happen to step away for a moment or two?"

"I don't go gadding about when I haven't permission, sir," Flossie said virtuously. "I know my duty. There's no time to slip away anyhow. Run off my paws, I am in this place. We get all sorts in here, sir. Gentlemen dripping horrid things onto the carpet—*and* growling—*and* thinking they're too good for the restaurant and wanting their meals carried up to them on trays. And always getting underfoot, or else sending you off on mysterious little errands. *And* foreigners, of course. Well anyway, it's better than the cats. Cats are really *very* trying, sir. They want everything just the way they like it, and they hiss something dreadful if you get one little thing wrong, and they turn their noses up at all the food and stick their paws in their teacups. And the blankets smell like catnip for weeks after."

"What would you say, Miss Yapper," Edgar inquired, minutely studying her face, "if I were to tell you that Mr. Ollie Muddypaws positively informed me that his brother had been in your company last night—Friday, that is—and not on Thursday?"

"I would say, sir, that Ollie was not making marvelous progress at finally learning the days of the week."

"And what would you say," Edgar persisted, "if I told you that a valuable silver heart-shaped locket engraved with the monogram 'E.R.' had been stolen from a guest here last night?"

Flossie shrugged imperturbably, but Edgar was certain he had seen a look of startled panic flash across her face. "I would say it was nothing to do with me, sir. Dead drunk half the time, the gentlemen here are, I tell you. Stumbling in at all hours and talking nonsense. One of them probably ate the locket by mistake. I've seen gentlemen eat worse. A gentleman here once—a husky, he was, and I'm sure I always thought he was perfectly steady and respectable, but you never really know with huskies, do you? Because they look so stalwart and aloof, I mean, but then you get to know them—well anyway, he ate a whole plate of mice on a dare from a cat, just swallowed them down one after another after another, tails and all—and then he was sick all over the floor—and then the cat coughed up a hairball with laughing—and then who do you suppose had to mop it all up?" She looked back and forth between them with a grimly triumphant expression.

"Do you know anything," Chase interjected while Edgar was still rallying from this, "about a dangerous Australian coiner who has been staying here under the alias 'Mr. Herder'?"

"We mustn't take up any more of Miss Yapper's time," Edgar said quickly. "Thank you, Miss Yapper; you have been most informative."

"I can't catch a criminal," Chase said, looking very put out, "if you won't let me ask any questions."

"There's a criminal staying here?" Flossie queried, her ears perking up visibly. "Here in the hotel? Criminals make the best tippers, I expect. Because they've gold bars and things, haven't they, just lying about like chew toys?"

"Well, this one will give you fake coins. He escaped here from a prison in Australia. Probably."

"*Inspector Chase!*" Edgar said in an undertone. "May I remind you that slander—"

"He's probably in league with Tommy. He probably has a whole network of criminals all over England. Using the Adelphi as a base, I shouldn't wonder. Burying their nasty forged money under the floorboards."

133

"Miss Yapper," Edgar said, turning to the saucer-eyed Flossie with a courteous little bow, "I imagine you have work to get back to. There will be no need to distribute any details of this conversation amongst the hotel staff. I wish you every happiness in your friendship with Mr. Muddypaws."

"I don't suppose," Chase said casually, as Flossie turned away, "that when you saw your *friend* Mr. Muddypaws on Thursday, he happened to mention his plans for last night? Off to see another girl, I expect," he added, with what Edgar imagined was probably intended as an attempt at an avuncular chuckle.

Flossie reached for the doorknob. "Yes, that's right, sir," she said, very innocently. "He said he was going to see a girl he had once cared for. He said he had finally worked out a way she could be useful."

She passed through the doorway, leaving Edgar and Chase staring after her in wide-eyed perturbation.

* * *

The walk back towards the Chases' house was brisk and grim. "I might have known it from the start," Chase said darkly, glaring at a passing seagull. "Not a pennyworth of truth in his little alibi. He ought to have tipped Flossie off before we got to her. Or perhaps he did," he added as an afterthought, "but she's cross with him for skulking under other girls' windows in the dead of night, and now she won't cover for him."

"Perhaps he should have brought her more bouquets."

"Oh, very funny, Mr. Beagle—very funny! Do you know what could have happened just now, while we were wasting our time talking to that girl? Tommy Muddypaws could have gone looking for my sister. Thank goodness Barks is with her."

"We have no indication that Mr. Muddypaws is of a particularly dangerous temperament, or that his intentions towards Miss Chase are dishonorable."

"You heard what he said about her. Useful indeed!" He shook his head in disgust.

"I heard Miss Yapper's report of what he said," Edgar corrected. "For all we know, she may not be a reliable source of information. Perhaps, as you said, she has developed some grudge against Mr. Muddypaws—quite easily done, I should imagine—and has hit upon the scheme of slandering him to the police."

"She didn't say it until I asked her that last question," Chase said unhappily. "She was on her way out the door."

"There is no reason to assume that Miss Yapper was even referring to your sister," Edgar said. "She did not specify a name, and Mr. Ollie Muddypaws indicated that his brother has a wide and varied selection of female acquaintances. Is that true, would you surmise?"

"I do not make a career of keeping up with Tommy Muddypaws' romantic accomplishments," Chase said in his grandest voice, "so I am afraid I cannot supply you with the latest gossip."

"I thought you might be able to hazard a guess, on the basis of your knowledge and experience of him," Edgar explained wearily.

"Oh, I don't know!" Chase snapped. "I never knew what anyone saw in him. How he even got this Yapper girl is a mystery, let alone—But everyone these days gets girls, apparently. Him and Mr. Herder both. *I* never even meet any girls," he added mournfully.

"That is not an accurate statement, Inspector Chase; apart from anything else, might I remind you—"

"Do *not*," Chase said, holding up a peremptory paw, "go bringing Miss Scott into this. Anyway, let's say Tommy has had every girl in Liverpool at his beck and call; what difference would that make? You don't believe in ridiculous coincidences, Mr. Beagle—I know you don't. Surely you can't be suggesting that Tommy was under some *other* girl's window last night."

"It does, on the face of it, somewhat strain credulity," Edgar admitted. "But perhaps there is some other aspect of the case which we have not yet discovered."

"Oh, yes," Chase said. "Perhaps it will turn out that Tommy Muddypaws has perfectly innocent motives for slobbering under my sister's window, and perhaps we will learn that we have always been wrong in our idea that midnight is for sleeping and not for paying social calls, and perhaps trespassing will stop being a crime, and then we can all go have tea and biscuits and wag our tails. Or *perhaps* we ought to face the truth, which is that my sister is in danger. Tommy snuck back after the party, for some horrible reason, and got that pestilential brother of his to lie to you."

"How do you account," Edgar inquired, "for the second trespasser?"

"Maybe somebody decent was passing by," Chase said, glowering, "and saw him lurking under the window, and realized he was after Emily and that he was up to no good."

"And how would this hypothetical passer-by have divined Mr. Muddypaws' intentions?"

"No one who lurks under girls' windows is up to any good. Don't you know *anything* about criminals by now, Mr. Beagle?"

"You mistake me. Mr. Muddypaws was not actually under your sister's window; how would anyone have known that he was looking for her, specifically?"

"Perhaps he was muttering her name," Chase suggested, perking up a little, "in a strange, mad voice. And biting the flowerbeds and foaming at the mouth. He always looks as if he has rabies," he added irritably. "Bulldogs are like that."

"Furthermore," Edgar said, disregarding this hypothesis, "if Mr. Muddypaws' nocturnal explorations led him to your family's house, then when would he have had the opportunity to acquire that locket last night?"

"It mightn't have been last night," Chase said. "He might have had it for ages, and just not shown it to Ollie. I wouldn't show anything nice to Ollie either. He's probably a licker."

"I formed the impression that Mr. Ollie Muddypaws rummages through his brother's possessions with some regularity," Edgar said. "I rather think he would have come upon the locket right away. Besides, I should imagine that Mr. Muddypaws either takes his little acquisitions straight to the pawnbroker's, or else consigns them to some secret hoard under his bed; it would be both profitless and imprudent for him to carry them about in his overcoat for days on end."

"Well, where did the locket come from, then?" Chase demanded.

"Before we engage in conjecture, Inspector, can we with certainty exclude any possibility that Mr. Muddypaws might have unlawfully obtained it from your sister?"

"You said the initials were 'E.R.', Mr. Beagle," Chase said. "Even in Liverpool, we do not spell 'Chase' with an 'R.'"

"I am quite aware of the rules of orthography," Edgar said with dignity. "I only thought that perhaps your sister had a second name."

"Indeed she does," Chase rejoined, "and it is 'Imogen'. Do you know, Mr. Beagle, I wish the locket *were* hers. That would mean that Tommy had already got what he wanted out of her, and that he wouldn't come back. But it's no good running away from the truth, Mr. Beagle—reaching for silly ideas just because we're worrying."

"I am not doing any such thing," Edgar said, more hotly than he had intended. "I am merely attempting to logically assess all of the potential possibilities within the scope of our conjecture. I do not permit personal anxieties to cloud my investigative efforts, Inspector Chase. I consider it a stroke of fortune that Mr. Ollie Muddypaws happened to describe the locket to me, and—"

"What's that?" Chase interjected sharply.

"I said, I am merely attempting to logically assess—"

"No, not *that*. The bit about Ollie. *Described* it, you say?"

"Yes," Edgar said blankly.

Chase groaned and buried his head in his paws. "Well, then," he said, "we might as well not know anything at all. I thought you had seen it for yourself. How much store do *you* set by Ollie's reading skills?"

"The gentleman does not strike me as a voracious consumer of literature," Edgar conceded, "except perhaps in the most literal of senses, but I assumed he had attained basic literacy."

"Well, you assumed wrong. I lived next door to Ollie for years, Mr. Beagle, and it was the biggest surprise of my life when he finally stopped swallowing his socks every morning. That locket could say anything at all. Anyway, I say we go and arrest Tommy before he can make a run for it—or a waddle, more like, with those stubby legs. There really is something ridiculous about bulldogs, isn't there? Like Mr. Waggins at the Tail & Whiskers. One doesn't like to point and stare."

"I am not entirely certain that we can make an arrest at this juncture," Edgar said.

"Who's going to stop me? If anyone tries, I'll tell them they're welcome to wire the Metropolitan Police and report me to the Detective Chief Inspector if they like. See how long it takes them to work it out. Anyway, we've got to go to the Muddypaws' house no matter what; I want to see that locket for myself. I'll bet it *does* say 'E.C.'"

"Is a monogrammed locket likely to belong to your sister?" Edgar inquired delicately.

"How should I know? She's clever enough to remember her own initials without needing to hang them around her neck—but, I am told, that is *not* why girls wear these things. It isn't like the tag on Barks's collar; it's only for decoration."

"You mistake me. I hope I may point out without offending you, Inspector Chase, that monogrammed lockets are not everyday purchases."

"They're a waste of money, you mean?" Chase panted along beside him. "That's all the more reason to think it might be hers. Herder could have bought it for her; it sounds like just the sort of frivolous nonsense he *would* buy. Might as well chew your money right up."

"Any number of guests at the Adelphi Hotel are also likely to own lockets, I would imagine."

"Haven't rich folks anything better to do than collect shiny bits of metal like a magpie?"

"It is common, I believe, to develop sentimental attachments to material objects."

"Well, buy some chew toys and a velocipede, then. Don't

make some girl look as if she hasn't the brains to remember her own name. Anyway, I might have known it was Mr. Herder's fault somehow. Shouldn't go loading anybody up with fancy gifts, when there's a thief in the neighborhood."

"He could hardly have known that Mr. Muddypaws was a thief," Edgar said.

"That's not my fault, is it? I told everyone. I told them *years* ago. They ought to have listened, and then they could have warned anybody who came to town—or just have tossed him into prison and had done with it. Do you know, Mr. Beagle, I never realized it before, but that evil feeling that I got from Herder is nowhere near as bad as the one I've gotten from Tommy all along."

"Violent, irrational dislikes are quite common among puppies," Edgar said. "In fact, in Dr. Snuffles' latest report on the psychology of the adolescent—"

"It wasn't irrational! Come now, Mr. Beagle, you've met him yourself. He was always exactly like that, only worse. You wouldn't have liked him any more than I did."

"Be that as it may, it is not usual," Edgar said, smiling slightly, "to retain an obsession with one's puppyhood nemeses into adulthood."

Chase stopped walking and wheeled around to face Edgar. "It is *not* an obsession!" he said shrilly. "When you put aside all emotion and look only at the facts of the case, Mr. Beagle, it comes down to this: he is a criminal, and I am a police dog. It is my duty to track him down and see him made to answer for his crimes. Go on—you *like* putting aside all emotion. As soon as you consider the thing clearly, you'll see that my motives have only to do with justice."

"How extraordinarily commendable of you."

"I can tell when you're doing sarcasm, you know," Chase said plaintively. "I figured it out *years* ago. Your mouth goes all twisty. It's what we, in the police force, call a *tell*," he added, puffing out his chest. "And now—as a member of the police force—I am going to go and arrest a criminal. You may accompany me if you like."

"We need not go very far," Edgar said.

"What, do you mean that criminals are everywhere?" Chase said in disgust. "For the thousandth time, Liverpool is not—"

"No, I mean that Mr. Muddypaws is waddling up behind you—that is to say, approaching from the west—at this very moment."

Chase whirled around. His gaze raked Tommy's raised hackles and thunderous expression. "Still getting underfoot, I see," he said, in an unnaturally loud voice. "Well then, Tommy—have you come to give yourself up?"

"Oh, look," Tommy drawled, "it's little Gabriel Chase, still thinking that everything is about him. Calm down, Gabriel; I'm not here for you." He pushed past Chase and glared at Edgar. "Mr. Beagle, what do you mean by hectoring my brother? I had already told you: I was visiting a lady. If you were half the gentleman you look, then you would have left the whole thing alone. But that's the worst of scent hounds—always thrusting their noses into everyone else's affairs—always trying to root out things that are none of their business!"

"Step away from Mr. Beagle," Chase said in a dangerous voice. "Perhaps you ought to remember who I am these days, Tommy, before you go persecuting my sister and my dearest friend within twelve hours of each other."

Tommy glanced in his direction and hoisted up one drooping eyebrow. "Persecuting your sister? I'm afraid I don't know what you're talking about. All I did was accept your parents' invitation to supper. If I hadn't gone, then the whole street would have thought I was still mooning over her and couldn't bear to see her with another fellow, and then they would have gossiped about it all night, and then you would have blamed me for that instead. You always did like blaming me."

"Do you deny," Chase demanded, "that you went back to see Emily in the middle of the night?"

"Of course I deny it. If your sister invites fellows over at odd hours, then it's nothing to do with me."

"What are you implying?"

"Nothing—nothing at all! Maybe she just fancied an innocent little chat with a gentleman friend in the moonlight. I expect they were talking about art, or books. A really *philosophical* discussion." He leaned very close to Chase. "But she always was quick to point out everyone else's faults, you know. Looked down on all of us, like she was the angel off the Christmas tree before Ollie chewed on it. And I'll tell you something for free: it's dogs like that who have the most to hide. So before you go sending scent-hounds to howl on my doorstep, maybe you ought to ask her a question or two."

"Do you know," Chase said conversationally, and quite pleasantly, "that I've hated you ever since we were puppies? Even before I knew you were a thief. Everyone treated me like I was mad, but I could see all along that you were rotten through and through. Well, today the world will finally find out that I was right. All of them trying to convince me that you were so well-mannered and charming! Imagine their faces when they find out what you get up to at night."

"Go on and tell them, then," Tommy said, just as pleasantly.

"You'll never be able to prove I was doing anything wrong last night—because, of course, I wasn't. But go ahead; see if they believe you this time. I'll bet they all laugh in your face, as usual. Or maybe pity you, by now. Still spinning tall tales about me, after all these years! Really, Gabriel, why don't you have better things to do?"

"You will address me," Chase said, breathing hard, "as *Detective Chief Inspector Chase.*"

"Do you know, Gabriel, I rather think I won't."

"Perhaps, Mr. Muddypaws," Edgar said, physically interposing himself between Tommy and Chase, "you might care to either confirm or deny your brother's account of your activities last night. He says you were with a Miss Yapper at the Adelphi."

Tommy groaned theatrically. "Well, you've found me out alright, Mr. Beagle! Keeping your nose to the ground pays off, I suppose. But why it should make any difference to you whether I care to take a pretty friend for a walk on her evening off—"

"But last night was not her evening off," Edgar said, very gently. "I shall be able to verify that quite easily. You see, Miss Yapper reports that she has not seen you since Thursday. We have already questioned her about you."

Tommy's bulging eyeballs flickered away from Edgar's face for the barest of seconds. "As I told you this morning, Mr. Beagle, girls are sly."

"Slyness," Edgar said, "generally implies a motive. I confess, Mr. Muddypaws, I am hard-pressed to imagine a reason why Miss Yapper would have lied."

"Exactly because it was *not* her evening off, alright? She slipped away to meet me. I promised her I wouldn't tell a soul.

143

They'd turn her out of her job."

"Perhaps she would have been more prudent to delay the inestimable pleasure of your company until her next incidence of permitted leisure time. But then, of course, she must have been impatient to present you with that little sentimental remembrance."

"That *what?*"

"Oh, I beg your pardon!" Edgar said, studying Tommy's face carefully. "I had assumed that the silver locket you acquired last night was a romantic token from Miss Yapper. Of course, in order for her to give it to you as a gift," he added, almost as an afterthought, "it would have to have been her property in the first place."

"What are you talking about?"

"During my pleasant conversation with your brother, I happened to learn that a silver locket materialized in your overcoat last night."

Tommy's paw began to dart towards his pocket, then stopped abruptly. "Do you have siblings, Mr. Beagle?" he asked lightly.

"I do not consider my familial situation to be of any relevance."

"Well, if you do, then you know what they're like. Always trying to get you into trouble. Thinking it's funny to tell tales to the police."

"I am afraid that is not a universal experience, Mr. Muddy-paws."

"Did you actually *see* any locket?" Tommy parried.

"Are you suggesting that your brother fabricated its existence?"

"What is there to stop him?"

"An utter lack of creative imagination coupled with an inability to improvise, I should think."

"I don't like your tone, Mr. Beagle. And I don't like your face much either. What do you think about that?"

"To be perfectly candid, Mr. Muddypaws," Edgar said in his most polite voice, "your own physiognomy is not entirely to *my* tastes. Fortunately, we need not be friends."

Behind Edgar, Chase made a peculiar choking sound.

"Fine—you don't like me. Gabriel's gotten to you. If I were you, Mr. Beagle, I shouldn't make a habit of believing everything he says. I was with Flossie last night, and I don't know anything about any lockets."

"Then why," Edgar said, very gently, "did you come looking for me, just now? You were distressed to learn that I had spoken to your brother, and anxious to stop me from doing so again. Were you seeking to ascertain whether I had grasped the significance of what he had told me? Or trying to scare me away, before he could tell me more? I wonder what secrets you are guarding so vigorously, Mr. Muddypaws."

Tommy's gaze flickered between Edgar's impassive face and the paw-cuffs at Chase's waist. "You don't scare me," he said. "You haven't any proof of anything."

And, with that, he wheeled around and waddled away at top speed.

"That settles it," Chase said at once. "He's evading arrest. I'm going after him. Hold my hat, will you?"

Edgar lay a restraining paw on his arm. "He is quite right," he said. "We have no proof. As far as we know, he has not committed any crime."

"Then who," Chase demanded at the top of his voice, "was in the garden last night? And where did Tommy get that locket?

You can't mean to tell me that you believe he's innocent. He seems guiltier than anyone I've ever seen."

That, Edgar supposed, was perfectly true. Tommy gave off an unmistakable air of being guilty. But guilty, Edgar wondered, of *what*? He did seem to be a of decidedly unpleasant type—but it did not follow that he must be dangerous. Edgar was perfectly prepared to believe that he had taken liberties with his neighbor's garden, and perhaps selected his female acquaintances on the basis of their willingness to be light-pawed around valuables, but that was not at all the same sort of thing as intending bodily harm to Chase or to Emily. If anything, Edgar would have imagined him to be rather cowardly. His empty bluster was not particularly menacing; it was much easier to imagine him pilfering trinkets at the Adelphi Hotel than lurking under windows and collecting jagged rocks. It was perfectly possible—and, in fact overwhelmingly probable!—that he had been telling a passable version of the truth all along; he might have conveniently omitted certain locket-related details, but he had not fabricated an entirely false account of his nocturnal activities. For that matter, it did not defy belief that Ollie had, as Tommy said, invented the locket altogether — that Tommy was guilty of nothing more than encouraging his lady friend to slip away from her job — that Tommy, in fact, had every right to be outraged by Edgar's intrusion into his privacy!

Then why, Edgar demanded of himself, was he unable to shake the unfounded, irrational belief that Tommy was lying?

It would be absurd to let emotion run roughshod over a cool, clear-headed, logical assessment of the situation. His impulse to keep investigating was probably rooted in nothing more than Chase's lifelong dislike of Tommy. Really, Edgar thought, he was becoming dangerously suggestible! Chase was, upon occasion, quite a passable judge of character, but Edgar had seen more than enough counterexamples to fuel any amount of skepticism. It was bad enough that he had permitted Chase to drag him to Liverpool to meet Mr. Herder, who was probably perfectly law-abiding, albeit inexplicably changeable. Only a fool would trust Chase's judgment for a second time. And it was of absolutely no relevance, Edgar told himself sternly, that Chase would be overjoyed if Tommy turned out to be guilty. One did not pursue criminal convictions to please one's friends, or even to console them for the termination of their sisters' engagements. Ridiculous, really, all the things he had done for Chase in the last twenty-four hours! He glanced at Chase out of the corner of his eye. It was strange, now that he thought about it, to see Chase away from the accustomed backdrops of London. Strange to look at him with fresh eyes—not to discover something new, but to remember all the qualities to which Edgar had, for better or for worse, become thoroughly habituated.

Strange to find himself considering, after so many years, what Chase was really like.

Loyal, stubborn, hot-tempered Chase, prone to injured pride and lavish self-dramatization. Talkative, over-friendly Chase, always eager to regale Edgar with all the unnecessary details of any story. Gallant, sentimental Chase, pathetically noble in his stalwart idealism, clinging with both front paws to his own peculiar code of honor.

Chase, who had never, after all, provided altogether satisfactory specifics as to *why* he had hated Tommy for so many years.

At the very back of Edgar's mind, something was stirring.

147

A half-remembered scrap of Mrs. Chase's gossip. A casual word from the concierge at the hotel. A matter-of-fact observation by Ollie Muddypaws.

Cautiously, Edgar permitted a theory to take shape. Insubstantial figures passed like shadow puppets across the canvas of his thoughts. It was unlikely, but it was not impossible.

If he was wrong, of course, Chase would be terribly insulted—probably even angry. Gentlemen usually got angry over this sort of thing.

But he did not think that he was wrong.

"Inspector Chase," Edgar said carefully, "I wonder whether you might tell me something about Miss Roughcoat."

Chase stared at him in disbelief. "You must be joking," he said. "Not you too. What do you want to know about her, Mr. Beagle? How sweet she looked in her little bonnet with the roses? How soft her paw felt in mine? How I dreamed about her every night for months? Well, I'm afraid I cannot satisfy your curiosity. I have not thought about her in many years, you see, and so I remember very little."

"Actually," Edgar said. "What I want to know is this: is 'Nora,' by any chance, short for 'Eleanor'?"

Chapter Nine

For a moment, Chase merely looked puzzled. "It is, as it happens," he said. "But why you should care whether a girl you've never met is named 'Nora Roughcoat' or 'Eleanor Roughcoat' is more than I can—*oh.*" He froze, his eyes wide. "'E.R.'—but, Mr. Beagle, why should that locket be *hers*? I'll bet there are hundreds of girls in Liverpool with those initials. Loads of things start with 'E' or 'R.' Anyway, her family doesn't have the money for that sort of nonsense, now the East India Company's broken up."

"Perhaps not," Edgar said, "but do you remember what your mother said last night?"

"Do you think I listen when my mother talks?"

"She said that Miss Roughcoat was receiving extravagant gifts from her new beau."

"What, Roddy Mastiff?" Chase snorted. "His idea of a nice present would be a handkerchief without any slobber on it. He can't afford to go lumbering around to jewelers and having things engraved."

"Yes, I quite see the difficulty," Edgar said. "But your mother mentioned later on, you may recall, that Mr. Mastiff is employed as an assistant at Mr. Schnauzer's shop. Sold second-paw, the locket would be significantly less expensive.

Besides, perhaps Mr. Schnauzer gave him a special price. At any rate, your earlier point was quite correct: 'E.R' is a not an uncommon monogram. It does not strain credulity to imagine that young Mr. Mastiff, happening to come upon a piece of merchandise fortuitously emblazoned with the very initials of his ladylove and priced within his means, may have felt inspired to present her with it."

"Even if all that is true, how would Tommy have gotten hold of the locket? If the Roughcoats' house had been burgled last night, we would have heard by now."

"There is a very obvious hypothesis to be made, Inspector," Edgar said quietly, "and I imagine it has already crossed your mind."

"I'm sure I haven't any idea what you mean." Chase's face was wooden. "And I've certainly said nothing that should make you go forming *hypotheses*."

"That is exactly the trouble: *you have said nothing.* Inspector Chase, you tell me *everything*. Every time someone bumps into you in the street, or is rude to you in a shop, or forcibly ejects you and Constable Barks from a pub, you recount every detail to me. I know the name of the schoolmaster who scolded you when you were ten years old, and the landlady who turned you away when you first came to London, and the sergeant who said you had too many biscuits in your pockets."

Chase scowled. "I'm very sorry if I've been *boring* you all these years—"

"No, you mistake me. I merely find it curious that, in nearly a decade by your side, I should never have heard the barest syllable about Mr. Muddypaws, your puppyhood enemy."

"He wasn't worth mentioning," Chase said shortly.

"Furthermore," Edgar went on, "you have provided me with

the flimsiest of explanations for your undisguised hatred of him." He held up a paw to forestall Chase. "Yes, yes, I know! You have accused him—quite correctly, it seems— of petty theft. But your work as a police dog has brought you into contact with plenty of thieves, and you never gave them a second thought. Your persistent antipathy towards Mr. Muddypaws does not seem indicated. Why should you take his criminal predilections so personally? After all, it is not as if he had ever stolen anything from *you*."

"That's all you know."

"All the more reason, then, for you to have told me about him."

"You don't understand, Mr. Beagle," Chase said miserably. "I couldn't tell you about him because then I would have had to tell you about *her*, and I couldn't tell you about her because— well, because I made a promise."

"Yes, I thought you might have," Edgar said. "You cared very much for Miss Roughcoat, I imagine."

"Cared for her?" Chase gave a hollow little laugh. "I was clean mad for her. The prettiest girl anywhere in England, I thought. There was a sparkle to her—vivacious, you would call it. I'd never seen anyone like her."

"And the lady did not reciprocate your sentiments?"

"I thought she did. She never said anything definite, but there were little things—looks from across the room and nudges with her paw—you know how girls are. Well, probably *you* don't, but maybe you'll have read about it in Dr. Snuffles or something. We were awfully young, Mr. Beagle. But I meant to ask her to marry me, someday, and everyone knew it. Tommy used to tease me for being so stuck on her. He had a different girl on his arm every week."

151

"Including Miss Roughcoat?" Edgar inquired delicately.

Chase turned anguished eyes on him. "They were kissing when I found them," he said. "I walked right in and saw them; Tommy had arranged it so I should. Nora was terribly frightened when she realized I was there. She said she would be ruined if anyone found out. The neighbors would gossip, she said, and no one would ever marry her. She begged me to promise I would keep it a secret. She was *crying*, Mr. Beagle— she just kept crying and crying. So I promised—and I never told—and then I went to London, and that was the end of it. She had never kissed *me*," he added bitterly. "You mustn't tell anyone, Mr. Beagle. I don't suppose telling you counts, not really."

"Because of my profession?"

"No, because you had guessed most of it already. And also because of you being my best friend, and a perfect gentleman."

"If we keep our silence," Edgar said, "then you will find it very difficult to prove anything against Mr. Muddypaws. Not half an hour ago, you were determined to arrest him at any price."

"Well, we *are* going to keep our silence. I gave a girl my word, Mr. Beagle."

"That is not," Edgar said, "nearly as important as pursing justice."

"Of course it is—are you mad? But anyway, all that's in the past. Twelve years ago. You can pursue as much justice you like in the here and now. Why go digging up old memories?"

"Because," Edgar said, "if I am correct in thinking that the locket was Miss Roughcoat's property, then I am afraid that 'all that,' as you term it, is *not* in the past. As you said, we have heard no reports of a burglary, and I very much doubt that

Mr. Muddypaws is suited to stealth operations. The most plausible explanation for Mr. Muddypaws' acquisition of the locket is this: Miss Roughcoat bestowed it upon him last night. He called upon *her* after the party, not Miss Yapper. He lied to his brother, or else instructed his brother to lie on his behalf; it *was* a fictitious alibi, just not for the intrusion into your parents' garden. Miss Roughcoat, presumably, does not want her beau to learn that she is receiving after-dinner visits from another gentleman. Or perhaps his brother, having found the locket, merely jumped to a false conclusion regarding its provenance."

"But why should Nora want to give Tommy anything? She's practically engaged to Roddy Mastiff."

"I assume she has succumbed to Mr. Muddypaws' doubtful charms nonetheless. It would not, after all, be the first time."

"He never even cared about her," Chase burst out suddenly. "He only went after her to prove he could steal her from me. Threw her over for another girl not a month later. And then three years ago, when my father got promoted, he started sniffing around Emily—I suppose he thought she would pilfer the imports for him, or maybe he just wanted to ruin my life again. And nobody believed me when I said she should keep away from him, and they thought I was perfectly mad when I said he was hanging around her to get at *me*—and I couldn't explain how I knew he was no good, because I had *promised* Nora—"

"It has been a heavy burden for you to bear," Edgar said gently.

Chase glared at him. "Don't you go getting sentimental on me, Mr. Beagle," he said. "I did stop loving her eventually, you know; I haven't been mooning over her for the last twelve

153

years, no matter what my mother thinks. I hope she and Roddy Mastiff will make a match of it."

"Unlikely, I should think, if she persists in distributing his gifts to other gentlemen."

"Look, I'm sure it wasn't like that. Even if she were still keen on Tommy after all these years, why should she go giving him jewelry? It's not as if he were going to wear it. And besides, she would have the dickens of a time explaining to Roddy where it had gone. The Mastiffs are awfully old-fashioned. They wouldn't stand for anything like that."

"I rather assumed," Edgar said, "that she was familiar with Mr. Muddypaws' passion for visiting the pawnshop. According to his brother, Mr. Muddypaws only maintains his friendship with young ladies if they assist him in his endeavors. Perhaps Miss Roughcoat has discovered that the occasional locket is the price for Mr. Muddypaws' continued affections."

"Dash it all, Mr. Beagle—Nora isn't that sort of a girl!"

"Forgive me, Inspector. I had inferred, based on her betrayal of you, that integrity was not the lady's strong point."

"And goodness knows," Chase said, over him, "she needn't bribe anyone to court her. I got a glimpse of her at the Wolfhounds' Christmas party last year, and she's still the loveliest thing I've ever seen. Anyway, if she and Tommy have been secretly carrying on for twelve years, then why shouldn't she just marry *him* instead of messing Roddy Mastiff about?"

"Mr. Muddypaws does not strike me as being inclined toward matrimony. Besides, he may have instructed Miss Roughcoat to encourage Mr. Mastiff's lucrative advances."

"She isn't like that, I tell you," Chase said stubbornly. "I know you never trust my intuition, but do you think I am a fool altogether?"

154

"I think," Edgar said, "that your former regard for her may be blinding you to the truth. I have constructed a perfectly logical hypothesis; your assessment of Miss Roughcoat, which is clearly rooted in sentiment, is not sufficient to refute it."

"You don't understand. She wasn't the type of girl you are imagining; she didn't happen to love me back, was all. She was fond of me, and she was flattered by my attention, but she never pretended there was more in it, not really—I can see that now. In time, I think, she would have grown to care for me. But Tommy came waddling in and swept her clean off her paws before she had the chance. She was always awfully impulsive, and she never thought things through ahead of time. We herding dogs are like that, I suppose." He gave Edgar a slightly melancholy smile. "Life works out for the best, Mr. Beagle. If I had married her, I would have settled down here, and never moved to London. Instead of which, she has a beau who probably suits her better than I ever did, and I have—well, I have all the advantages of having moved to London. If we could not be happy together, then at least we are happy apart. I have put the whole sorry affair well behind me."

"That," Edgar said, as delicately as he possibly could, "does not seem to be entirely true."

"And what is *that* supposed to mean?"

"Your persistent antipathy towards Mr. Muddypaws—"

"He *is* a thief; I didn't make it up!"

"—which, only this morning, evidently manifested itself in a refusal to call upon him, even though you are generally eager to participate in my investigations, particularly when you have a personal stake in the case, as exemplified by your insistence upon interviewing Miss Yapper straight away—"

"I had to go to the bank."

"You could have gone an hour later."

"Well, you could have gone to see Tommy an hour later," Chase rejoined, scowling.

"Would you have accompanied me if I had?"

"No, but it isn't what you think. I'm man enough, I hope, to call upon Tommy Muddypaws without quaking like a whippet or punching him in the head or whatever you're picturing."

"Such a notion never crossed my mind—"

"Don't be grand."

"—and yet, I confess myself somewhat bewildered as to why you should have declined to join me, if not for—"

"Isn't it bad enough," Chase demanded, very loudly, "you'd seen my mother and Mr. Dewlaps and all?"

"I have thoroughly resigned myself," Edgar assured him, "to enduring your relations and acquaintances. One more or less will hardly make a difference. Besides, I was going to see him whether you accompanied me or not."

"No, that's not—" Chase tossed his head and pawed moodily at the ground. "There's a reason I never asked you home with me for Christmas, alright?"

"I assumed it was a merciful impulse upon your part."

"You are *not*," Chase said, with an irritable sideways glare, "as witty as you think. Look, when you first meet a fellow out on his own, without seeing how the folks in his life treat him— well, you're bound to have such and such thoughts about him, aren't you? And maybe those aren't the same thoughts you would have had if you had seen that straightaway—or, I mean, the thoughts you would keep on having, perhaps, if even now you were to see—do you follow me?"

"No."

"Well, you saw it yourself just now, after all. The way he talks to me, I mean. You can understand, can't you, why I hadn't wanted—" Chase sighed, loudly and heavily. "No, never mind, let it go—alright? Talk to me some more about the locket or something."

"Alas, how can I," Edgar said, slightly bewildered by the change in topic, "when you persist in rejecting my every suggestion out of paw?"

"It is not out of paw! I know Nora and you don't. You have no reason to think she's the least bit likely to get mixed up in something sordid."

"I rather wondered whether Captain Mastiff's interrogation of her acquaintances might be predicated on any definite and founded suspicion."

"Captain Mastiff *what* now?"

"Your mother told us about it last night," Edgar said patiently. "She said that a Captain Mastiff had interviewed her regarding your erstwhile friendship with Miss Roughcoat."

"Well, I don't remember that at all. I must have been down the other end of the garden."

"No, you were standing right next to me. It was just before I was introduced to Mr. Herder and his friends."

"What, while Ollie was digging that hole and Tommy was standing there drooling?"

"Yes, I suppose it must have been."

A very peculiar expression was spreading across Chase's face. Edgar could not tell whether it was anger or triumph.

"We are going to the Roughcoats' right away," he said.

"I beg your pardon?"

Chase heaved an impatient, theatrical sigh. "We—that is to say, you and me—"

"You and *I*—"

"Stop that; you know perfectly what I mean. You and *I*—there; are you happy now?—are going to go and have a talk with Nora Roughcoat."

"My dear Inspector Chase," Edgar said, "while I can fully understand your desire to pay a visit to Miss Roughcoat, I should imagine it would be more judicious to stay well out of this situation."

"I am a *police dog*," Chase snapped. "Why do you always try to stop me from investigating crimes? It's all you've done this weekend."

"Why," Edgar parried, "do you persist in misidentifying your emotions as evidence that a crime has been committed? If Miss Roughcoat has been given this locket as a gift, then it is hers to dispose of as she pleases. And if she has chosen to, in turn, give it to Mr. Muddypaws, then it is his property now, and he has a perfect right to pawn it if he likes. Furthermore, your mother mentioned that Mr., Mrs., and Miss Roughcoat are all suffering from kennel cough at present. You may, perhaps, be acquainted with Dr. Snuffles' monograph about the transmission of airborne respiratory illnesses—"

"If we get kennel cough," Chase said viciously, "we get kennel cough. I'll bet he's there with her right now. Come *on.*"

Edgar hurried along in Chase's wake. He was suddenly, and unhappily, aware that he had been rushing back and forth all day, engaging in utterly pointless conversations just to humor Chase. If he were in London, at this hour on a Saturday, he would already have gone for his walk—a nice measured one along a predictable route, not all of this unnecessarily frenetic dashing through dingy back streets!—and accomplished several hours of work. Was this what Chase's life was like, whenever Edgar was not with him—forever running in circles and barking at strangers, with no fixed plans or attainable goals, spurred to action over and over by every piece of nonsense that popped up along the way? Perhaps herding dogs were simply born with a boundless reserve of energy. Perhaps, if they did not continually find ways to expend it, they would devolve into outright mania. And why, for goodness' sake, could Chase not see what was perfectly plain: that he had been deceived in the character of his former beloved, and that his headlong rush to visit her today was impelled only by the most ridiculously sentimental of motives? At least, Edgar thought bitterly, Chase was consistent; apparently, he had always selected his lady friends injudiciously!

"Come *on*," Chase said again, darting off down a side street. "It's just this way."

"Perhaps," Edgar suggested, panting to keep up with him, "you might care to smooth down your ears and permit me to fix your cravat before we call upon Miss Roughcoat."

"Whatever for? This isn't a social call." He stopped in front of a large, rather weatherbeaten house, and reached for the knocker. "And anyway, I'm done with trying to impress her."

An elderly tabby in a threadbare cap and apron opened the door. She goggled at Chase and Edgar with big green eyes, and her whiskers twitched with interest. "If it isn't Mr. Gabriel Chase, all grown up!" she exclaimed. "I remember when you used to come sniffing around here every day. Do you know, I always thought you and Miss Nora would—"

"Never mind about that," Chase said urgently. "He's here, isn't he? Tommy Muddypaws?"

"Yes, sir, he got here a few minutes ago, and they're sitting in the parlor. But how on earth did you—"

"And he was here last night, wasn't he? Probably around

nine or ten. He sent you up to Miss Roughcoat with a note, perhaps, asking her to come and talk to him—and her parents are in bed with kennel cough, so they were none the wiser. Never mind—I'll bet Miss Roughcoat told you not to mention that to anyone." He shouldered past the parlormaid, ignoring her startled, high-pitched meow. "Let's go, Mr. Beagle. We haven't any time to lose."

Edgar followed him at a more sedate pace. The foyer, he half-consciously noted, was papered in a cheerful, modern design of questionable aesthetic merit. Silk curtains, their once-bright colors only slightly faded, hung over the windows. Chase, striding ahead down the hallway with a thundercloud expression, seemed to know exactly where he was going. Edgar idly wondered whether this was the first time he had been in this house since the fateful day he had come upon Tommy and Nora. How very like Chase to have sworn a ridiculous oath, all those years ago. It was oddly reassuring to know that Chase had, as it were, always been Chase. Despite all his chaotic bursts of energy and fantastical theories and ill-starred romantic endeavors, Chase really was, on the whole, quite comfortingly predictable. Edgar found himself hoping, rather fervently, that Chase would finally be able to avenge himself on Tommy—*no*, he told himself; hoping that justice would finally be served. A perfectly reasonable thing to hope for. Tommy had, after all, presumably been enticing young ladies into a life of crime, not to mention pawning stolen goods and ravaging his neighbors' flowerbeds, for *years*. He was, when one stopped to really consider him, a menace to the community. Chase's personal history with him—and any second-paw outrage that a more susceptible dog than Edgar might have experienced on Chase's behalf—was, of course, of

160

no real consequence.

They were nearing the end of the hallway. From behind the closed door in front of them, Edgar could just make out an indignant female voice. "I *won't* tell lies to the police, Tommy," it said. Chase growled low in his throat and lunged for the handle.

"My dear Inspector Chase! Without even knocking? Consider the impropriety—"

But Chase had already shoved the door open. Inside the parlor, two figures were seated in front of the fire.

"Oh look, Nora," Tommy Muddypaws drawled, barely even deigning to glance up at Chase. "Your old admirer has burst in on us *again*. He's even brought a spectator this time."

Nora Roughcoat jumped up at once. A pale blue silk wrapper, edged in delicate white lace, set off the striking curves of her statuesque figure, and her luxuriant brown and white fur was noticeably rumpled; she had, Edgar supposed, been unexpectedly summoned from her sickbed upon Tommy's arrival. Edgar had imagined that she would be chagrined, or even angered, by Chase's sudden intrusion, but her limpid eyes and the exquisitely molded lines of her pointed face displayed only fear, and the tips of her elegant triangular ears were trembling violently. "Gabriel!" she breathed.

"Hello, Nora," Chase said, more quietly than Edgar had ever heard him say anything. "This is my friend Mr. Beagle, a private investigator from London. Mr. Beagle, Miss Roughcoat."

"I am delighted to make your acquaintance, Miss Roughcoat," Edgar said.

"I feel as if I already knew you, Mr Beagle." Nora turned back to Chase, smiling a little. "Do you know, your mother used to come round and read your letters out loud? Trying to show me what I had missed, I suppose. Tommy *said* you would realize he had my locket, sooner or later. But I supposed you would just send over a constable, not come to see me yourself."

"Did you think he wouldn't jump at the opportunity?" Tommy sneered. "I suppose he got the idea that you and I had renewed our friendship, and thought you might be able to spare a kiss or two for him this time."

Nora gave no sign of having heard him. She took a few steps forward, her gaze fixed on Chase's face. She might almost, Edgar thought, have been sleepwalking. "Gabriel," she said again, and seized Chase's paw. "Tommy wants me to lie to you and say I gave him the locket freely, but I know I needn't. You'd never do anything to harm me. You'll protect me, won't you?"

"At any cost," Chase said. "I always have, haven't I?"

Edgar resisted the impulse to audibly sigh. For goodness' sake, he thought, why must Chase always be so susceptible to young ladies of the adventuress variety?

"Gabriel, I don't know what to do." Nora's voice trembled, and she let out a slight cough. Edgar took a hasty step backwards. "I'll run out of things to give him, soon enough. And then he'll go straight to Roddy's father—I know he will."

"My God," Chase said, in a low, dangerous voice, stepping around Nora and advancing on Tommy with a look of pure disgust. "I always knew you were a thief and a scoundrel, but blackmail is low, even for you. I suppose you overheard my mother at the party, and then came waddling right over here."

"Blackmail's an ugly word," Tommy said, smiling agreeably. "Shall we say instead that Nora has decided to thank me for my discretion regarding our amorous history?"

"That *is* blackmail," Chase said, through tightly gritted teeth.

"Well, I never forced her to do anything. She decided of her own free will that the price was worth it to her. Just a little business arrangement between old friends."

"That's still blackmail."

Tommy's grin never wavered. "And if it is, then what are you going to do about it? Arrest me?"

"Can you give me one good reason why I shouldn't?"

"Because it will all come out during the trial," Nora broke in desperately, coughing again.

"If Roddy loves you as he should," Chase told her, scowling, "then he won't give a hang about all that."

"His family will."

"He ought to choose you over them. If you had been mine, I would have chosen you over all the world."

Nora's gaze softened. "You were always terribly sweet, Gabriel. I see you're still a romantic."

"I am *not*—"

"But this is real life. Roddy isn't going to let his family disinherit him just so he can marry me."

"He doesn't deserve your paw in marriage, then."

"I suppose you think," Tommy interrupted, smirking, "that she ought to run away with you to London instead."

Chase flinched visibly. "No," he said, "I don't. I only want her to be happy."

"How noble of you. You always did think you were better than the rest of us."

"Well, I'm certainly better than *you*," Chase said.

"What, because you've got a flash address in London and a friend with deep pockets?"

"No, because I don't seduce girls and then blackmail them

163

over it. Now then, Tommy: this is going to stop. Tell your ridiculous story to every mastiff in England, for all I care. Everyone will just think you're a liar. You haven't a shred of proof. I kept my promise to Nora; no one ever knew."

"Nora ought to have thought of that before she gave me the locket," Tommy said softly, "I have proof *now*."

"What, proof that you're a blackmailer?"

"No, no. Proof that the Mastiffs shouldn't let Nora marry their precious son. What's to stop them from believing me if I say that she gave me the locket as a token of affection?"

"What's to stop the local police from believing that you stole it from her?" Chase parried. "You've certainly stolen enough other things. Ollie can tell everyone all about how you like to go to the pawnshop."

Tommy dismissed this with an airy wave of his paw. "Stolen it from her? Do use your brain for once, Gabriel. How would I have gotten hold of it? Anyone can see there hasn't been a burglary here. I suppose she kept it in her bedroom; for me to have an opportunity to steal it, she would have to have taken me up there in the night. And if you go to the police with a story about *that*—well, all I can say is, can you blame the Mastiffs if they draw their own conclusions about her?"

"You understand, I hope," Chase said, breathing hard, "that if you do anything to harm Nora, I'll never rest until I've found a way to destroy you."

Tommy laughed outright. "The thing about threats," he said, "is that you have to be someone who can back them up. Your shiny badge doesn't fool me. I've known you since we were puppies—and frankly, *Inspector*, I am not impressed." He turned to Nora and grinned. "Did you know," he said, "that little Gabriel Chase told all the other boys that he was going

164

to marry you when he grew up? He said it for *years*. We all laughed at him, of course."

Chase's hackles rose visibly, and his front paws curled into fists. Edgar felt himself tense. Surely Chase was not so monumentally injudicious as to instigate a physical altercation! Gentlemen of Tommy's type were, in Edgar's experience, often cowards when it came to violence—but, on the other paw, Tommy was somewhat larger than Chase, and possessed of rather more impressive muscles—and Constable Barks was not here—and there was Tommy's lip, lifting into a decided snarl, and a faint growl humming at the back of his throat. Edgar made some hurried, and decidedly unreassuring, calculations regarding his own pugilistic abilities. He would have to think on his paws instead. If only he were armed, right now, with a definite fact! A solid accusation regarding Tommy's criminal activities would, he imagined, alarm Tommy enough to draw his attention away from antagonizing Chase. He turned the morning's events over and over in his brain. There was *something*, he thought, but he could not grab hold of it—not quite yet. Perhaps, in a moment, it would take definite shape.

And perhaps, in the meantime, a guess, or perhaps even a mere bluff, might be enough.

"Mr. Muddypaws," Edgar said very casually, sounding for all the world as if he had no idea he was interrupting anything, "it strikes me as curious that your friend Miss Yapper seemed alarmed when I mentioned the locket; given that you got it from Miss Roughcoat, Miss Yapper cannot have been involved."

Tommy startled and glared. "What about it?" he demanded. "Flossie's a funny girl."

"I further wonder," Edgar continued imperturbably, "how Mr. Schnauzer's second-paw shop, whose usual wares are apparently typified by flea-ridden cravats of dubious quality, should have come into the possession of so valuable a piece of jewelry. Mr. Schnauzer was evidently willing to price it within Mr. Mastiff's means, indicating that it was not a special purchase on his part; he probably obtained it from one of his regular suppliers. One might, perhaps, conjecture that you and Miss Yapper stole the locket from a hotel guest on some earlier occasion and took it to a local pawnshop; that Mr. Schnauzer is in the habit of buying that pawnshop's unclaimed acquisitions; and that, having extracted it from Miss Roughcoat, you intended to pawn it a second time and start the whole sorry cycle over."

He was gratified to see sudden panic flashing through Tommy's eyes.

"Even if that were true," Tommy said, scowling, "which it is *not*, you haven't any evidence."

"Oh, I imagine Miss Yapper could be persuaded fairly easily to betray you, particularly once she is under arrest for snapping up unconsidered trifles in hotel rooms," Edgar said, smiling. "You do not seem to have inspired any extravagant measure of loyalty in her."

"She's only a servant. You would take her word over mine?"

"Of course I would. Your word, if you will forgive me, appears to be worth very little."

"At least *I* never lied about important things," Tommy said, very haughtily. "*I* never told everyone I was running off to London to be a police dog just because it was *so exciting* there and *not* because I had finally gotten it through my head that I wasn't wanted at home. And *I* certainly never talked about

166

a girl as if she were a perfect saint, when I knew full well she was going around kissing another fellow behind the parlor door and under the staircase and up against the silver cabinet and—"

And, with dizzying suddenness, there it was. Edgar could almost hear the piece click into place in his brain. He barely stopped himself from heaving an audible sigh of relief. "Inspector Chase," he said, laying a firm, restraining paw on Chase's arm, "how far from here is the nearest pawnshop?"

Chase looked at him with considerable irritation. "I know you like to make a map in your head everywhere you go, Mr. Beagle, but this is hardly the time. I was just about to throttle this damned—"

"*There is a lady present!*" Edgar said severely. "Could one travel, do you suppose, to any local pawnshop, conduct one's business, and return in approximately an hour?"

"How should I know? *I* don't go about nicking other dogs' things and selling them."

"Hazard an educated guess."

"I should think there would be one over at Everton, and that's about an hour either way on paw. You could take a cab from here to there, though that would be awfully expensive, but I don't suppose you could find one there to get back here afterwards; it's not that sort of a place. But *why* you should want to know that—"

"So," Edgar said, with an air of quiet triumph, "Mr. Muddy-paws did not have time to visit the pawnshop before I called on him this morning. Nor did he have time afterwards, before his encounter with us in the street."

"What does that matter? I suppose your point is that he hasn't had a chance to pawn the locket, so it's still at his house.

But the locket doesn't do us any good." Chase set his jaw firmly. "You can save your little speech about justice trumping sentiment, Mr. Beagle. I am not going to destroy Nora's life."

"You misunderstand me," Edgar said gently. "Indeed, the locket is still at his house—*and so is your parents' silver ladle*. We may reasonably infer from Miss Yapper's account that he went to the party with the express intention of pilfering valuables. That, I take it, is the sense in which he meant that Miss Chase could be useful to him: by hosting an event at which the finest tableware was sure to be brought out, and at which no one's attention was likely to be on him, she had unwittingly given him a perfect opportunity. There is no obstacle to arresting him. Plenty of witnesses saw him in attendance. He cannot even attempt to blame his long-suffering brother this time; he was not wearing gloves at the party, and I doubt he had the foresight to wipe his paw prints off the ladle after he had taken it home. Once he is standing in the dock for petty theft from his neighbors, I imagine that any slanderous stories he cares to spread about Miss Roughcoat will be received with a healthy measure of skepticism. You are, after all, an extremely high-ranking officer at the Metropolitan Police; your word will carry considerable weight should you choose to vouch for the lady's character."

"You believed me about the ladle?" Chase asked, very softly, "I thought *nobody* believed me about anything Tommy did."

"Unlike everyone else in this city," Edgar said. "I am not in the habit of underestimating you."

The corner of Chase's mouth twitched into a grin. He drew himself up very straight, lifted his chin, and unclipped the paw-cuffs from his belt. Edgar got the impression that he might have rehearsed this before, perhaps upon multiple occasions

168

over the course of several years. "Thomas Muddypaws," Chase said, "I arrest you for theft."

Tommy merely snickered. "I'd like to see you try. What's to stop me walking right out that door?"

"Although I would prefer not to resort to physical violence," Chase said, very grandly and officially, "I must warn you that, if you insist upon forcing my paw—"

"Do you know," Tommy interrupted casually, "Nora never gave a toss about you? You were such a scrawny, pathetic little thing. Fancy you thinking you were good enough for her! And here you are, still sniffing around above your station—"

"As it happens," Chase snapped, abruptly reverting to his normal voice, "Nora is *not* above my station. I run the Detective Division of the Metropolitan Police."

"Oh, I didn't mean her," Tommy said, smirking. "I meant this gentleman you've attached yourself to. Years of writing letters home about your *splendid, clever* friend, trying to convince everyone that you were worth taking notice of! Everyone just felt sorry for you, and sorrier for him. We all supposed he was just too polite to drag you to the pound." He heaved an elaborate sight. "One day, I hope, you'll finally learn to know when you're not wanted."

"Well, as you can see," Chase said, through tightly clenched teeth, "I am *not* not wanted. Mr. Beagle came all the way from London just to help me catch *you*—didn't you, Mr. Beagle?"

"Certainly, Inspector, I have come to Liverpool pursuant to your investigative activities."

Tommy chortled humorlessly. "Lucky for you he was free this weekend. You couldn't have pinned a thing on me if he hadn't stepped in to save you." He peered craftily at Chase through his deep-set eyes. "That was *not* an admission of guilt.

I needn't talk to the police if I don't want."

"Who do you think you've been talking to all this time?" Chase snapped.

"Oh, yes, you mentioned—you're a *police dog* now. Made many arrests by yourself, have you? Standing on your own two back paws? Really putting your nose to the ground and tracking down dangerous gangs of trained assassins and international criminals?"

"What are you getting at?"

"Oh, nothing—nothing! It's only—well, you couldn't even catch *me* on your own, could you? I'll bet you've been picturing your big arrest for years; I suppose you thought I would just die of terror, and then Nora would throw herself into your arms, and then the Queen would jump out from behind the bushes and make you a knight, and then there would be a big parade with trumpets and an elephant. Instead of which, you've turned out to be just as hopeless as you always were, and someone cleverer had to do your job for you—and, by the way, Nora *still* doesn't want you, though goodness knows she's never been choosy—"

Chase reared back his fist and struck Tommy squarely in the face. Tommy gave an undignified yelp, tripped over his back paws, and sat down heavily on the carpet.

"I'll tell you what," Chase said, "I've been picturing *that* for years."

Tommy glared up at him, drooling balefully. "When we were puppies," he said, "I could have knocked you down with one paw tied behind my back."

Chase bent down and cuffed Tommy to the leg of the armchair. "I grew up," he said. He straightened up, threw out his chest, and turned to Nora. "I think you will find," he said, very grandly, "that this gentleman will not trouble you any longer."

"That was perfectly splendid," Nora breathed, her eyes shining.

"All in a day's work for the Metropolitan Police."

"Well, all the same, I think you're awfully brave. Shall I ring for the maid and send her to fetch a constable or two?"

"It is a pity," Chase said with great regret, "that my own particular constable is not here. I should have liked to introduce you to him. Mr. Beagle, ought I to dash back to the house and fetch Barks and bring him back here, do you think? No? Alright—I suppose it will be quicker to get the local constabulary. I ought to have a word with them about Flossie Yapper anyway. Go on and send for them."

The police arrived quickly. Edgar stood to one side, covertly spectating as Chase, with his chest still puffed out self-importantly, barked out orders and made brisk, decisive gestures. Really, Edgar reflected, Chase was growing more mercurial every day! Baffling to be so exultant over this arrest, when they had not escaped the constant, looming danger of the nocturnal intruders, when Chase's sister had been abandoned practically at the altar, and when they were almost certainly incubating kennel cough. And incredible that Chase's confidence should be bolstered by the straightforward capture of an adversary so blatantly undeserving of respect. Surely Chase's estimation of himself was not predicated on his ability to best his puppyhood rivals—not when he had effected so many noteworthy arrests, and risen to such heights in his profession!

"Congratulations on your victory, Inspector," he ventured, once Mr. Muddypaws had been removed, just in case Chase was, for some unaccountable reason, mentally cataloging this as one of his triumphs.

"No one ever believed me," Chase said viciously. "I can't wait until my mother hears about this. So long, Nora, and don't forget to invite me to your wedding. If anybody else bothers you, you just let me know."

"You've turned out to be simply marvelous, *Inspector Chase*," Nora said. "Goodbye, and thank you for everything."

Chase took a few steps towards the door, and then turned back abruptly. He took a deep breath, squared his shoulders, and pricked his ears all the way forward. "Nora?" he said.

"Yes?"

"If not for Tommy, would you have married me?"

"Never, Gabriel," Nora said, very kindly, and without a second's pause. "You were sweet—you really were. But you ran in circles all the time, and you talked too much about squirrels. I already did enough of that myself. I don't think herding dogs should marry each other, do you? We're loyal, I grant you, but we never stop dashing about. No household needs two of those. It's better for us to marry someone strong and steady and floppy-eared—like Roddy Mastiff." She cocked her head, and her expression softened. "All the same, I was awfully fond of you, and I didn't mean to break your heart."

Chase smiled at her. "That's all I wanted to know," he said. "I hope you and Roddy will be very happy together. Goodbye, Nora."

Chapter Ten

E dgar expected Chase's self-congratulatory mood to last, but it fell from him like a mask as they walked away from the Roughcoats' house. His shoulders slumped, and he scuffed his shoes moodily along the pavement.

"Is anything the matter?" Edgar ventured.

"What's that?" Chase gave Edgar a quick smile. "No, no. It's only—well, I always thought I'd feel different, was all. If I ever managed to arrest Tommy, I mean. Or if Nora ever thought I had done something impressive. I used to daydream about saving her from all sorts of dangers, you know. Pirates and monsters and highway-cats and things. Real life is awfully disappointing sometimes. I say, did you really mean that thing you said? About not underestimating me?"

"Certainly, Inspector, I should say that my assessment of your abilities is quite accurate."

"No, I mean, do you think I—never mind." He gave a gusty sigh. "Listen, we needn't talk about all that, alright? Let's just get to work. I have a theory about Herder."

"Another one, with such dizzying speed?" Edgar asked politely. "By all means, tell me all about it."

"It's only this: why shouldn't Tommy have gotten to him

too? A fellow like Tommy only has room in his head for a couple of ideas. We have seen that he likes getting his paws on expensive gifts that his former lady friends' new beaux have given them—very well. Emily has plenty of expensive gifts from Herder; maybe Tommy tried to blackmail *her*. He could have threatened to go to Herder with a pack of lies, to make Herder think there was more between her and Tommy than there ever was. And a proud, truthful girl like Emily wouldn't go along with such a thing, so Tommy went ahead and slandered her to Herder, and Herder was fool enough to believe him and broke off the engagement."

"A remarkably inventive hypothesis, Inspector—but do you imagine Miss Chase to be undergoing selective amnesia? Surely she would have told us about any such conversation with Mr. Muddypaws. Besides, Mr. Herder indicated that the fault was all on his own side."

"And how would you know that?"

"By Miss Chase's express invitation," Edgar said cautiously, "I read the letter in which Mr. Herder terminated the engagement."

"Oh, you did, did you?" Chase scowled. "She didn't expressly invite *me* to read anything. At any rate, maybe there's a way around all that. My theory would explain everything."

"As a general principle," Edgar said, "if adhering to a theory necessitates willfully ignoring the facts in one's possession—"

"Oh, don't be so infuriating. *Listen* to me. Maybe Tommy never actually talked to Emily about it. Maybe he *was* in our garden last night, after he left Nora. His little scheme had worked so well on her that he thought he would try it out on Emily too. But he never got the chance, because some other dog came by and dragged him away, so he thought he would go visit Herder this morning and just offer to sell him information about Emily instead, and instead of taking the bait, Herder—who is, after all, a thoroughly bad lot—jumped to his own conclusions and threw Emily over."

"This is pure conjecture, Inspector Chase, and is exceedingly difficult to reconcile with the sentiments expressed in Mr. Herder's letter. Besides, unless Mr. Muddypaws possesses hitherto unsuspected powers of teleportation or has a bizarre habit of paying visits at unsociably early hours, he scarcely could have had the opportunity to call upon Mr. Herder this morning. I was at his house just after breakfast time, you recall."

"Then," Chase said, glowering, "who the devil—alright, *alright*, Mr. Beagle, I beg your pardon; you needn't look at me like that!—was in the garden last night?"

"Any one of the other hundreds of thousands of dogs and cats in Liverpool, I should imagine."

"You needn't reject all my ideas out of paw," Chase snapped. "Dash it all, I was right about Tommy, wasn't I?"

"Indeed you were, and I congratulate you on your perspicacity, but it does not logically follow that you are an infallible expert upon every subject."

"Neither are you. You were completely wrong about Nora—"

"I have never claimed omniscience, Inspector—"

"—and I'll bet you'll turn out to be wrong about Herder too."

"Quite possibly," Edgar said. "Nevertheless, I propose that we return to your parents' house, say our farewells, collect your luggage, and be on our way."

Chase turned wide, astonished eyes on him. "Go home, you mean? What—*now*? Surely we owe it to poor Emily to figure out what happened with Herder—or, at the very least, to knock him down."

"Actually, I imagine that Miss Chase would prefer that we leave Mr. Herder strictly alone—but in any event, Inspector, I am rather more concerned with last night's mysterious intruders. We have not satisfactorily ruled out the possibility that you were their intended target. It is imperative that we return to London at once, before they can make a second attempt. Lest your would-be assailants follow us, we can station some constables outside your building. Or you can stay with me for a few days, if you will promise not to disarrange my cravat drawer again."

"I only did that the once," Chase said, scowling, "and it was years ago, so you needn't go on and on about it forever. Anyway, Mr. Beagle, I haven't any intention of turning tail. I hope you do not imagine that I am such a coward as to desert my sister in her time of need."

"I fail to see what steps you could possibly take to help her. It is over, Inspector Chase."

"I'll bet you want to find out what really happened, though. You *always* want to find out what really happened."

"Not at the expense of your life."

"Do you know, Mr. Beagle," Chase said gleefully, "you are becoming very dramatic."

"I see no reason to insult me, Inspector."

"Well, what do *you* call it, then? I still say you haven't the least reason to think that I'm in any danger." He darted a sudden, sidelong glance at Edgar. "Do you know what I think? I think that you are afraid that you will not be clever enough to figure out what happened with Herder and bring him to justice, so you are running away instead of trying."

"Your attempts at manipulation are, as always, far too heavy-pawed to be effective. Besides, this is not a question of justice. There is not, nor has there ever been, a particularly compelling reason to think that Mr. Herder has committed any crime. And, should Miss Chase care to accuse him of breach of promise, she has ample evidence already; she will require a solicitor, not an investigator. Shall we ask the lady how she would like us to proceed? It would be decidedly unchivalrous for us to continue our investigations against her wishes."

Chase gawked at him. "Since when do *you* rate chivalry higher than knowledge?"

"I was attempting," Edgar said, keeping his temper with no little difficulty, "to use a line of reasoning that would appeal to your disorganized system of ethics."

"Who's being manipulative now?"

"I am endeavoring to save your life. Some slight subterfuge is, I believe, permissible. It is for your own good."

Chase regarded him with bright, hurt eyes. "*Please*, Mr. Beagle," he said, "not you too. You said you weren't under-estimating me, but here we are. Despite what everyone in Liverpool seems to think, I am not a puppy anymore."

"I fail to see the connection—"

"My life is not in any danger—and if it were, I would be able to look after myself without you having to put any elaborate stratagems over on me. Have you any idea how patronizing that is?"

"My dear Inspector Chase—"

"Don't you 'my dear Inspector Chase' me. You always assume you know better than I do. I'm not as clever as you, of course, but that doesn't mean I'm useless altogether. I got Tommy, didn't I? Even though everyone said I was wrong about him?"

"You certainly did, but—"

"Well, I'm going to get Herder too. I don't care what you think. You can come with me or not, just as you please. I *can* do things on my own, you know. I don't need you to make *all* my arrests for me." He turned on his heel, making the tips of his ears quiver, and marched away.

"If you object to my methods," Edgar said, hurrying after him, "I shall be delighted to discuss them with you upon some future occasion—one, ideally, on which we are not standing in the middle of the street. I do not understand why you are experiencing negative sentiments towards me, Inspector."

"Of course you don't."

"I accompanied you to Liverpool at your importunate request, made an earnest attempt to aid your sister, and assisted you in your investigation and capture of Mr. Muddypaws. I have undertaken every single task that you have set me. My only crime, it seems, is to care about your safety."

Chase stopped walking and wheeled around. "What do you suppose I do when you are not there, Mr. Beagle?"

"Mostly daydream about squirrels, I should think."

"No! I live alone without starving to death or setting the furniture on fire, I put my clothes on the right way up every morning, and I go off and work at a highly prestigious and demanding job. I even manage not to fall prey to assassins. I don't need you following me around like a nursery maid."

"I never said you did."

"You didn't need to say it; it's quite enough that you want to drag me away from my family and my investigation and send me scurrying back to London with my tail between my legs. I can tell perfectly well what you think of me."

"I think that you are to be protected at any cost. So that you can go on pursuing justice, that is, in your *exceedingly* impressive capacity as Detective Chief Inspector at the Metropolitan Police. I deem this one investigation, such as it is, to be less important than all of your future endeavors."

"You are not anything like you think you are," Chase said mutinously.

"I beg your pardon?"

"Well, you never stop howling on about logic and reason—"

"*Howling on?*"

"Yes, howling on, you heard me—but the moment you have an actual emotion, you panic and make bad decisions just like anyone else. You think you're so much better than the rest of us. Well, we may all be idiots compared to you, but at least we're honest."

"I do not see, Inspector, how honesty enters into the matter. I assume you are referring, however obliquely and disparagingly, to the fact that I place a high value on rational thought. From this fact, it does not logically follow that you should accuse me of—"

"Did you really think I didn't know? You lie to yourself every minute of the day. Telling yourself that you haven't got any feelings."

"I am afraid I haven't the faintest idea—"

"Trying to fool yourself into thinking no one can ever hurt you again," Chase said, over him. "You'll be in for a nasty shock, one of these days."

Edgar went very still. "If you do not wish to be treated like a puppy," he said icily, "you ought not to behave like one. You cannot expect me to stand back and watch you be killed; as a seeker of justice, I have a moral imperative to prevent crime, and I am afraid it outweighs the dictates of your fleeting, irrational emotions. You are at perfect liberty to ignore me, if my society is so wearisome to you."

"Mr. Beagle, I didn't mean—that is, I only meant—"

"I believe you have made your meaning perfectly clear."

"Oh, don't be like that. I'm sorry, alright? I didn't know you would get so upset."

"I am not upset in the least. I am perfectly calm."

"Haven't I just said, you don't fool me with that nonsense?"

"Perhaps," Edgar said, ignoring this, "you might deign to acquiesce to my earlier suggestion of returning to your parents' house and asking Miss Chase how she would like us to proceed. If, that is, you are not too busy insulting me."

He set out towards the house, without glancing back to see whether Chase was following him. From all the panting and scuffing sounds, it seemed fairly certain that Chase was. So, Chase had grown weary of Edgar's prudence and logic and cool-headed intelligence—of all the qualities, in short, that made Edgar of any use to anyone! It had been, Edgar thought dispassionately, only a matter of time. Chase was—or had been!—moderately fond of him, and had, perhaps, once entertained the slightest tendencies towards hero-worship, but Edgar supposed he ought not to have been under any illusions beyond that. Friendship, for a police dog and a private investigator, was merely a convenient term for a straightforward system of mutually beneficial collaboration. After all, why should Chase, whose interests ran towards dashing about frenetically and keeping local pubs in business, have derived any actual pleasure from Edgar's society? No doubt Edgar had been boring him half to death, these many years. Chase had, he supposed, tolerated him in exchange for his professional assistance and his powers of ratiocination. Well, Chase had already climbed as high in the ranks of the Metropolitan Police as he was ever likely to; and he had, evidently, stopped wanting Edgar's help; and so the transaction was over. It would be foolish for Edgar to mourn; there had been nothing for him to lose. It was better this way. His affection for Chase, which had evidently been one-sided all along, had been threatening to become a liability. He never ought to have let his guard down; he never ought to have told Chase any details of his personal affairs, never ought to have given Chase, or anyone, the barest glimpse into his mind. His natural impulse to keep the world at arm's length had, it turned out, been quite correct. He could trust no one but himself, in the end. Let Chase get on with investigating Herder, Edgar thought, with a sudden, sharp jolt of puppyish anger. Let him go and vent his nonsense at somebody else, for a change; let him make a fool of himself in front of all of Liverpool, prattling on about coining and gambling and atmospheres of evil; let him see exactly how far he could get without Edgar! Why should it be Edgar's job, anyway, to protect Chase's dignity and shield him from professional missteps and go poking around his family's distasteful personal affairs? Chase could stand on his own back paws, for once. Maybe he would finally learn something.

The house was just up ahead. Edgar held the door for Chase with scrupulous politeness. He hoped he would be able to make it upstairs without encountering Mrs. Chase. His mental faculties would probably benefit significantly from a few moments alone in the spare room, with no border collies expecting him to humor them or puzzle out their emotional vagaries. Perhaps volatility was simply in the nature of the breed.

But, like a pantomime demon, Mrs. Chase popped up at once, silhouetted ominously in the doorway to the parlor. "*Now* where have you been, Gabriel?" she barked.

Chase strode forward and puffed out his chest. "We—I mean, *I*—have just arrested Tommy Muddypaws," he said.

Mrs. Chase goggled at him with her pale, protuberant eyes. "You've *what*? Gabriel, I have to see his parents every day! D'you know the ruckus they'll raise when they find out?"

"Well, if they don't like it, then they shouldn't have brought him up to be a thief. It isn't *my* fault. He *is* a thief, like I always said. I've got loads of proof."

"Has he?" Mrs. Chase demanded of Edgar.

"I am quite sure that Inspector Chase knows what he is doing," Edgar said stiffly.

Mrs. Chase chortled. "Well, he never has before."

Out of the very corner of his eye, Edgar rather fancied that he saw Chase wince. "Your son has effected a remarkable capture," he told Mrs. Chase hurriedly. "It turns out he was entirely correct about the nefarious Mr. Muddypaws all along."

"That's more than *I* know," Mrs. Chase sniffed. "Tommy always seemed like a perfect angel. Anyone would have thought it would be Ollie who would get in trouble. At any rate, Mr. Beagle"—here, she dropped her voice to a rather carrying whisper, and stepped away from the parlor door— "can you guess who's here?"

"Almost certainly, I cannot."

"Well, I'll tell you: it's Mr. Tenterfield. He's sitting in the parlor right this very minute, waiting to see Emily, and I'm sure I haven't any idea what he wants with her. Maybe he has

182

a message from Mr. Herder, but why Mr. Herder shouldn't have come round himself is more than I know."

Chase nudged Edgar, and then, evidently remembering that they were quarreling, withdrew his arm with lightning alacrity. Presumably, he had managed to infer that Mrs. Chase was unaware of the broken engagement. "Is Miss Chase out?" Edgar asked, ignoring him.

"She dragged that awful Airedale into the house a few hours ago, and then marched right back out again. Off on one of her walks by the river, I shouldn't wonder. Maybe she can pick up another fiancé, since she's gone off hers. I don't know what the world is coming to—girls are so foolish nowadays. When *I* was a girl, we used to brush out our ears and read our Bibles before bed, not go gadding about with foreign millionaires. Thank goodness, I hear her at the door now—no, it's only Angus, wanting his tea." She pushed past Edgar and Chase and seized her husband by the arm. "Angus, what do you think? Mr. Tenterfield is here."

"Splendid," Mr. Chase said heartily. "I've been wanting a talk with him. He's an awfully pleasant fellow."

"Don't be so silly. Can't you see what this means? I'll bet he's come to tell her that Mr. Herder has gotten sick of all Emily's sulking and moping, and is calling off the engagement."

"That's alright," Mr. Chase said. "Let her be well clear of him, if he's not the dog she took him for. She can find another millionaire; she found this one, didn't she?"

"*No*, Angus, she can settle down with a nice local boy, if anyone will have her after this, not go reaching above her station and mixing herself up with dogs whose families we don't know. I always *said* no good would come of meddling with foreigners. Oh, *there's* Emily. Emily, do you know who's here in the parlor this very instant? It's Mr. Tenterfield. Go in and talk to him."

"Good afternoon, Miss Chase!" Mr. Tenterfield said, stepping out of the parlor right on cue, with his habitual air of detached amusement. Edgar deemed it overwhelmingly probable that he had heard everything.

"Good morning," Emily said dully. "I suppose you have come for the ring." She began reaching into her pocket.

"Not at all—not at all! I have come, if you will excuse the liberty, to see if I can make amends."

"How very kind of you. If Mr. Herder had come to make amends himself, perhaps that would be of some use."

"No, you misunderstand me. I am not here at his instigation. I merely felt it my duty to see whether I could patch up the lovers' quarrel and resuscitate the engagement."

Mrs. Chase gasped theatrically. "So, he *has* jilted her," she said at the top of her voice.

"Of course he has," Chase said, "and I don't know why you're so surprised. I *said* he was exactly the sort of vicious, low-down scoundrel who would jilt her, didn't I?"

"No," said Mrs. Chase, "you didn't. You're much too old to tell lies to make yourself seem clever."

"Well, I knew it all along," Chase retorted, "even if I never said it. Nobody else knew it, did they? Not even Mr. Beagle."

"The colloquial term 'jilt,' Inspector," Edgar said, feeling rather stung, "carries with it a connotation of dishonesty or caprice, emanating from, and simultaneously indicative of, a flawed sense of honor. Therefore, your adoption of it in this context, being predicated on no concrete evidence but, presumably, propagated to your ratiocination solely by your much-vaunted, and little-proven, intuition, constitutes an

184

inference of only the most irresolute fortitude."

"Is he talking French now?" Mrs. Chase demanded of her son.

"No, he's just showing off," Chase said. "He doesn't know French. He didn't even go to Eton, remember?"

Edgar caught himself flinching—an absurd response, he told himself furiously. It made perfect sense that Chase's latent insecurity about his own inadequate schooling, together with his natural tendency towards puppyish spite, should express itself in aspersions against Edgar's educational credentials. There was certainly no call to take it personally.

"Never mind about where he went to school," Mrs. Chase said stonily. "Here's what I should like to know: what on earth I am supposed to say to the neighbors? If Mr. Herder was going to jilt her, he ought to have done it before we sent out the invitations."

"The neighbors!" Chase scoffed. "Poor little Emily standing here with her heart broken to bits"—Emily bristled visibly—"and you only care for what the neighbors will think!"

"When you have lived in one place for as long as I have, Gabriel," Mrs. Chase said, turning and regarding him evenly, "instead of in your rented rooms in London with new lodgers in the building every fortnight and goodness only knows what growlings and yowlings and carryings-on, you will know how important it is to avoid a scandal and to keep your neighbors' good opinion."

Chase scowled and muttered something. It sounded very much like "the neighbors can be damned," but Edgar was certain that he would not have been so impolite.

"Might I have a word with you in private?" Mr. Tenterfield asked Emily pointedly.

"Oh, what's the use?" Emily said, at the same time as Chase announced, "Anything you have to say to my sister, you can say in front of me."

"But not in front of everyone," Mr. Tenterfield countered, with a delicate little glance towards Chase's parents. "Shall we step into the parlor? I assure you, my news is well worth the hearing."

"If you insist," Emily said, following his gaze. "Mr. Beagle, would you mind joining us? Yes, *alright*, Gabriel, you can come too, if you must."

It was evident that the parlor was seldom used, except as a storehouse for the wares that came in and out of Mr. Chase's harbor. Edgar had to pick his way between weatherbeaten crates and odd, knobbly sacks, all bearing unfamiliar, and not altogether pleasant, aromas. There was a sheet-draped settee, upon which Chase promptly flung himself with a level of petulant force that made the sheet come cascading down around him, a sideboard in need of varnishing, and an assortment of other pieces of mismatched furniture, possibly accumulated by the previous piermaster. Mr. Tenterfield waited until Edgar and Emily had seated themselves on the two narrow chairs. Then, he closed the door behind himself, very carefully, and took a few steps forward. His face was the very picture of gentlemanly solicitude, and, as he turned his head to address Emily, the tips of his ears quivered as if in sympathy.

"Miss Chase," he said, "I have debated what to do, and, though it may be dishonorable to betray my friend's confidence, I am certain that I would be rendering him an even greater disservice were I to deny him the opportunity to be redeemed through the love of a good, sweet lady such as yourself. And yet, I fear, it may already be too late—unless, that is, you are prepared to take immediate action. Even the most virtuous among us have our vices; I hope you can find the compassion to look upon his without condemnation. In any event, I am afraid you must brace yourself for a very great shock." He took another step into the room, and stood gazing sadly down into Emily's upturned face.

"It is my immense regret to inform you," he said, "that Mr. Herder has developed an addiction to gambling."

Chapter Eleven

For a long, tense moment, no one spoke. Edgar found himself struggling for air, as if an invisible St. Bernard were lying on his chest. He set his teeth and forced himself to breathe normally. So, Chase had been right once again—and would, Edgar thought bitterly, no doubt be insufferably pleased with himself for the foreseeable future!

"I knew it!" Chase cried, breaking the silence right on cue, and bouncing to his feet with a violent gesture that knocked the sheet to the floor altogether. "I said so all along."

"Did you?" Mr. Tenterfield inquired, looking utterly baffled.

"Yes," Chase said firmly, "I did. Why does no one ever listen to me? I saw him right away for what he was: just a worthless, wastrel blackguard son of mongrels—"

Mr. Tenterfield coughed politely. "Pardon me," he said, "but I am afraid I must object to hearing such coarse language in connection with my dear friend."

"Well, then," Chase retorted with some spirit, "you ought to have told him not to break my sister's heart."

Edgar caught himself reflexively half-rising from his chair, just in case the situation were to become progressively hostile. But Chase, of course, would no longer welcome his intervention. He sat back down and deliberately wrenched his focus to Emily, who was sitting very upright and still in the chair beside him, staring straight ahead with unnaturally bright eyes. Edgar permitted himself to wonder, with a sudden pang, what the future held for her: how many sleepless nights, tormenting herself with memories; how many unguarded hours, wondering why she had been deserted; how many lonely years, before she met someone worth caring for.

If he were a magician, Edgar thought, as Chase had once seemed to imagine, then he would be able to smooth her path with an airy wave of his paw, to grant her dreamless nights and clear-headed days, to banish the feelings that had made a chew toy of her heart.

Well, he was not a magician. He had never pretended to be.

But he was an investigator, and there was a chance— just a chance—that there was something here that could be investigated after all.

He stole a glance at Chase—bright-eyed and wild-eared, gesticulating with both front paws as he passionately apostrophized Mr. Herder's pedigree in a gratuitously loud voice and appallingly ungentlemanly terms. Chase had, undeniably, been right about Tommy and Nora. Could he have been right about Mr. Herder also? Edgar allowed himself to consider, for one bare second, the possibility that he had, after all, been underestimating Chase all along. What, he wondered, would that change? If he combed through every half-remembered conversation from the last twenty-four hours—if he took Chase at his word—if Chase had, for a wonder, been barking up the right tree—then what would it actually mean?

Edgar raised his chin, and sat very still. He pictured a smooth stone wall all around him, cleanly blocking out Chase and Mr. Tenterfield's raised voices and the clutter of the parlor and Emily's wet, despondent eyes. Insulating him, even, from the fruitless exclamations and senseless vagaries of his own emotions. It would not do to hurry his thoughts, to force them to a false conclusion for want of patience.

Slowly, gradually, he permitted the pattern to take shape in his brain. Tommy Muddypaws, ransacking gardens and extorting lockets and pocketing the silver at parties. A few chance words from Flossie Yapper—really, he ought to have listened to her more carefully. There was something there, if only he could remember it before it slipped through his paws. Three sorts of gentlemen—or maybe three particular gentlemen—three dogs in a hotel, for all the world like the nursery rhyme about the Labrador retrievers in the tub! It was a long time since anyone had recited *that* to him. His thoughts skittered reflexively away.

Parents—no, *families*—but why should the idea of families have come suddenly into his head? He sifted carefully through his memory. Yes, there was Mrs. Chase's querulous complaint. *Mixing herself up with dogs whose families we don't know*, she had said.

Growlers, and dogs who dripped onto the carpet—and the third dog—something about trays—something about foreigners...

In his mind, the mist shifted and swirled and resolved itself into discrete little slivers of meaning. The river, and the docks, where the great, billowing ships stood poised to set forth for every part of the world. The river, and the docks—and across from them, the house that always belonged to the current piermaster. And Emily, who was unsuited to be a millionaire's bride; Emily, who was no more and no less than the piermaster's daughter. Emily, who was looking at Edgar

190

now, with her head cocked, probably wondering why he was staring so fixedly at a blank stretch of wall. She was reasonably observant; she was reasonably discerning. More intelligent, perhaps, than average. But when all was said and done, she had known her fiancé for a few bare months. She had been, no doubt, too trusting and open-hearted not to have taken his account of himself at face value. And Edgar had seen him, after all, only through her too-wide eyes—had gotten all his impressions second-paw. He had merely let Emily paint a picture for him, of a gentleman who would never gamble, never speculate, never so much as set a paw on unfirm ground. A gentleman who was a paragon of unimpulsiveness. Studiedly innocuous. Nothing like a herding dog.

Mr. Herder, with his perennially hunted expression. Mr. Herder, who had gone walking by the piers, pretending to be lost; Mr. Herder, who had first approached and then precipitously courted the piermaster's daughter. Mr. Herder, who had traveled to England to conduct some unspecified point of business, and found a pretty reason to prolong his stay.

Mr. Herder, who had, for some mysterious reason, been parted from his dear friend Mr. Tenterfield for years.

Mr. Herder, whom Chase had thought evil.

And, looming always by Mr. Herder's side, Mr. Mongrel, with his overt air of menace—Mr. Mongrel, whose friendship with Mr. Herder seemed never to have been explained to anyone. He pictured the deep scratch that Mr. Mongrel's cruel claws had carved into the dining room table.

Anyone would have thought it would be Ollie who would get in trouble, Mrs. Chase had said, just a few moments ago.

Yes, he supposed. Yes, anyone would have, and well they

191

might have done so. Obvious answers were not necessarily wrong, not in real life.

They were not, of course, necessarily right either.

Tommy's too clever, Ollie Muddypaws whined, at the very back of his mind. *Tommy doesn't let them see.*

Ollie and Tommy and Mr. Herder and Mr. Tenterfield and Mr. Mongrel. They whirled around and around in his head like merry-go-round horses, smearing together into bright, featureless shapes.

And, all in a flash, Edgar realized.

Australia—yes, of course, Australia! Blast it all—why couldn't he have listened to Chase, for once?

But if it were really *that*, then surely he could prove it. It would be difficult, without Chase's cooperation, but on the whole, he rather thought it could be done. A telegram, perhaps, to the Australian police. A letter to the Commissioner at Botany Bay.

Edgar's thoughts parted and cleared. It was almost surprising to find the room still standing around him. He took a deep breath, the tips of his ears and tail quivering, and then another, and glanced over to make sure that Chase and Mr. Tenterfield were still occupied. "Miss Chase," he said, very quietly, "may I ask you a question concerning Mr. Mongrel?"

"You needn't ask me whether he's one of those wolf hybrids," Emily said tonelessly, "because everyone I know has already asked me that, and I still haven't any idea. Ask Mr. Tenterfield, if Gabriel ever finishes shouting at him."

"I find myself wholly uninterested in the gentleman's pedigree," Edgar reassured her. "I wish to know only this: have you ever heard him speak?"

A flicker of astonishment broke through Emily's numbed

expression. "Well, I must have, I suppose, mustn't I?" she said. "I mean, he must have introduced himself to me. But I can't remember, really. It's not as if he routinely brimmed with witty conversation. He growls like anything, of course," she added nonchalantly, "but I haven't noticed any howling, so perhaps he *isn't* a wolf hybrid after all."

"Howling is not synonymous with being a wolf," Edgar said, rather stiffly.

"Oh, I didn't mean it like *that*! Do you really think I would say a thing like that to a hound? I only meant—well, all wolves are sure to howl, aren't they? At any rate, Mr. Beagle, why should you care whether I had heard him speak?"

"Well, you see," Edgar began, "he might not actually sound like—"

"Miss Chase," Mr. Tenterfield said at this juncture, unexpectedly striding over and claiming the nearest corner of the settee, "forgive me for interrupting you. I must, you see, prevail upon your better nature; you have, I know, suffered greatly at my friend's paws, and you would be quite within your rights if you never wished to so much as hear his name again. And yet—"

"What do you want?" Emily said.

Mr. Tenterfield bowed his head. "I must first beseech you to pardon my impertinence in asking anything at all of you. But I have seen my poor friend pine for you, with his ears downcast and his tail between his legs; I believe that, for your love, he might learn to be a better dog. Now that he has given you up, he has nothing to hope for, no reason to amend his life and save his soul. His paws are set now upon the dark and thorny path to destruction—but, you, I think, might rescue him from his worser impulses. Not for my sake or his sake, but in the name of compassion itself, I entreat your assistance. If you went to him now, even now—if you forgave him and wept over him—then he could not, I think, continue in his resolve to leave you."

"No thank you," said Emily, and turned away.

"No?" Mr. Tenterfield echoed. He slipped off the settee, knelt at Emily's feet, and panted appealingly up into her face. "Miss Chase, surely you cannot be so hard-hearted. I tell you plainly, his salvation lies within your paws—"

"Oh, leave me alone!" Emily cried, her voice breaking. "Don't you understand? I was mistaken all along. The dog I knew—the dog I wanted to marry—was nothing like this Mr. Herder. I can see quite clearly now that he never existed. The gentleman at the Adelphi, who shares his name, is a perfect stranger to me."

"If you will only come along with me—"

Emily rounded on him, her eyes burning. "If you had any decency in you," she said, "then you would let me mourn in peace, not torment me by seeking to drag me into the presence of the creature that has taken the place of the dog I loved. But I suppose Gabriel was right—you have been dragging James around to casinos."

"Upon my honor, no, Miss Chase!"

"I expect you have no honor," Chase said moodily, leaning against the wall with his arms clenched across his chest. "Why not take your blackguard and your wolf and clear out of Liverpool?"

"Miss Chase," Mr. Tenterfield said desperately, glancing around as if he expected Chase to hoist him bodily out the window at any moment, "are you so indifferent that you have no wish even to hear his own account of his infirmity? Will you not wonder, always, who he really was, and what he really felt for you?"

"But why," Emily asked, with a bright, brittle laugh, "should I care what a stranger felt for me?"

"He is *not* a stranger, Miss Chase—he is your own James still, only afflicted with a malady that he is too weak to bear without your aid—"

"Emily," Chase interrupted, suddenly crossing the room towards her with an odd expression on his face, "I think perhaps you ought to see him."

"Oh, not you too!"

"No, you don't understand. I don't give a hang about reforming him. But if you can only find out what really happened—well, then you won't have to spend twelve years wondering about it and breaking your heart imagining what could have been, will you? You might as well skip straight over all that rubbish."

"Why twelve?"

"It was only an example."

Emily smiled at him, very slightly. "But you see, Gabriel," she said, "I do know what happened. I was half a puppy still, and I imagined there was perfect sympathy between us. I ought to have realized that no one half so wonderful could really exist. Next time, I shall know better."

"Surely you still love him, Miss Chase," Mr. Tenterfield said, stepping towards her with a degree of alacrity that bordered on desperation. "And you have my word upon it that he loves you. Why not come and talk to him, if only for five minutes? You could do him some good. You must realize, surely, that it is your duty—"

"Mr. Tenterfield," Edgar said firmly, "the lady has made her wishes quite clear. But, for my own part, I would be delighted to come and have a word with Mr. Herder."

Across the room, Chase's head turned sharply towards Edgar.

"He may have gone out," Mr. Tenterfield said. "Probably ran straight to the card table, poor fellow."

"In that case, perhaps you might conduct me whither I might await his return."

"He'll turn up at the Adelphi eventually," Emily said, in a clipped voice, "unless, of course, that was a lie as well, and he has been living under the nearest bridge this entire time, like a vagrant—"

"Or a water rat," Chase offered darkly.

"—But I can't imagine what you want from him."

"The truth, Miss Chase," Edgar said. "Merely the truth."

And, stepping deftly around Mr. Tenterfield, he passed out of the room.

It took about twenty minutes to walk to the Adelphi Hotel. Chase, fuming *sotto voce* as he marched grimly along and fixing his burning gaze straight ahead, was as intent of purpose as Edgar had ever seen him. Apparently, Edgar thought with a touch of resentment, Chase still considered himself automatically permitted to tag along on Edgar's investigations—and probably to take the credit for them, too! Or perhaps Chase had mentally decreed himself the splendid hero of an epic revenge quest, as Chase *would*. In Chase's head, Edgar was probably the one tagging along. Edgar eyed Chase uneasily. He wondered whether Chase understood that the normal laws concerning grievous bodily harm applied even to splendid heroes of epic revenge quests. He was intensely, pricklingly aware that he ought to be going over his plan for what to do at the Adelphi; ought, in fact, to be forming his plan in the first place! He would need, after all, a calculated progression of maneuvers. Advertising a different suspicion, perhaps; there were certainly enough for him to choose from. Poising himself to uncover Mr. Herder's secrets with the delicate precision of a trowel skimming the soil off a golden artifact. And then, with all the pieces in their proper place—

Chase barked viciously at a passing squirrel, stumbled over his own shoelace, and then glared at Edgar as if everything had been his fault. Really, how was anyone supposed to think, with Chase around? And mentally rehearsing, Edgar noted, with tight irritation mounting in his chest, would be pointless anyway. Chase, after all, was just going to get underfoot, and wreck his meticulously laid plans—and then, no doubt, blame Edgar for the ensuing failure!

Besides, who could say which version of Mr. Herder was waiting at the Adelphi? Emily's adoring lover, or last night's taciturn supper guest, or someone else altogether? Someone whose first care all along, perhaps, had been to outrun and to obscure his past.

Too many permutations; too many branching possibilities to wrestle into a definite script. Too many hairpin turns to be made in the moment.

There was, Edgar told himself very sternly, no need to panic.

Behind Edgar and Chase, Mr. Tenterfield bobbed miserably along, with his ears and tail drooping pitifully. He did not break his silence until they had stepped over the hotel's threshold.

"I wonder," he said, lightly laying a solicitous paw on Edgar's arm while the uniformed Manx at the door hissed his disapproval of Chase's return, "whether I might be so bold as to appeal to your innate sense of reason. And yours too, of course, Inspector. You see, my friend—poor fellow; poor fellow!—has not, alas, what one might term courage. When confronted with his misdeeds, he is in the habit of denying them, even to the point of inventing fantastical alternatives. It is not his fault; he is, in many ways, a puppy still, and not all gentlemen's upbringings promote strength of character. The last few years of his life, in particular—well, in the event that he should furnish absurd excuses or regale you with wild tales, I implore you to consider them through the lens of dispassionate logic. It is playacting, nothing more. Besides, you two are gentlemen of good breeding, and, I am sure"—here, he looked at Chase very pointedly—"will be able to find it in your heart to pity rather than antagonize or censure him. After all, who among us can claim to be without vice?"

"Mr. Beagle," Chase said reflexively, and then proceeded to look extremely cross with himself.

"What? Oh—yes, no doubt, no doubt! But I was speaking rhetorically." He flashed Chase a charming smile.

"Well, you shouldn't ask questions if you don't want the answers," Chase retorted. "Damn fool thing to do."

"Let us go up," Edgar interjected, uncomfortably aware that Mr. Dewlaps was gawking at them from across the lobby, "and see what we can do for Mr. Herder. Young gentlemen are wont to have their little diversions, I am informed; I should not dream of holding any youthful misdeeds against him."

Mr. Tenterfield coughed sharply, nearly walked into a pillar, and pushed his way past Edgar and Chase, towards the sweeping staircase—"*not* manners," Chase muttered—with his gaze locked on the landing and his ears quivering with some indefinable emotion. What in the world, Edgar wondered, did Mr. Tenterfield imagine was going to take place upstairs—a melodramatic confrontation, perhaps, or even a vicious physical scuffle? If only terriers were not so inclined towards histrionically darting about and yipping, Edgar thought resentfully, watching Mr. Tenterfield sprint up the stairs, it might be possible to make some headway! He caught Chase's arm and drew him to one side, at the base of the staircase. Chase jerked away at once, with an expression of irritation. "What do you want?" he demanded.

"I only wish to discuss our plan, so that we may present a united front when we come into Mr. Herder's presence," Edgar said meekly.

"*We* have no plan. *My* plan is to break his damned neck, and you may do whatever you like."

"May I propose an alternative course of action?"

"No."

"I believe, Inspector, that I am very close to uncovering the truth. I implore you to refrain from giving way to your vengeful impulses; I rather imagine that breaking Mr. Herder's neck will hinder him from answering my questions."

"Don't you go getting high-pawed with me, Mr. Beagle," Chase said, scowling and beginning to ascend the stairs. "This is no concern of yours. It is not *your* sister who has had her heart broken."

"Believe me," Edgar assured him, "I shall be acting in your sister's best interests."

"Well, so will I! Why is your plan so much better than mine?"

"Because mine may well result in Miss Chase's future happiness, whereas yours leads to nothing but a prison term."

"I shan't *actually* kill him, Mr. Beagle," Chase said impatiently. "I wasn't being literal. But I shall handle this matter however I see fit, whether you like it or not. I may not have my paw-cuffs anymore, but I can still arrest him if I want to. Somehow."

"Breaking an engagement is not an arrestable offense."

"Well, I'll get him on something else, then."

"We have no evidence that he has committed any crimes."

"Oh, I'm sure he has. He's a thoroughly bad lot. And they have loads of convicts in Australia, you must remember."

"I assure you, I have not forgotten that. I fancy it may be of the utmost relevance."

"You're doing it again," Chase said, almost plaintively.

"Doing what?"

"Being all mysterious. As if you know something that I don't."

"You have access to the same information I do," Edgar said politely. "You are at liberty, of course, to draw your own conclusions from it."

"I *have* been drawing my own conclusions. And do you know what? I was right all along. So you needn't go on treating me like a fool or an amateur."

"I have the utmost respect for your intelligence and your suitability for your chosen profession, Inspector Chase."

"I can *tell* when you're lying, you know. You aren't very good at it. You do a funny thing with your eyes, and you fiddle with your cravat."

"In any event," Edgar said, hastily lowering his paw, "do you remember what Miss Yapper said about the Adelphi Hotel's clientele?"

"What, that the cats are never satisfied with anything? I already knew that. A cat moved into Mr. Basset's old rooms last month, and I can hear him yowling at all hours."

"No, that—"

Chase yanked sharply on Edgar's sleeve and pointed upwards. Mr. Tenterfield had reached the top of the stairs, and was already scurrying down the hall. "Never mind about Miss Yapper," he said. "Let's get after him. Otherwise he may warn the scoundrel, and then they may go out the window, and then where would we be?"

"Out of prison," Edgar was sorely tempted to reply, but he forbore.

Mr. Herder's sitting room was a catalog of luxuries— imposing mahogany furniture; heavy damasked curtains with a tasteful sheen and a profusion of golden tassels; a real Turkish rug of such decadent plushness that Edgar could feel his paws sinking into it. But Mr. Herder seemed indifferent to his surroundings. Edgar could hardly recognize him as the stiff, self-contained dog of the night before; he was untidily slouched in an armchair, still wearing his dressing gown. His head lolled indolently against the wall next to him. Out of the corner of his eye, Edgar saw Chase's lip curl.

"Look, James," Mr. Tenterfield said with forced cheerfulness, hurrying over to him, "here are visitors for you! They have come to effect a *rapprochement* between you and your ladylove."

"Well, tell them to go away again," Mr. Herder said, in unexpectedly sepulchral tones. "There is nothing to be done."

"You must not distress yourself so," Mr. Tenterfield said comfortingly, laying a gentle paw upon his shoulder.

"We will not impose too presumptuously upon your time," Edgar said, taking care to keep his voice very level. He had once read that one could steady an over-dramatic herding dog by using a calm, even tone, but it had never worked on Chase,

201

and it did not appear to be working now.

"What do you want?" Mr. Herder demanded.

"Only to speak with you. I should like to resolve a few questions, if I might."

Mr. Herder laughed, long and wild and utterly mirthless. He really was not, Edgar reflected, notably similar to the gentleman Emily had described. Perhaps there was something the matter with his reason.

"Amateur theatrics," muttered Chase.

"I would like," Edgar persevered, "to clear up a few little points about Mr. Mongrel. Where is he, incidentally? I rather thought he would be by your side."

A flash of unmistakable panic darted across Mr. Herder's face. "I haven't any idea," he said defiantly. "I don't keep him on a leash."

"Perhaps you ought to," Chase said.

"I rather imagine," Edgar said, very pleasantly, "that he is concealed somewhere in this suite."

"Well, if he likes to get himself stuck under the furniture, that's his affair."

"You mistake me. You may, perhaps, have anticipated an unpleasant visit from the gentleman relatives of your onetime fiancée. Or, of course, you may have some obscure reason of your own to fear visitors. Some secret, perhaps, that you will undertake any desperate measure to keep from the public gaze. I imagine that Mr. Mongrel is concealed *with your full knowledge*, and by prior arrangement; I imagine, Mr. Herder, that he is waiting to strike. Crouched in the armoire, perhaps, or waiting just on the other side of the bedroom door—to which, I notice, you are sitting very close—or lurking behind the curtains."

"I can at least sit where I please, can't I? What would you have me do, Mr. Beagle—rearrange all the furniture lest any chairs stray close enough to a door to awake your suspicion?"

"Right, the bedroom, then," Chase said, stalking across the room and wrenching the bedroom door open. Mr. Mongrel, hulking menacingly in the doorway, fixed him with malevolent, bulging eyes and launched into a long, low growl.

"Good afternoon, Mr. Mongrel," Edgar said brightly.

Mr. Mongrel shifted his gaze to Edgar, bared his teeth further, and growled again.

"Oh, I beg your pardon," Edgar said. "Is it good evening already?"

Mr. Mongrel emitted yet another growl.

"That's all you'll ever get out of him," Mr. Herder informed Edgar, "so you needn't waste your breath. It's best to just pretend he isn't there."

"Oh, *Jimmy*," Mr. Tenterfield put in, reproachfully. "How *can* you be so unkind about our old playmate—who was always so devoted to you—who only ever wanted to protect you and assist you? When you consider that his behavior springs from pure affection, you cannot possibly think him your inferior. You are clever; well, he is strong and loyal, always eager to walk just behind you with his teeth bared against any eventuality. It takes, they say, all types to make a world. Have you forgotten everything from when we were puppies? Such adventures as we used to have!"

"It is a curious notion," Edgar mused, "that the three of you should have played as puppies."

"Why?" Mr. Tenterfield demanded protectively. "Because fate placed Mr. Mongrel in a different class? You believe, perhaps, that, born as he was to labor with his paws, and

203

deprived of the schoolroom, he is not fit to associate with more fortunate gentlemen such as Mr. Herder and myself."

Chase shot Edgar a swift, indecipherable glance from across the room.

"I believe nothing of the sort," Edgar said, very firmly. "I merely meant that, in light of his grizzled muzzle, he is plainly—forgive me, Mr. Mongrel!—some decades your senior."

"Well, strain can do that to a chap at any age. Goodness knows, after so many years of—well, not having a very pleasant time, you can hardly expect him to be the picture of health. But there—I should not like to expose a friend's private concerns or bygone misadventures to the world!" He leaned very close, gazed earnestly at Edgar, and lowered his voice. "You wouldn't, of course, be able to see anything like that on a dog like James, for instance—since cattle dogs' muzzles are so gray and blotchy already."

Edgar did not permit the least trace of emotion to pass over his face. He had mentally catalogued all of the possibilities already. But all the same, he wondered; he very much wondered.

At least, he thought, he might be able to confirm a piece of it.

"Does Mr. Mongrel's painful history also explain his reticence?" he asked.

Mr. Tenterfield shot him a sharp, quizzical glance. "How do you mean?"

"I could not help but notice, you see," Edgar said mildly, resting an innocent gaze upon Mr. Mongrel, "that he never speaks."

"He isn't very sociable with strangers. What about it?"

"Is that the only reason?" Edgar pressed.

"What other reason could there be?"

"Well," Edgar said, "he might be keeping his silence so as to conceal some distinctive feature of his speech. For example, he might not have an Australian accent."

"Why shouldn't he?"

"Perhaps he did not come to Australia until he was an adult. That would, of course," Edgar added, almost apologetically, "mean that the story about his puppyhood friendship with you and Mr. Herder, which both confers a reputational advantage and affords him a facile explanation for his incongruous presence by Mr. Herder's side, was a lie."

"And why, according to you, should he lie about his past?" Mr. Tenterfield inquired, his smooth, polite voice turning icy.

Edgar looked innocently from Mr. Tenterfield to Mr. Mongrel and back. "Because he was a convict, of course," he said.

Mr. Mongrel emitted a deafening snarl. He raised his hackles, flattened his ears against his head, and let forth an explosive stream of profanity from between his sharp yellow teeth. Even Chase—whose own vocabulary, Edgar had been pained to observe over the years, was not always strictly that of a gentleman—looked absolutely scandalized. Mr. Mongrel did not, Edgar was grimly pleased to note, have an Australian accent, but quite an unrefined English one.

"Alright, alright—what of it?" Mr. Tenterfield interposed, making frantic shushing gestures towards Mr. Mongrel. "Must the shame of it stalk after him like a bloodhound all his life? It may be that he has some episodes in his earlier life which he wishes to keep private—and which, I may say, it is not altogether gentlemanly for you to endeavor to drag into the public gaze. Is it not perfectly plausible that I, as a charity to a penitent sinner, should have consented to put forth a harmless fiction about having been puppies together, for the sake of his reputation? Having been once in prison, it is terribly difficult to take one's proper place in society. And yet, poor fellow, does he not deserve a second chance to make good? I am sure that an enlightened gentleman such as yourself, Mr. Beagle, believes that it is possible to rehabilitate criminals."

"I should hardly cite him," Edgar said, glancing over at Mr. Mongrel, who was skulking and scowling against the wall with a mad, murderous gleam in his close-set eyes, "as an exemplar of rehabilitation."

Surly, inarticulate mutters and growls rumbled between Mr. Mongrel's slavering jaws.

"My dear fellow," Mr. Tenterfield told him, smiling pleas- antly, "perhaps you ought to step back into the other room. He's very sensitive," he added to Edgar, *sotto voce*, as Mr. Mongrel, with a final, baleful glare, retired into the bedroom. "He doesn't like to be reminded of his past. Poor soul—poor soul! Well, who can blame him? All those years in prison would have been enough to drive anyone mad. I keep the closest eye on him I can, you understand. For his protection, and, well—for everyone else's. One doesn't like to say these things about one's friends, but there it is." He heaved a charming little sigh, and very gently shut the bedroom door.

"Is he staying here, at this hotel?" Edgar inquired.

Mr. Tenterfield wrinkled his brow in perplexity. "Quite so."

"In that case," Edgar said, "I congratulate you on your care of him. Under your guidance, his reintegration into society has evidently been a brilliant success, at least from a pecuniary standpoint; the Adelphi is, I gather, quite a costly establishment."

"Why should you concern yourself with that, Mr. Beagle?" Mr. Tenterfield asked, with a bemused little smile.

"Oh, no reason—none at all!" Edgar hastened to assure him, smiling back. "Far be it from me to pry into the gentleman's personal affairs. The state of Mr. Mongrel's finances is of absolutely no consequence to me. Nor, of course, are the outsize sums that have—coincidentally, I assume—been regularly disbursed from Mr. Herder's bank account ever since Mr. Mongrel arrived here."

"How do you know about those?" Mr. Herder demanded.

"Ah," Edgar said, with a sidelong glance at Chase. "Let us not pause now to marvel at the English passion for justice. In any event, it hardly seemed likely that those sums were for gambling debts."

"*Gambling* debts?" Mr. Herder's wild laughter rang out anew.

"Besides," Edgar continued, "it was easy enough to guess that the withdrawals had started only when Mr. Mongrel arrived in Liverpool. Easy enough, even, to guess that they were payments, of one sort or another."

Edgar found himself suddenly aware that Chase was staring at him, and probably had been for several minutes. Without turning his head, he could not begin to guess whether the gaze was resentful or admiring. Only this morning, he reflected bleakly, he would have placed some faith in Chase's ability to guess what was coming next—to, with no prompting or signaling, preempt any desperado's attempt at escape or retaliation. Now, perhaps, whatever sympathy between him and Chase had enabled the existence of that near-telepathic communication had been extinguished. He was on his own;

he would have to think on his paws. All the same, no brilliant bluff or stratagem sprang into his mind. With no hope of impressing Chase, it was difficult to summon up an adequate burst of showmanship or soupçon of flair.

Well, the simple facts, wielded with agile, delicate precision, would have to be enough.

He took a deep breath, and squared his shoulders. His heart was beating hard. He was vividly aware that Mr. Mongrel, in the bedroom, probably had his shaggy, unkempt ear pressed right up against the keyhole, and even more aware that Chase's only set of paw-cuffs had been taken away with Tommy Muddypaws inside them. If only Chase would think to stand guard by the door—if only Mr. Herder would behave sensibly—if only everyone would remain calm for just a few moments more! The whole affair had been a sordid muddle, but Edgar was nearly certain that he had guessed right—nearly certain that he was armed, now, with the clear, incisive light of truth to burn away the shadows. His gaze swept slowly all around the room.

"We must ask ourselves, gentlemen:" he said, "what sort of dog would employ a vicious criminal? What sort of dog would impetuously set sail from Australia, and obfuscate his reasons for so doing? What sort of dog has been inexplicably parted for years from his puppyhood friend? What sort of dog has reason to fear visitors? What sort of dog would approach a wholly innocent young lady, only to use her as a pawn in his own nefarious schemes? When all is said and done, sirs, what sort of dog possesses a personal manner that, even when he is behaving altogether unobjectionably, strikes nearby gentlemen—gentlemen, I may say, of great sensitivity and intuition—with a sense of evil?"

"Mr. Beagle," Mr. Tenterfield said, with a distinct bite in his voice, "I must ask you in no uncertain terms to stop slandering my oldest and dearest friend."

"But why," Edgar inquired, offering his most innocent smile, "should you imagine that I was talking about *him*?"

Mr. Herder stared up at him from the chair. One of his blotchy cheeks was twitching violently, and his mismatched eyes were stony. Edgar turned towards him and looked him full in the face.

"For how long, Mr. Herder," Edgar asked, very calmly, "has Mr. Tenterfield been blackmailing you?"

Chapter Twelve

For a moment, nothing happened. Then, Mr. Tenterfield's charming, debonair laugh rang out across the room. "You mean 'Mr. Mongrel,' of course," he said lightly. "I am afraid you have misspoken, in the emotion of the moment."

"I am happy to say I am not susceptible to such foolish mistakes, Mr. Tenterfield."

"Well, then, I suppose even detectives must have their little jokes, just like the rest of us. But really, Mr. Beagle, do I seem the least bit like a criminal?"

"Indeed you do not," Edgar promptly conceded. "I do not mind telling you that this affair has been worrying me a great deal. You see, it is so very difficult to envision you in the rôle of villain!"

"I am much relieved to hear it," Mr. Tenterfield said, laughing again and straightening his cravat. He seemed to be taking everything in genuine good humor. Edgar permitted himself a moment's doubt. The logic had led him here, of course—but, up against Mr. Tenterfield's frank gaze and friendly smile, it was seeming like nothing more than a pile of disjointed, nonsensical fragments. Perhaps he had made leaps that would not hold firm; perhaps his emotions had clouded his judgment; perhaps his fleeting impulse to protect Emily had made him over-eager first to construct a convoluted daydream that might exonerate Mr. Herder, and then to take it for fact.

Edgar shook out his ears firmly, and set his jaw. He was not, after all, so foolish as to let the weak, subjective impressions of the present moment outweigh hours of painstaking analysis."But, you see, Mr. Tenterfield," he said quietly, "Miss Chase found it ludicrous that Mr. Herder should be a gambler. I had two pieces of information that could not be reconciled: on the one paw, Miss Chase's knowledge of his character, and, on the other, your information as to his infirmity."

"Well, Miss Chase is not the first young lady who has ever been deceived in a gentleman. Anyway, she has known him only a few months."

"Yes, that is the simplest explanation," Edgar conceded. "But, on the whole, Miss Chase strikes me as a young lady of some perspicacity. And yet, if her assessment of him was even halfway correct, then your account could not be true."

"Mr. Beagle," Mr. Tenterfield said pleasantly, "I sense you are about to accuse me of being a liar."

"Of course you are a liar; you lied about Mr. Mongrel. It is only natural that I should wonder what other lies you have told me today."

"I cannot help but feel that you are carrying the joke rather too far, sir."

"I assure you, I am quite in earnest."

"Well then you've chewed the wrong end of the stick altogether. I openly admit, the payments were to me. But I certainly haven't been blackmailing anybody. James gave me the money quite freely."

Edgar raised one eyebrow. "How *very* altruistic and munificent of him."

"Call it a token of his friendship. Anyway, why should I have lied about him? I hardly hold it my practice, Mr. Beagle, to go about slandering my friends."

"I imagined that you knew the full story behind the cryptic termination of his betrothal."

"Well, what if I do?"

"Perhaps," Edgar said, watching him carefully, "there is something so monstrous in Mr. Herder's past or present life that the truth would, if it came to light, be more lethal to his reputation than a rumored weakness for gambling would. Or perhaps he had some reason to break off his engagement—one might guess that he was preparing to precipitously flee the city—and he needed some convenient excuse for his departure. I rather thought, at first, that you might have been spinning ridiculous fictions with the aim of shielding him."

Mr. Tenterfield stared, and then gave a brief, rueful laugh. "Quite so. You've caught me out. I would undergo any manner of injury or dishonor before I would reveal the least syllable of James Herder's vices, let alone his crimes. You see," he added, hanging his glossy head a little, "I'm awfully loyal. Jimmy, are you quite alright?" he inquired solicitously, as Mr. Herder let out a hoarse, racking cough.

"But," Edgar said, "if Mr. Herder has he some secret that renders him unworthy to claim Miss Chase's paw in marriage, then why should you have exhorted her to come and see him?"

"I handled matters clumsily, I admit," Mr. Tenterfield said sadly. "I am not very good at deception, you understand. I only wanted to give Miss Chase a chance to say goodbye, if she liked." He heaved a deep, pathetic, melancholy sigh. "If

212

I've made a mess of things, I'm very sorry. I have done my best to take the path of honor."

"By lying at every turn?"

"Barely even lies," Mr. Tenterfield said swiftly. "Harmless little fictions. I put it to you: if the world believes that Mr. Mongrel and I were puppies together, or that Mr. Herder's misdeeds are of an innocent nature—well, whom does it harm? I have acted only to protect my friends, Mr. Beagle. You can hardly fault me for that."

"It does not do, sir, to rate friendship higher than truth."

From the other side of the room, Chase gave way to a prolonged, dramatic yelp of exasperation.

"Perhaps you might try telling me the truth now, Mr. Tenterfield," Edgar suggested, ignoring this. "I wonder, for instance, whether you might finally care to explain how you really became acquainted with Mr. Mongrel."

Mr. Tenterfield shrugged charmingly. "How does anyone become acquainted with anyone, Mr. Beagle?"

"I have often wondered."

"We found ourselves in close proximity," Mr. Tenterfield went on, casting Edgar a slightly odd look. "We were neighbors, you see. We got to talking, as neighbors will, and we formed a certain sympathy between us."

"Was this before or after his term in prison?" Edgar inquired serenely.

"It is not to your credit, Mr. Beagle," Mr. Tenterfield said, suddenly severe, "that you harp on his tragic and bitterly repented past. He has amended his life; his every prayer is that he may forget those dark and dismal years. Have you no mercy in you?"

More coughing came from Mr. Herder at this juncture.

Edgar wondered whether he was consumptive, or else developing a case of kennel cough. He surreptitiously took a few steps away.

"Well, what do *you* want?" Chase demanded of Mr. Herder. "Making a noise like a cat with a dozen hairballs! If you have something to say for yourself, then you should have gone to my sister this morning and said it to *her*, face to face."

"I rather imagine," Edgar said, "that Mr. Herder was in no state to visit Miss Chase this morning. You see, his leg is injured rather badly."

"His what is *what* now?" Chase snapped. "Don't invent rubbish just because you're trying to show off."

"I am surprised," Edgar said coolly, "that the situation has escaped your keen attention; I should have thought it was quite obvious. For my part, I could not choose but observe that he remained in his chair when we arrived, even though good manners would dictate that he should rise to greet his visitors."

"He hasn't any manners, is all."

"I further noticed," Edgar went on, as if there had been no interruption, "that he was wearing his dressing gown, at this advanced hour in the afternoon. He does not strike me as particularly indolent, and he does not appear to be ill. It is not, I think, an altogether unreasonable leap to surmise that his unconventional attire is in some way strategic. Perhaps he is deliberately concealing something. Perhaps his leg is bandaged too heavily to permit him to dress; perhaps is wounded too badly to bear his weight. He was perfectly alright at the party yesterday, so something must have befallen him overnight." He turned to Mr. Herder, with a polite little bow. "I assume it was Mr. Mongrel who attacked you, around half past three?

Mr. Herder's eyes were very round. "How do you know *that*?"

Edgar found himself automatically pausing, just as if he were expecting an interjection such as this type of question was wont to prompt from Chase. "He knows everything," Chase might have said, yesterday, or a few hours ago. "He's the cleverest dog in the world."

Chase, of course, said nothing.

"I heard you in the Chases' garden," Edgar said, feeling very cross with himself.

"It was *him* in the garden?" Chase demanded, his lip curling with scorn. "*This*, Mr. Beagle, is the great danger that should make me flee the city? One weak-willed cattle dog and a mangy mongrel?" He crossed his arms over his chest and turned on Mr. Herder with narrowed eyes. "I *thought* it was you, loitering about to pester my sister. What kind of scoundrel stalks innocent girls in the middle of the night?"

"Believe me," Mr. Herder said, "it was never my intention to breach the bounds of propriety regarding Miss Chase. As a matter of fact, I was attempting to establish contact with Mr. Beagle."

"Oh, *were* you?" Chase snarled. "And what, exactly, did you want with Mr. Beagle at half past three?"

"As you may have surmised," Mr. Herder said, shifting uncomfortably in his seat, "I am in some difficulty at present. I wanted Mr. Beagle's advice."

"And why not mine?" Chase demanded.

"Indeed," Mr. Herder said earnestly, "I had initially hoped I might confide in you, Inspector Chase; I would have liked to talk things over with someone who cared for Emily's

215

happiness as much as I did. Knowing of your profession, I had always imagined you to be a gentleman of great perspicacity and judgment"—here, Chase preened himself slightly—"but then, of course, I met you. I watched you at that wretched supper party. You insulted the other guests and seemed to place no value on what they would think. From puppyhood, I have always had to plan out everything I say; I have steadfastly guarded my tongue against giving offense. It struck me as quite extraordinary that there seemed to be no intermediary step between your thoughts and your utterances. It was only too plain—begging your pardon—that I would be unwise to place faith in your discretion."

"And so," Chase snapped, "you decided that Mr. Beagle—who, this time yesterday, you did not even know existed—would be a safer bet than Emily's own brother, who heads up the Detective Division at the Metropolitan Police. Just because one of us can't think of anything to say at parties. Is that about the shape of it?"

"I did not intend to insult you—"

"Oh, I'm not insulted. I'm not insulted in the least. Why should I be insulted? If you weren't clever enough to realize that you should have come to *me*—if you think dogs must be cold and aloof in order to be worth talking to or trusting—then that's not my fault, is it? You can hold whatever peculiar ideas you like. It's nothing to do with me. If you think the middle of the night is the right time to pay social calls, then I don't set much store by your *perspicacity* and *judgment* anyway."

"That is hardly why—"

"And what the blazes were you doing, mucking about with all those rocks—building a model of Stonehenge? It wasn't very good."

"I was looking for pebbles to throw at the window to wake Mr. Beagle," Mr. Herder said humbly, "but all the ones I found were too big; they would have broken the glass. I tried to stack them all up so that they wouldn't be in anyone's way. I didn't mean to be a bother."

"Didn't—mean—to be a bother! Sneaking about in the garden—and getting yourself bitten—and then jilting my sister two days before your wedding—"

"I suppose, Mr. Herder," Edgar said, while Chase was busy sputtering, "that, Mr. Mongrel having compelled you to return to the hotel, your injury has kept you a prisoner here ever since. One wonders why you did not send for the police, and have the calamitous gentleman removed from the premises."

"He's usually good as gold," Mr. Tenterfield broke in. "But every few months, the madness surges up in him, and there is no controlling him. I do the best I can, you understand. He's only gotten out a few times so far. Comes back at daybreak, howling like a werewolf and all matted with blood. I never can tell whether it's his or someone else's. But I really shouldn't think he had gotten out last night. I am sure I would have heard him; I always have before. Someone else must have attacked James, and in the dark, he mistook his assailant for Mr. Mongrel. Anyway, this is hardly the place to sneak out unobserved. You can't stir a paw around here without practically tripping over porters and sommeliers and things."

"And chambermaids," Edgar said.

Mr. Tenterfield looked faintly and genteelly puzzled. "Just as you say. I am afraid I do not know exactly what staff the hotel employs. My point was only, someone would have seen."

"Someone *did* see," Edgar said. "I had rather an interesting interview with a chambermaid this morning. She gave me a perfect précis of the three of you, if only I had known. She mentioned that, in addition to gentlemen dripping unpleasant substances, there were gentlemen who perpetually growled, and gentlemen who required their breakfast on a tray. I imagined, at first, that she was speaking of multiple different classes of gentlemen. But, perhaps, she was complaining to me of *your* party, whose unpleasant behavior must have been all too fresh in her mind. A fanciful theory, of course. Nothing on which to found a firm accusation. Merely an idle toy which my remembrance caught up. But it fit too well to be disregarded altogether. An enthusiastic growler—well, that would be Mr. Mongrel, of course. Mr. Herder, stumbling in late, with his wounded leg dripping blood. So, by process of elimination, Mr. Tenterfield, *you* must be the third dog, ordering your meals brought up to you. Is it a custom of yours?"

Mr. Tenterfield gave a startled little laugh. "Do you see anything very sinister in that?"

"Well," Edgar said, "if it were *not* your custom, then I should query why you suddenly took it up now. Perhaps some particular acquaintance of yours arrived at the hotel, and you thought it expedient to avoid a rendezvous in the dining room."

"How perfectly ridiculous. As a matter of fact, I went down this morning and ordered Mr. Herder's meals brought up to him—he was having a bit of a lie-in after his midnight jaunt—so he wouldn't have to struggle down to the dining room on his injured leg."

"Very thoughtful of you."

"Well, I believe in being good to one's friends, whatever you may think of me. We've known each other all our lives, you understand. There was a professional relationship between

James' father and mine, and so we found ourselves often in each other's company. We were practically brothers." He turned to Mr. Herder with a warm, fond smile. "You used to say that all the time—do you remember?"

"That was a long time ago, Alaric," Mr. Herder said expressionlessly, "and it was mostly you who said it. You always did like to fancy yourself a gentleman," he added.

"How terribly unkind you have become," Mr. Tenterfield said quietly.

"Perhaps I have. Perhaps you taught it to me."

"I only ever tried to help you, Jimmy," Mr. Tenterfield said sorrowfully.

"Is *that* what you call setting that lunatic savage on me in the middle of the night, and then mucking about binding my wounds with cravats and things after he carried me back here dripping blood, instead of sending for a surgeon? It will be a a miracle if I haven't contracted rabies."

"Such uncharitable language," Mr. Tenterfield murmured, "for your dear old friend—"

"Enough of this nonsense." Mr. Herder turned his head sharply towards Edgar. "Mr. Mongrel is not my *dear old friend*, Mr. Beagle. I never saw him in all my life until three days ago, and I hope I may never see him again. Alaric picked him up in prison. Neighbors indeed! They were cellmates."

"I *said* we oughtn't to trust an Australian," Chase interjected truculently. "Perhaps somebody will listen to me some day."

"I see you are getting the wrong idea, gentlemen," Mr. Tenterfield said, stepping closer to Edgar and Chase with a pleasant, engaging smile. "Jimmy likes to shift blame; you might call it his speciality. As he has so ungallantly informed you, I was born into a lesser station than he. It was all too easy—alas!—for him to persuade the Australian police to imprison me for his crimes."

"That isn't *true*," Mr. Herder snapped.

Mr. Tenterfield raised an eyebrow. "Indeed? Do you deny, then, that you were a thief in Australia, some ten years since?"

"Certainly not." Mr. Herder set his jaw and lifted his chin. "I have never denied that, and I should not dream of starting now."

"And is it your claim that you *were* imprisoned for your crimes? Did you allow justice to be served, and humbly repent your sins in prison?"

"Stop it, Alaric."

"Or did you, perchance, wriggle out of trouble like a coward? Did you, for instance, save your own wretched skin by selling your only friend to the police?"

"I said, stop it."

"Or what—you'll have me arrested *again*?" Mr. Tenterfield wheeled around, turned his bright, ingenuous gaze on Edgar and Chase, and panted appealingly. "If I could only turn back the clock—if we could only be those two happy, carefree puppies, romping together though the fields and wagging our tails with pure affection! But alas—those halcyon days will never come again. We are all older and wiser, gentlemen, and we have all made mistakes of our own. I have been something too liberal with my love and trust. He has betrayed his dearest friend to prison. Nobody is perfect. Well—let us not harp on the past! I came here bearing forgiveness in my outstretched paws. I would have shielded him, as I always have before. But now, I see, he is determined that his worst deeds are to be dragged into the light. And so, I may as well abandon all flattering pretense and tell you the bare truth of the matter:

James Herder is a liar and a traitor. There is not one ounce of loyalty in his whole body."

"Herding dogs are seldom accused of disloyalty," Edgar pointed out.

"Well, let that be a mark of how warped and unnatural he is."

"But if, as you say, he has gravely ill-used you, then why should you have come to England for his wedding?"

"Perhaps *you* can turn off friendship and affection like a tap, Mr. Beagle. Perhaps one day, when *your* first friend goes to the altar, you will absent yourself in the name of bygone injuries. For my part, *I* endeavor to cultivate loyalty and forgiveness in my heart. It is my duty as a gentleman to choose the nobler course." He raised his short-furred chin and gazed pensively off into the distance.

"And why," Edgar persevered, forcing the irritation out of his voice, "should Mr. Mongrel, who is *not* Mr. Herder's friend, have accompanied you?"

The ghost of a smile flitted across Mr. Tenterfield's face. "If you knew what I know about Mr. Herder," he said, "you would bring a bodyguard also. I am no longer the trusting puppy who believed his pretenses of affection. He has already destroyed my life once. I meant to take no more chances. And you see, I was right; he is as vicious and depraved and under-pawed as ever. Accusing me of setting Mr. Mongrel on him! Trying to turn your opinion against me, just as he turned the police against me long ago!"

"If that is how matters stand between you," Edgar said, "then why should he have given you so much money?"

"I shall tell you all about it," Mr. Tenterfield said meekly, "and I suppose you will say that he paid me for my silence—but

221

that was never my intention—indeed, it was not, gentlemen! You see, when I first learned of his engagement, I naturally supposed that he had confessed his past to his bride-to-be; I thought him very fortunate to have found someone willing to overlook his terrible offenses. But when I arrived here for the wedding, I discovered that he had not told her, and that he never meant to tell her! Well, I could not for my honor stand by, knowing what I know of him, and permit so sweet and charming a young lady to put all her faith in his dissolute heart and tangle up her fate with his forever. I was perfectly aboveboard in my intentions, of course; *I* would never sneak about telling tales behind a friend's back. I informed Mr. Herder straight out that I meant to enlighten Miss Chase as to his true nature—and, would you believe it, he swore up and down that he had changed! He begged me not to ruin his happiness—me, who had known no happiness for ten long years! He said he still had all the old love and loyalty for me— only, he had been too frightened to stand by me when he was young. He said he was sorry I had gone to prison; he said he had wept over me; he said he had bitterly repented his treatment of me every day. Perhaps I am too easily persuaded, gentlemen; perhaps, even now, I am too trusting. But, you must understand, I had waited so many years for those words to cross his lips! I told him that, if he could prove his good faith by any token, I would not stand in the way of his future joy by telling the world what he really was. And so, he gave me a little money: reimbursement for my passage from Australia, since I had undertaken the journey for his sake, and room and board at this hotel. I thought, perhaps, that he had changed. But then, when he sent that letter to Miss Chase this morning, I realized what a fool I had been. He simply meant to sneak off with never a word of explanation or farewell; he meant to wriggle right out of one more hole instead of owning up to his sins for once in his life. Well, when I thought of that pretty young girl breaking her heart over him, I simply couldn't bear it. Why betray my sometime friend *and* cause Miss Chase unnecessary pain? I thought it kinder to feed her a palatable story, accusing Mr. Herder of a harmless little weakness that afflicts so many young gentlemen; better she should think him weak-minded than discover the true nature of his unspeakable offenses. I ask you—Inspector Chase—Mr. Beagle—what would you have done in my shoes?"

"Either told the truth like a gentleman," Chase said stoutly, "or stayed quiet altogether. Not invented a pack of lies and gone sneaking around like a cat."

Mr. Tenterfield's ears and tail drooped pitifully. "I implore you to forgive my prevarications," he said. "I have allowed my fear to govern me—my fear, and the lingering ghost of the love I once bore my dearest friend. I can do nothing but entreat your sympathy, and await your judgment. I hope you will not think too badly of me. I am guilty of nothing but an open heart and a too-trusting disposition."

"A very pretty story," Edgar said, leveling a cool gaze at Mr. Tenterfield. "I advise you to take it on the stage; with all its cheap attempts at pathos and its narrative flaws, it ought to suit the London public admirably. But, for my part, I am not so easily persuaded. I cannot be stirred by meretricious displays of emotion, nor dazzled by metatheatrical legerdemain. I seek the substance behind the form; I interrogate each detail; I search for logic even in the heart of chaos."

"That's why I stopped going to the theatre with you," Chase could be heard to mutter.

"Your story," Edgar persevered, "has been a lie from beginning to end. For a start, you did *not* come to England for Mr. Herder's wedding."

Mr. Tenterfield gave a few surprised, melancholy blinks. "I beg your pardon, Mr. Beagle?"

"You have just indicated that you journeyed here from Australia. You must have set sail long before the newspaper announcement was published."

"I *said* it didn't make sense for him to take the Liverpool paper," Chase interjected irritably.

"I can conjecture only that you were *already on your way* to pay Mr. Herder a surprise visit, for some reason which was wholly unconnected to his betrothal. Tell me, what innocent reason could you possibly have for concealing your true motivations in seeking him out?"

"You seem to be a dog of steadfast dedication; imagine if you will, how it might pain you to have been parted for ten years from some dear friend of yours. And yet, I have some pride, Mr. Beagle." Mr. Tenterfield cocked his head sideways appealingly, and gave Edgar a sad, wistful little smile. "Ought I to have told him outright that, even after all his mistreatment of me, I longed for his company and could not bear my loneliness any longer?"

"Come, sir! it is no use seeking to entangle me with facile charm," Edgar said sternly. "Your scheme has run its course; you have told one lie too many, and discredited yourself. I have arrived at my conclusions by putting my nose, as it were, to the ground, and following the path of logic wherever it led me. Do you think that now, at the eleventh hour, your silver tongue can sway me?"

"Probably not," Mr. Tenterfield said, with sudden, cheerful

equanimity, "but it's certainly distracted you nicely. Mr. Mongrel is right behind you."

Edgar whirled around. Indeed, the bedroom door was hanging open. The vast, menacing bulk of Mr. Mongrel stood a few paces from Edgar, all rolling eyes and pointy yellow teeth.

"You might have warned us he was sneaking up," Chase snapped at Mr. Herder. "Or aren't you on our side?"

"There are no sides," Mr. Herder said. His eyes were locked onto Mr. Mongrel, and his muscles were tensed so hard that he was trembling. "There are only normal dogs like us, who— God knows!—have their faults, but who would never dream of harming anybody. And then there are those who are pure evil. Rotten to the core. The walking embodiments of darkness and destruction through this bleak world."

"This is not helping," Chase informed him. He eyed Mr. Mongrel with undisguised unease. "Just as a point of interest, what was he in prison for?"

"Eating someone, I expect," Mr. Herder said gloomily.

"You ought to be ashamed," Mr. Tenterfield said, without changing his tone in the slightest, "to so openly display your propensity to assume the worst of your social inferiors." His debonair smile was still nailed to his face, and his eyes, Edgar was beginning to notice, were perhaps just a little too bright and too fixed to denote perfect sanity. "Why should you suppose him a cannibal? The poor fellow cannot help his personal manner. As a matter of fact, he did some services for a lady, several years ago. Ladies like to keep their paws clean, you know. So really, he was very chivalrous, if you look at it the right way round."

"What was he," Chase snapped, "a murderer for hire?"

"Certainly not!" Mr. Tenterfield gasped, sounding utterly scandalized. "Call him a set of teeth for hire, if you will. Useful when the lady wished to make a point. No murderous tendencies whatsoever. Of course, the deplorable state of modern medicine being what it is—well, some of these so-called surgeons are no better than veterinarians: fit to bandage up dingoes with sore paws, and nothing else. So is it any fault of *his*, really, if some upstart cannot manage to patch up a flesh wound competently, and an altogether unintentional and lamentable death ensues? The police take rather a dim view of these things, but I put it to you, gentlemen: if they are so bothered by unnecessary loss of life on the surgeon's table, then oughtn't they to go and petition for hospital reform, instead of skulking about and making deals with criminals, or whatever it is that the police really do?" He gave a sudden, supercilious smile. "But of course, Inspector Chase, you *are* the police. I had almost forgotten."

"Everybody *does*," Chase said.

"He's never attacked a police dog before," Mr. Tenterfield said thoughtfully. "But I think it's good for him to try new things, don't you? I wouldn't want his intellect to atrophy. At any rate, he ought to keep in practice biting. He hasn't any other skills to fall back on. So you can think of it as doing him a favor, if that's any consolation to you." He motioned very slightly with his paw. The tips of Mr. Mongrel's ears snapped to attention.

"Was that a threat?" Chase demanded.

"Of course it was; you're very stupid, aren't you? If it runs in your family, then no wonder your sister was fool enough to fall in love with Jimmy. Don't worry, though, he won't strike until I tell him to. Probably."

"*Alaric!*" Mr. Herder gasped with pain as he struggled and failed to stand up. There was a new sharpness in his voice. "Leave these gentlemen alone. You can hate me all you like—"

The mechanical smile remained implacably pinned against the contorted mask of Mr. Tenterfield's face. "And so I shall, for as long as I live," he said. "Did you think I would forget? Did you think I wouldn't know what you had done? You should have been the one in prison, not me; did you think I would forgive you? Did you think I wouldn't come for you, one day? But you ran from me in Australia—slippery as ever, aren't you? I tracked you all the way across the sea, and do you know what I found? Can you guess? That's right: little Jimmy Herder the thief, dressed up in fancy frock coats and stuffing his lying mouth with imported biscuits and lazing about a shiny new hotel. And, of course, all set to be married—married to a damned pretty girl!"

"For God's sake, leave Emily out of this."

"Don't worry, I shall be very attentive to her. She will need a devoted friend to console her, now that you have broken her heart. How convenient that there is already a point of sympathy between us: we are both your victims."

"I never meant to hurt you, Alaric. This isn't *fair.*"

"Well, the world isn't fair, Jimmy," Mr. Tenterfield said pleasantly, his smile never wavering. "You know that better than anyone. Go on, Mongrel. Get rid of the hound first; he's the one with the brains."

Mr. Mongrel's mad, staring eyes snapped onto Edgar. He gnashed his jagged incisors with a fur-raising rasp. He took a slow, menacing step forward, and then another step, and another. Edgar could, he thought frantically, reach the door, perhaps, several feet to his right—although Mr. Mongrel would probably spring straight across the room and seize him between slavering jaws while he fumbled with the doorknob. Or he could try to outwit him somehow, to dodge around Mr. Mongrel's blocky, clumsy limbs. Out of the corner of his eye, Edgar saw that Chase was fiddling with something by the window. Apparently he was quite content to leave Edgar to his fate. Well, that was perfectly alright; Edgar did not require his assistance. Edgar's intelligence was more than a match for Mr. Mongrel's bulk and strength—if only he could think about it properly—if only he could move! But nauseating panic was racing through his body and rooting him in place. Mr. Mongrel snarled and gave a long, thunderous growl.

"Right, then," said Chase, dashing back from the window with something—Edgar blinked fuzzily and squinted hard; it was the heavy brass window pole—clutched in both front paws. He looked Mr. Mongrel up and down, which required craning his head back, and then swung the pole sideways and unceremoniously slammed him into the wall. "I should say it's well past time you went back to prison."

Edgar stepped hurriedly backwards, before Chase could accidentally hit him with the end of the pole, and took a long, steadying breath. There was an interval of scuffling and cursing and grunting, as Chase alternately fended Mr. Mongrel off with the pole and herded him forcibly back into the bedroom. At length, he slammed the door shut, dropped the pole with a deafening thud—Edgar hoped that a legion of servants and inquisitive guests, headed up by the fuming concierge, was not about to burst into the room—and then grabbed one of the ornate, high-backed mahogany chairs and wedged it firmly and triumphantly under the doorknob. On the other side of the room, Mr. Tenterfield lounged against the wall with his arms crossed, staring daggers.

"Thank you," Edgar mouthed to Chase. Chase shot him one indecipherable glance—it might, Edgar thought, almost have been confusion—and then proceeded to ignore him utterly.

"You haven't won, Jimmy," Mr. Tenterfield announced, very calmly. "All the ruckus up here—do you imagine that Miss Chase will escape hearing the inevitable gossip about your *dear friend* Mr. Mongrel's arrest?" He detached himself from the wall and took a few sinuous steps towards Mr. Herder. "What do you suppose she'll think of you, once she knows you associate with criminals? Poor girl—poor pretty little fool—breaking her heart trying to puzzle it out!"

"My sister isn't a fool," Chase informed him, still breathing hard. "And why should she have to puzzle anything out? Did you think I wouldn't tell her all about it?"

"For pity's sake, don't tell her Alaric's version," Mr. Herder beseeched. "Please—you mustn't repeat all those poisonous lies to her. I deserve nothing but your scorn—but I was never as bad as he says I was. I'll swear it on anything you like." He sagged suddenly against the wall in despair.

"Sit up properly, and be a man," Chase growled. "You aren't a Shar Pei puppy. If you want us to know what really happened, you'll have to tell us about it, not flop over and whimper."

"Indeed, Mr. Herder," Edgar said, not ungently, "I should very much like to hear the full story."

Chapter Thirteen

M r. Herder looked from Edgar to Mr. Tenterfield, with a blank, frozen look that might have been defiance or might have been terror, and then sat up ramrod-straight, visibly set his jaw, and swallowed hard.

"First off," he began, holding himself so rigidly that he trembled a little, "you'll have to know about when we were puppies. I don't know how much Emily told you about me, but my father was one of the richest dogs in Australia, and I was his only son and heir. The ranch has been in the family since my great-grandfather came to Australia. It was already quite prosperous when my father inherited it, but he had a knack for business that I have not, and it flourished under his paws; it was as if everything he touched turned to gold. That meant, of course, that he was much absent, and much taken up with his work even when he was home. My mother had faded away when I was a very small puppy. Most of the boys of my acquaintance seemed to hold me in awe, or perhaps merely in envy, and never had the least disposition to be my playfellows. But for all that, I was never lonely, because, for as long as I could remember, Alaric had been there. He was the son of my father's crofter. That's all the *professional relationship* our fathers had; his father paid rent to mine, and sometimes chivvied some cows back and forth."

He paused, licked his lips, and glanced with trepidation at Mr. Tenterfield. The terrier's expression was hard and brittle, and his arms were still folded across his chest. "Go on, Mr. Herder," Edgar said. "You are doing splendidly."

And Mr. Herder went on.

"Alaric was always the clever one, you understand. He was absolutely charming, even as a puppy; he was always everyone's favorite. Even my own father adored him and had very little use for me. All the servants and the townsfolk used to say it was a pity he wasn't the heir to the ranch, instead of me—oh, I could hear them whispering behind their paws when we went about together! He could win the heart right out of everyone he met, you see; he always had the perfect witticism or compliment right on the tip of his tongue—but as for me, I never knew what to say to anyone. Clothing that looked rich and dashing on him somehow turned into nothing but sackcloth as soon as I put it on. He could swim and dance and caper up and down all day, but I was always a yard behind him, scrambling to catch up and tripping over my back paws. It was as if everywhere we went, he was made of some glittering metal, and I was merely a lump of stone by his side. Everyone thought I was stupid, or sullen, or shy, or maybe all three. And I suppose I *was* stupid—because I trusted Alaric! He was such a wonderful friend to have. So witty, and full of ideas—so clever at coming up with games and getting into mischief! And a damned sight too clever at getting out of trouble afterwards—I see that now. I never knew how it was, but every time we had done something we ought not to—nothing dreadful, you understand—only such usual scrapes as puppies get themselves into—chewing the furniture or digging up fenceposts or what you will—he never took any of the blame! He would be a mile away by the time the trouble was discovered, with his paws freshly washed, looking as innocent as you please, and somehow I would still be on the spot! And it was always, 'Oh, Jimmy, no one minds what you do because you'll be rich one day, but they'll send me away if they find out I was in it too—you must save me, Jimmy!' He says I am a liar—I do not deny it—but I am *not* disloyal. I became a liar for *him*, because I couldn't bear the thought of losing him. I lied to my father, to Alaric's father, to neighbors, to shopkeepers—I am ashamed when I think of it now. But every lie I ever told was to protect him."

"Oh, leave off playing the injured martyr, Jimmy," Mr. Tenterfield sneered. "Tell them what you really did. Furniture and fenceposts indeed! You were a horrid little common criminal."

There was a mounting desperation in Mr. Herder's face, but, behind it, a sort of stolid calm that Edgar found himself admiring. "Gentlemen," he said, "I should not dream of contradicting my sometime friend's accusations, and my shames are too heavy for me to beg your indulgence or seek to escape your censure. All I ask is your patience while I confess my crimes to you—so that, when you proceed to judge me, you shall at least do it on the correct grounds. I was, as he says, a thief. He drew me into it—no excuse, I realize, particularly for a dog of my pedigree and station! But, whether I was too honest or simply too dull, I assure you I never should have dreamt of it on my own. I thought, I suppose, that our exploits would make me bolder, or more dashing—more like him. I was only a puppy—maybe twelve or thirteen when it started. He told me all puppies our age did such things. It was shameful to lag behind, he said. And I did not want him to think me a coward." He drew a deep breath. His ears were drooping, and his eyes were flat with utter misery. "It was just little things from the shops, at first. Chew toys, or a tennis ball, or what you will. Alaric would talk to the shopkeeper, with that disarming smile of his—he could talk to anyone about anything, and everyone would look at him like he was the only thing in the world—and meanwhile, I would nip around back and pocket our loot. Everyone thought me so slow and stodgy and dull; they never would have suspected me. Alaric said if I was ever caught putting something in my pocket, I could just say I had forgotten to pay for it, and tell the shopkeeper to put it on my father's credit account. I was not nearly so stupid as all that, but I suppose everyone would have believed I was. Alaric was like a magpie; he insisted on saving everything, under the loose plank beneath my bed—because of course it would not have done for *him* to be caught with it!—and he would look at it triumphantly. But after a year or two of this, he got more ambitious. He was tired of amassing cheap little toys, he said; toys were for puppies, and he was growing up now. He wanted cash from the till. The thing couldn't be done, I said—not in our usual way. Even if he were somehow to lure the shopkeeper away to the other side of the store, I never would have had the nerve to dash in and grab the cash at the right instant, and I certainly could not have brazened it out if I had been caught. Yes, yes, Alaric said— he had already thought of all that. This time was not to be like our other little adventures. We were going to break into the greengrocer's shop after dark. Alaric, it turned out, had been teaching himself to pick locks on the sly. He picked the lock on my bedroom door then and there to demonstrate, and my resulting awe and jealousy, gentlemen, is a mark of how warped and debased I had become in his company. I wish I could say I had at least protested, but I did not. It seemed such a foolproof plan; the greengrocer's was on a little side street, which was sure to be deserted at night. There might have been some little trouble sneaking off the property after dark, but my father was away on business again, and the servants would not have dared to stop me, and Alaric's father never seemed to care what he did. And it seemed so grown-up and dashing to be having an adventure so late at night—so thrilling to be defying all the rules! You will ridicule me, gentlemen, if I say I fancied myself a second Robin Hood, even though I had no such noble aims for the money. Indeed, I did not want the money at all; that was not the point of the thing. I was wicked and foolish, but at least I cannot number avarice among my sins."

"That is because you were rich," Mr. Tenterfield snarled. "You already had everything your heart desired."

"You needn't posture as a beggar," Mr. Herder said wearily. "You know my father was always very generous to you."

"It was merely a charity. The money was never really mine."

"And you imagined the money from the greengrocer's till would be?"

"At least I would have worked for it."

"Setting aside Mr. Tenterfield's idiosyncratic outlook on personal property," Edgar broke in, "I am very interested to hear what happened the night of the burglary."

Mr. Herder gave a little shiver. "Very well—very well! It is easy for you to hear all this, I suppose. It is not easy for me to tell it. I have done my level best not to think about it these ten years."

"Oh, I am sure you were having a fine time drowning your sorrows in Bordeaux, while I was picking oakum until my paws were sore—"

"Mr. Tenterfield!" Edgar said sharply, drawing himself up and raising his chin. Out of the corner of his eye, he could just see Chase reaching reflexively towards the spot on his belt where his paw-cuffs usually hung. "You have already had your say. Mr. Herder, if you please?"

Mr. Herder was trembling, but he continued. "It was as dark and as clear a night as one could have hoped for. I met Alaric down by the gates. I had a dark-lantern, and by its light, I could see that he walked lame, and that one of his front paws was wrapped in bandages. 'I turned my ankle in a wombat hole and toppled right over,' he growled. 'Damned bad luck.' 'Are you able to walk?' I inquired. I was mostly anxious, you understand, not about the success of the robbery, but about my friend's wellbeing. And I was surprised at his misadventure, too; I was the one who was always falling down and getting hurt! 'Quite—quite,' he said. And then he gave a little yelp of pain and stumbled, clutching at me for balance. 'We ought to give over the robbery until you are better,' I said. He looked at me scornfully. He was always looking at me scornfully. 'And wait until your father comes back from his trip? Besides, the weather is perfect tonight. We may never have such a piece of luck again. I am perfectly alright; I shall lean on your arm for support,' he told me. It was a little thrilling, of course, thinking that he needed me, for once. But there were obvious problems. 'We cannot get through the door of the shop together,' I said, 'and one of us must have both paws free to open the till.' I saw him realizing that I was right—and that, of course, was pretty thrilling too! 'I suppose I must lean on something else, then,' he said. 'Half a minute—I think my father has a walking stick somewhere about. I'll just sneak back in and pinch that.' 'No, no, you'll wake him!' I cried. And then my eye fell on a long, sturdy stick, just lying on the ground—by Providence, it seemed to me. I picked it up and held it out to him. 'Here's your walking stick!' I said. I was very proud of myself. I had never been so quick-witted before; he was ever the opportunist. He was gratifyingly pleased. Together, we made our way through the silent streets. It was a fine, cool night, the stars twinkled jovially above us as if they approved our enterprise, and my heart was beating like a trip-hammer, but I had never been happier. Finally—finally!—I was earning my friend's esteem! And as we walked, he complained of the wind, and shivered— he had forgotten a hat—so I gave him mine, and my scarf for good measure, and I was so pleased to be of use to him a second time that the cold bothered me not a jot. We got into the store quite easily; Alaric's lock-picking skills were every bit as good as he had boasted. It was an easy thing to open the till. But, just as I was beginning to slip banknotes into my pocket, he stumbled again—I supposed he had forgotten about his injury and tried to take a step without the stick—and fell into a display of oranges. They bounced and burst as they fell, and the noise they made seemed to me like thunder, but Alaric only laughed at my dismay. 'That isn't nearly enough to wake them,' he said. 'Don't be a sniveling little coward!' 'Wake whom?' I said. 'The greengrocer and his wife, of course. They live above the shop. Didn't you know? Well, never mind. I'm sure they won't suspect a thing—and anyway, I heard her say he had been laid up with lumbago all week. Go on and finish clearing out the till, and we'll go.' But just then, we heard footsteps, coming down the stairs at the back of the shop. Fainthearted as I was, I nearly swooned. Alaric grabbed me and pulled me down behind some boxes just as the greengrocer's wife appeared on the scene. She walked across the shop, turning her head from side to side, sniffing for intruders. I had known her all my life; she was a kindly, grandmotherly, shaggy sort of dog. She had given me sweets for free, two or three times, and she had never treated me as if she thought me stupid. It came into my dim little brain, for the very first time, that we would be doing her and her husband an injury by depriving them of the day's takings. I do not know whether you will believe me, gentlemen, but I made my mind up then and there: once she was out of sight, I would have nothing more to do with the robbery—or, if I had to, then I would come back the next day and leave a packet of money somewhere about the store to make up for it. My conscience felt much easier after that. It was all going to be alright. But, as the greengrocer's wife passed by our hiding place, Alaric sprang out. He took his makeshift walking stick, and he coshed her on the head with it. She screamed—I had never heard anyone scream so loud; the sound has haunted me in my dreams these ten long years—and she took one step backwards—and then she slipped in the oranges, and down she went among them. Alaric flung down his stick and tore out of the shop without a backward glance. It did not strike me, in the moment, how spryly he moved for someone who had been limping all night. I supposed he assumed I would be at his heels. But I looked at the greengrocer's wife, and she was lying very still. I hardly knew what to do. If I stayed, I would surely be found. And she was not in any danger; her husband must have heard the noise, and he would come down in a minute and attend to her. But no—Alaric had said he was laid up with lumbago! I looked at her again. It was hard to tell in the darkness, but I fancied her head was bleeding. Of course I couldn't leave her there like that. Whatever you may think of me, gentlemen, I am not such a monster. I knelt down beside her—I got oranges all over my britches, but it was no matter—and I began fumbling through my pockets, looking for my handkerchief to staunch the blood. That was when the police arrived. They collared me at once, of course—I had been found right at the scene of the crime, crouching over her body, with my pockets bulging with banknotes—and they took me down to the station. They were astonished when they realized who they had gotten—the heir to the Herder fortune, scrabbling in tills like a little street rat and hitting defenseless old ladies over the head! They insisted that I must not have acted alone. Surely, they said, such a horrifying crime could not have been of my conceiving. They demanded my accomplice's name. Will you believe that, even after that hideous attack, I defended him still? I could not pretend I had been alone—I was tired and frightened and not such an accomplished liar as all that, for all my years of practice shielding his puppyish peccadilloes—but I said that I was the son of a gentleman, and that it would not be a gentlemanlike action to peach on my comrades. They were too clever for me; they changed tack straightaway. They said that, because of my father's position, *et cetera*, they were disposed to look kindly on me. I had not, they were sure, meant to do anyone any harm. They were quite prepared to make a bargain with me, by which they would let me walk free if I would only disclose the real assailant's name. But if I did not, they would be forced to send me to prison for years and years and years. They had, they told me, all the evidence they needed. It lay in my own power to decide my fate. I was only fourteen, you understand, and I believed every word they said. My head filled right up with dreadful images of myself languishing away in a dungeon until my fur was grizzled. All the same, my impulse, at first, was to protect Alaric even at my own expense. We herding dogs are awfully loyal, you know. But before I could open my mouth, and quite against my will, the memories all came flooding into my mind at once— how for some eight or nine years, I and I alone had suffered scoldings and punishments for deeds he had instigated, while he sat smiling by. It was the nature of the world, though, I told myself, as I had so often told myself; it would have been disloyalty in me, or so he had always said, to have called down a harsher fate on his head than on mine. I tried to think only of the good times—how clever he was, and how easily I laughed in his company, and how proud I had always felt if he looked at me with approval in his eyes. But the memories just kept coming and coming, until I felt half drowned with them. And then, at the end of the whole catalog of injustices I had undergone for his sake and at his entreaty, I remembered how tonight, he had let me think myself so clever in handing him the stick—the stick which was just the right length for walking and just the right heft for striking a deadly blow, which I had foolishly imagined fortune to have dropped by our gate! I remembered how he had taken it with his bandaged paw. I realized in that instant—and the realization nearly made me sick—that my paw-prints, and mine alone, were on that stick. He had contrived to dress up in my hat and scarf, to cover his face in case anyone saw us—or, perhaps, so that, should the greengrocer's wife recover consciousness, her last, blurry impression would have been that I was her attacker! And, of course, he had cast the stick right down next to me before he abandoned me. He had never been lame at all. All this time, you see, I had been comforting myself with the idea that Alaric had never meant for anything so drastic to happen—surely he had simply panicked and lashed out, with no intention of causing actual injury, and then fled in horror at what he had done. But the facts—the facts all showed quite plainly that he had planned this all along. A dog who can walk perfectly well does not encumber his burglary equipage with a stick unless he means to use it later. No—from the start, he must have meant to attack the greengrocer's wife. And, from the start, he must have meant for me to take all of the blame. That, I supposed, was the real reason he had hidden our cache of stolen goods under my bed: so that the police might see that this was not my first crime. Which meant, of course, that he had been planning this for more than a year, or maybe even for our entire lives; that even as he had laughed and joked and sported with me, and put his arm around my shoulders and said he wished I were his brother—all that time, in the poisonous little recesses of his brain, he had been going over his plot to send me to prison! I ask you, gentlemen, how you would feel if the one dog you trusted were to betray you utterly. For my part, it struck me to the very heart. I felt something shattering all to pieces inside me. If I was less than nothing to him, then why should he be the whole world to me? Why should I go to prison to protect someone who had dreamed all along of destroying me? I gave the police his name, and I walked free."

"Had he *murdered* the greengrocer's wife?" Chase asked, saucer-eyed. Edgar threw him a look of some impatience.

"No, no, she recovered in hospital and has been perfectly well ever since."

"What happened after the police released you?" Edgar asked, before Chase could interrupt again.

"There was the trial. I gave evidence, but my name was kept out of the papers, because of my father's position. Even under oath, and even knowing what I knew, I painted Alaric as softly as I could without lying outright. He went off to prison—only ten years, because he was so young—and, I suppose, because he charmed the magistrate, as he had always charmed everyone! I missed him bitterly, and I was utterly friendless. I never stole again, of course, and Heaven knows how sorely I have repented my crimes. My father died in an earthquake five years later, and I came into my money and set to work managing the ranch. It was the greatest surprise to me when I discovered that, without Alaric by my side, I was not nearly so stupid and dull as I had always thought. The years passed by. I thought of him often—though, of course, I tried never to think of that night! And would you believe, gentlemen, that when he finished his sentence and turned up on my doorstep last winter, I was happy to see him?"

"And did you think I would be happy to see you?" Mr. Tenterfield snarled, clenching his front paws into fists. "Did you think I had come in friendship to you—I, who had starved and sweated and sustained myself only with dreams of revenge, while you gorged yourself on the fat of the land like a little prince? You never deserved one bit of what you had. It was only a mistake of nature that you were born into luxury instead of me—you should have been the crofter's son! You weren't fit to be a gentleman. I saw you wearing your little tailcoats and trying to give the servants orders—it was like watching a dingo tottering about on its hind legs. Everyone could see it, and they all laughed at you behind their paws.

241

Your father never cared tuppence for you. He was ashamed to have you as his heir. If you had been carted off to prison instead of me, you know perfectly well that he would have disowned you and adopted me in your place, and then I could have gotten everything I had always known I deserved. It was a clever plan, Jimmy—even you must be able to see that it was a clever plan! Years and years of training you to lie for me and always take the blame. You had been a fool all our lives—how was I supposed to know you would choose that night to finally grow a brain?"

"I opened my house to you," Mr. Herder said, turning to him with an expression of utter heartbreak. "I begged you to forgive me, even though I had done only my duty in testifying, and had done barely that. I offered to make it up to you, to receive you as a brother into my home and my fortunes. But you—you are nothing but a demon. Your only desire was to torment me."

"Well, it seemed unfair to me," Mr. Tenterfield said with venomous sweetness, "that the entire town should hold you in esteem, when I knew what you really were. I was—how did you put it?—doing only my duty when I said I meant to disillusion them."

"You need not have blackmailed me. I would have given you the money freely."

"I am afraid, Jimmy, my silence cannot be bought. *Some* of us do not enter into dishonorable bargains for our own gain. It was really the least you could do to provide me that little income while I was debating whether I should make you known to the townsfolk."

Mr. Herder turned back to Edgar and Chase. "I fled from him, gentlemen," he said wretchedly. "You may call me coward, if you like. But I could not live with the constant reproach in his eyes, and always the little digs and veiled threats calculated to torment me. All the old feelings of horror and guilt and betrayal I had tried so hard to dam up now broke upon me like a tidal wave and threatened to drown me utterly. I booked passage on a clipper to Liverpool—I knew nothing about England, but it was the first ship I could find—and I slipped away in the night without telling a soul. My overseer could manage the ranch quite well in my absence. I thought that perhaps Alaric would tire of his little game before I got back. I meant to keep to myself for a month or two, then write home and see whether he was still hanging about. But then, all my plans were disarranged. I was walking along by the river, feeling as if the world was utterly hopeless, and I happened to catch sight of a girl—the sweetest, dearest, loveliest girl who ever walked this world!"

"I see you still need somebody to worship," Mr. Tenterfield said, through his teeth.

Mr. Herder's agonized gaze flickered to Mr. Tenterfield, but he went resolutely on. "Practically as soon as I had spoken to her," he said his voice trembling very slightly, "I knew what I meant to do. I would turn my back on my past and my country; I would sell the ranch, and build a new life here in England. I would finally put my money to some use, instead of buying stocks and repairing fences and paying off filthy blackmailers. I was happy—happy for the first time in ten years! I bought a house in Mayfair, and I booked a wedding tour of the Continent, and I sent Emily jewelry and flowers and sweets. I would have thrown the whole world down at her paws if it had been mine to give."

"You might have given her the truth," Chase snarled.

243

Mr. Herder bowed his head. "I was not that thoughtless puppy anymore. I meant to begin afresh. And I knew her brother was high up in the police; it was not the sort of family to let wrongdoing slide. But I would have told her, for all that—I did intend to tell her, gentlemen! I meant that there should be no secrets between us. And now, you may call me coward once again—because, before I could confess my crimes to her, she told me a story of a lad who had courted her once. She said she had been inclined to fancy him at first, but then she had found out that the flowers he was bringing her had been stolen from his neighbor's garden. And she told me, with a look of scorn I had never seen on her face before or since, that her heart quite froze up towards him that instant. She told me that she could never respect, let alone love, a common little thief like that. I should have confessed everything then and there, and let her send me away—I know I should have. But I was weak—I suppose I have always been weak—and I could not lose the only thing I had ever really wanted: the love of the most wonderful girl ever made. I assure you, gentlemen, that was my only lapse of honor concerning her. I would have been true to her until my dying breath—and so, I suppose, I shall, though I never see her again." His whiskers drooped pathetically.

"And then what happened?" Edgar prompted.

Mr. Herder gave a low, mirthless laugh. "And then Alaric showed up, of course! Right in her house one evening, just a few days ago. I have never had such a fright in all my life. Apparently, after I disappeared, he hung around the dock asking questions until he worked out which ship I had sailed on, and then followed me at once."

"Not quite at once," Mr. Tenterfield corrected. "I had to

wait for Mongrel to get out of prison." He gave a feral, sharp-toothed smile. "I had to be sure you wouldn't be able to just run from me again. He was in a hurry to get back to England anyway; he was willing enough to trade his services for his passage. *We* didn't take a clipper ship, of course. Not everyone has that sort of money to throw around. We sat below decks for *months*, just dreaming of the look on your face when we turned up here. I was a little worried, I confess, about how I was going to track you down. For all I knew, you might have moved on from Liverpool. You would have, if you'd had a particle of sense. But luck was on my side, for once! Do you know what I saw, the very day after I arrived? Last week's newspaper, just lying around in a restaurant—with a great big announcement about your upcoming wedding to the piermaster's daughter! It was as if Providence *wanted* me to find you."

Mr. Herder groaned and buried his head in his front paws.

"You were afraid I would come for you, weren't you?" Mr. Tenterfield snarled. "That's why you didn't put your picture in the paper, wasn't it? I knew I still had you, the minute I saw that. I pictured you thinking of me and cowering and praying you could sneak past me, and do you know what I did then? I laughed and I laughed and I laughed. Did you really think you could stop me from finding you? You should have kept yourself out of the papers altogether, Jimmy. Didn't you know I would spot your name at once?"

"As it happens, I did not," Mr. Herder said faintly. "I never imagined you were mad enough to stalk me halfway across the world and then comb through every page of the local newspaper; I see my error now. Keeping my picture out of the newspaper had nothing to do with you. I did not wish for anyone in England to recognize me, because—"

"Because you are a *criminal*—"

"Because my father was well known here, and I did not wish to have any of his old business associates turn up and ask me awkward questions about why I had abandoned the ranch."

"Afraid of blackmailers, were you?" Mr. Tenterfield sneered.

"*But,*" Mr. Herder persisted miserably, "my name is not unusual; without my photograph, which would have marked me by my breed as Australian, why should anyone imagine I was *that* James Herder?"

"Why should anyone ever have imagined it?" Mr. Tenterfield said. "Well, your talent for passing as a commoner has finely come in useful; congratulations."

"*Yes*, Alaric," Mr. Herder said, rounding suddenly on him with fierce desperation, "we all know you think you ought to have been the son of the house. Perhaps if you hadn't turned out to be a thief and a liar and a vicious little thug and gone to prison, my father would have loved you best one day."

"It's better to be whatever names you like to call me," Mr. Tenterfield said, panting very hard, "than to be a cowardly, treacherous, spineless little idiot like you."

"Well, he didn't turn out to think so, did he?"

"I wonder, Mr. Herder," Edgar remarked, very pleasantly, as a snarl reverberated low in Mr. Tenterfield's throat, "whether you might answer my earlier question. What happened when Mr. Tenterfield and Mr. Mongrel arrived in Liverpool?"

"Alaric set about being poisonous, exactly as you would expect," Mr. Herder said, still glaring at Mr. Tenterfield. "He greeted me very sweetly, and spouted some rubbish about being my best man, and then promptly gave me a little jab about telling Emily all my puppyhood wrongdoings. And ever since then—well, my life has been hell. I am ashamed to admit to you, gentlemen, that I have been in constant terror. You will tell me, I suppose, that a full-grown dog ought not to be struck dumb with fright when confronted with an old foe, especially one who is half his size. I have often told myself that very thing. And yet, gentlemen, I beseech you to believe me: I could not converse in front of him. All the words I wanted to say were trapped inside me, just going around and around in my head. Beside him, I found myself a puppy again, tongue-tied and clumsy. It was just at it had always been: Alaric spoke, Alaric smiled and jested and charmed, and I was silent and dull. But this time, of course, he was not content to outshine me; he wanted to torment me too. He may tell you what pretty stories he likes, but the truth of the matter, gentlemen, is that he has been blackmailing and threatening me outright. He knew perfectly well that, if he had told Emily about me, the look in her eyes would have killed me where I stood. Besides, her mother was always going on about what the neighbors would think. It was plain enough that, if anyone found out she was betrothed to a criminal, her reputation would be ruined forever. For three days, I tried to puzzle out what I should do. All the time, I could see her growing more and more unhappy with my demeanor, and it stabbed me to the heart. I was half-expecting her to decide she preferred Alaric; everyone else always did, so why not the girl of my dreams also? I thought, of course, of going to her, in secret. The conversation was different every time I imagined it. Sometimes I threw myself upon her mercy, like a weakling—as if she ought to be saddled with my shames! Sometimes I lied to her and made her hate me, so she would not pine for me. Sometimes I told her that Alaric had escaped the madhouse, and that if he came to her with any outlandish slander, she should dismiss it as the ravings of a lunatic. Sometimes, she even forgave me. But, of course, I never got to talk to her at all—because as soon as Alaric suspected what was in my mind, he told me he would set his pet assassin on me. Oh, I know what you are thinking, Inspector Chase! I am a herding dog myself, you must remember. I had all those glorious ideas too: that a gentlemen ought to deem his lady well worth any desperate measure; that I might take the noblest course by sacrificing my blood for her; that my love for her ought to make me strong enough and brave enough to take on a whole pack of Mongrels. It is easy enough to be a hero in your daydreams, when no one's teeth are grazing your throat. I did my best. As usual, it was not good enough. I wished every moment that I had some clever friend I could confide in, but I was all alone. Forgive me my intrusion last night, Mr. Beagle; I was desperate for someone to advise me."

"It is not up to him to forgive you," Chase interjected. "It is *my* parents' house. Anyway, I still say you should have come to *me*."

"But your powers of discretion…" Mr. Herder began helplessly.

"As if I wouldn't have found out anyway! Mr. Beagle would have told me everything straightaway, wouldn't you, Mr. Beagle?" He shot Edgar a wide-eyed, appealing sidelong glance. Edgar supposed, with a sudden stab of irritation, that Chase, for some almost-certainly ridiculous reason of his own, did not wish to reveal that he and Edgar were no longer friends. Nothing but lies and playacting and keeping secrets, this last twelve hours. No one who would just say what they meant; everyone stepping like tin soldiers through the insipid motions of their little unspoken rituals. Why bother talking so much and saying so little? And why should he, as if infected with the ambient impulse towards amiable deception, permit himself to be dragged into whatever absurd subterfuge Chase was planning? He remained resolutely silent.

"Well, anyway, you should have told me all about it," Chase informed Mr. Herder, darting another glance at Edgar. His eyes were wide and bright with some vivid emotion. Edgar supposed it must be annoyance, although it did not match the pattern that Chase's features usually formed when he was annoyed. A good thing, really, Edgar thought, that he had understood the situation so clearly! If he had not known better, he would have taken Chase's expression for pain. Perhaps, Edgar theorized, dogs' physical manifestations of emotion changed when they had not gotten enough sleep. Dr. Snuffles had probably written something about it; Edgar made a mental note to check the bookshop when he got back to London—if he ever got back to London! Surrounded by dogs who were all brimming with some violent emotion, and stranded in unfamiliar terrain, it was difficult for him to conjure up any images of his house. The world seemed to have shrunk to this little room, overflowing with a murky jumble of emotions, flooding and clogging the delicate machinery of Edgar's brain. Edgar gave his head a firm shake to clear it.

"What happened after Mr. Mongrel induced you to return to the hotel last night, Mr. Herder?" he asked.

There was a haunted look in Mr. Herder's mismatched eyes. "Alaric was sitting up waiting, of course. He laughed at me; he told me no one would have believed me anyway. He said I was still as clumsy as ever, crashing around and probably waking half the neighborhood; he said he wished the police had heard the ruckus and picked me up, so I could see what it was like being tossed into a cell. And then he refused to send for a surgeon, and he confined me to this room and set Mongrel to guard me. He got the chambermaid to bring my meals upstairs, lest I try my luck with anybody in the dining room. And he followed her right up the stairs and into my room at breakfast *and* lunch *and* tea—like having a bloodhound nosing at your heels—no offense to hounds, Mr. Beagle—in case I should pour out my whole sorry tale while she was setting down the tray."

Edgar became aware that there was the barest whisper of a sound coming from the other side of the door. Probably Flossie Yapper herself, with her pointy ear to the keyhole. He wondered whether she had heard about Tommy's arrest.

"Well," Mr. Herder continued mournfully, with no apparent realization that Edgar's attention had become diverted, "all my avenues of hope had been blocked off. I turned the thing over and over in my head, and I realized there was only one course I could undertake. I spent all my wit in finding a way to slip the chambermaid a letter to Emily, right under Alaric's nose, breaking off the engagement. I had to protect her from scandal, you see, and I had to set her free to find someone worthier of her than I. But the porter downstairs saw the chambermaid giving it to the baker's boy, and went running to Alaric as soon as he got a chance; I suppose Alaric had bought his loyalty—with my money, of course! Alaric was furious when he realized what I had done. I thought perhaps he might kill me, but I was past caring by then. A strange sense of peace had settled into me. No catastrophe or injury could possibly cause me greater pain than the knowledge that I had broken Emily's heart—and so, there was nothing more that I needed to fear. I let him rage awhile, but he wearied of it when he saw I was unmoved, and went storming off—to go and slander me as a gambler, apparently! I suppose he thought that, if he could lure Emily over here, then I would weaken and beg her to marry me after all, and he would regain all his power over me. But I would have remained steadfast. Setting her free was the only honorable thing I could do—the only honorable thing, perhaps, that I have ever done. I will have, at least, her memory to comfort me, as I sit in the darkness with my arms too empty and my heart too full, through the long, silent years that lie before me. These past few months must last me the rest of my life. I have no one but myself to blame: I was arrogant and foolish all along. The moment I saw her, I might have known she was too good for me—I might have known I had no right to reach for a chance at happiness. How could I ever have thought I deserved her; how could I have deluded myself that a girl like that could ever be mine?" He heaved a long, heartbroken sigh, and his mouth curled into a melancholy little smile. "I suppose it is a mercy that I will not have to see her face when she learns the truth about me. Tell her I will always love her, won't you? Tell her my heart and soul belong to her forever."

The door crashed open. Edgar glimpsed a flash of black and white, darting across the room too quickly to be resolved into shapes—and then he heard a rustling of skirts—and then Emily was kneeling on the floor by Mr. Herder's chair, with her bonnet half off and tears streaming down her face. The diamond ring had reappeared on her paw. "You fool—you fool!" she cried. "Did you really think I would care what mistakes you made when you were fourteen? Or that I would mind one bit what the neighbors thought? As if there were anything in the world that could make me forsake you!"

A strangled sob broke from Mr. Herder. Emily seized both his front paws in hers, and stared directly into his eyes for a moment. Then, she rose and wheeled on Mr. Tenterfield, and threw back her head. Edgar was reminded of his initial impressions of her: she might have been a young pagan priestess in an oil painting, performing mystic rites by dawn. She held herself very straight, and her eyes shone like stars.

"Now, sir," she said to Mr. Tenterfield, "you have no more hold on my future husband. As I believe the quotation goes: you may publish—publish, and be damned!"

But Mr. Tenterfield did not stay to publish, or to be damned. He sprang across the room like lightning, eluding Chase's desperate, outstretched arm, and, before Edgar had even finished gasping, vanished through the still-open door. Chase let out a long, low growl and tore after him, as Chase would. Edgar supposed that in about thirty seconds, Tenterfield— past master as he was in the dubious art of scavenging for makeshift weapons!—would probably catch up the nearest heavy object and hit Chase over the head. As he turned to follow, he was intensely aware of Mr. Herder's astonished gaze boring into his back, and of the sound of Emily's panting as she struggled to regain her composure. He gently shut the door behind him, and broke into a run. Even through two closed doors, he could plainly hear the forsaken Mr. Mongrel striking up a ragged, sinister, melancholy howl.

Chapter Fourteen

E dgar sprinted down the hall, acutely conscious of the way his fitted jacket dragged across his shirt and rumpled his fur as it resisted his movements. He could hear the light staccato clicks as Tenterfield darted across the parquet floor of the lobby, doubtless scattering guests and turning heads as he went—and then the heavier percussion as Chase pelted frantically after him—and then a shout, and a crash, and a crescendo of horrified gasps. A lady's voice yowled something about sending for a surgeon. Edgar's heart juddered violently against his ribs. Really, he must be in worse physical condition than he had thought! He hurried around the corner to the landing. Chase lay flat on his back on the floor. Edgar could not see the rise and fall of his chest. Beside him, a potted fern lay desolately on its side, shedding soil across the parquet. In the distance, Tenterfield was making frenetic, unobstructed progress towards the front door.

"Stop that terrier!" Edgar fully intended to command the assembled onlookers, as he raced down the stairs. But instead, he heard himself crying out "Inspector Chase! Are you hurt?" A few guests exchanged alarmed glances and stepped hurriedly out of his path.

"Vicious little blighter hit me and ran," Chase wheezed. "Get after him, will you?"

"Do you feel faint? Are you bleeding?"

"Will you stop fussing over me?"

"How many paws am I holding up?"

"Stop it. He hit me in the chest, not in the head—and no, I haven't got a cracked rib." Chase sat up, with some effort. "I was only winded. I'll be quite alright in another minute or two." He turned his head sharply, and assumed his most gallant, stalwart expression. "It's alright, everyone, I shan't need a surgeon." He gave an airy wave of his paw, winced a little, and then turned sharply back toward Edgar. "Why on earth didn't you go after him? You could have caught up with him outside, if you had run."

"And leave you lying injured?"

"Don't be dramatic; there are dogs and cats all around. Someone would have gotten me to hospital if I had really been hurt. And since when do you prioritize ministering to the wounded over catching criminals?" He peered crossly up into Edgar's face, still breathing hard. "But I had forgotten; according to you, I am helpless and weak, so I suppose it was your moral duty or something to make sure I didn't just crumble into a pile of dust on the spot."

"Certainly not," Edgar said, more hotly than he had intended. "I value the wellbeing of any dog or cat injured in the pursuit of justice. It would be the height of dishonor in me to behave as if we were less than strangers, merely because we are no longer more than acquaintances."

"Wait, wait—because *what*?" Chase scrambled laboriously to his feet.

"Kindly keep your voice down," Edgar said, very stiffly. "You have made your position perfectly clear, and this is hardly the moment to discuss it further. We are in public."

Chase spared a single, contemptuous glance for the few guests who were still lingering around the perimeter of the lobby. Mr. Dewlaps, behind his desk, was leaning so far forward that drool fell perpendicularly to the floor. "Never mind about that lot. Just tell me what on earth you're talking about."

"You need not strain yourself in attempting to spare my feelings; I hope you at least hold me in enough esteem to deal plainly and directly with me. I quite realize that you have no further use for my society."

"I have...what now?"

"*Please* keep your voice down. You need not be insulted; I am not accusing you of anything. Your sentiments are entirely understandable. After all, although I was able to successfully conclude some small part of the matter upon which you engaged my services, I have failed to prevent Mr. Tenterfield's escape."

"Engaged—your—services?"

"Do not be alarmed; I have no intention of sending you a bill."

"*No*, that's not what—"

"In future, I would like, if I may, to associate with you upon occasion, in a strictly professional capacity, so that I may continue to further the aims of the Metropolitan Police. Nonetheless, should you prefer to consult a different private investigator—"

"What the devil should I want to do *that* for?"

"—then we can, of course, simply shake paws and part." His voice, he was grimly pleased to see, did not waver in the slightest.

"Shake paws and part! I say, don't you have any—"

"Yes, I am aware that a few personal effects of yours are in my possession. Upon my return to London, I shall send them to you by post immediately."

"What are you going on about?"

"You left your hat and umbrella in the hall last week, and your handkerchief on the floor of the sitting room the week before that."

"No, no, I know *that*, but—"

"I have, of course, had it laundered and pressed for you," Edgar hastened to reassure him.

"That wasn't what I was—"

"Ah, I see," Edgar said. "You are primarily concerned not with your handkerchiefs, but with your dignity. Quite right. Please do not alarm yourself; I have already realized that the severing of our association may cause you some little degree of embarrassment amongst your social circle here in Liverpool. After all, you would not wish to lose face after having used our connection to your reputational advantage for years. Accordingly, as a mark of my former collegial regard for you, I am prepared to keep up the fiction until my departure, as I gather you were intimating—"

"Mr. Beagle, are you going mad, or am I? Maybe I *did* get hit in the head."

"There is no need for this charade of consternation," Edgar said coldly. "Our mutual utility has run its course."

"But Mr. Beagle! I haven't any idea what—" Chase paused, took a deep breath, and swallowed hard. "I mean—well, that is to say—oh, dash it all, don't you like me anymore?"

"My personal sentiments do not enter into the matter."

"Alright, but that's just what you *would* say—"

"I have known all along, of course," Edgar persevered, "that we were not suitable companions. The—what shall I call it?—exuberance of your temperament could not long be satisfied alongside what you no doubt consider to be my coldness."

"Mr. Beagle, w*ill* you stop trying to be grand? I know you too well, I say—"

"Perhaps that is the problem," Edgar said, before he could stop himself. "You know me too well to tolerate my company. My better parts are wearisome to you. You have tired, at length, of the investigator's logic and expertise and caution, and now all that is left is the dog himself, you see nothing that merits your regard."

"Mr. Beagle! I'm sorry if—"

"You need not pity me," Edgar assured him.

"Mr. Beagle—"

"Indeed you need not; never reproach yourself on my account."

"Mr. Beagle—"

"I am not prone to loneliness, and I shall do quite nicely by myself."

"Mr. Beagle—"

"Having once experienced friendship, I may safely strike it from my roster of phenomena necessitating empirical investigation. Accordingly—"

"*Edgar*!" Chase broke in at the very top of his voice. "Sorry—sorry, *Mr. Beagle*! Only—*will* you just stop talking nonsense for a minute and listen to me? We had a quarrel, is all. Haven't you ever had a quarrel before? Of course we're friends. Unless—" He hesitated for a moment, and a curious look flickered through his wide, bright eyes. If Edgar had not

257

known better, he might almost have taken it for fear.

"Unless?"

"Unless you don't—I mean, of course we're not *suitable companions*, but, well, look, I never told you any lies, did I? So it's not my fault if you were disappointed when you came here."

"I could hardly be disappointed," Edgar said, bewildered, "when my expectations were so low."

"No, that's not—" Chase took a deep breath. "Look, I told you right when I met you that my father worked in a dockyard, and that I hadn't gone to any fancy schools. I'm not like Tenterfield; I don't go about pretending to be a gentleman and leeching off of rich folks. You seemed to think we were headed for the slums, so it's not as if I tricked you into thinking I was any better than I am. But maybe you were picturing something quite different—some balderdash about the noble poor, with empty pockets but full hearts, all huddled together in their dim little house and loving each other as hard as they can, in between bouts of rabies. All very touching and artistic. I suppose you weren't prepared for real life; I might have guessed. You didn't know what my family and my neighbors would actually be like."

"I should never dream of holding their irritating peculiarities against you."

"*No*, that's not what—" He broke off, and panted plaintively into Edgar's face. "Fancy gentlemen—gentlemen with famous fathers and university degrees and houses in Piccadilly—well, they don't hang about with dockpaws' sons, do they? I suppose being here made you think about it a bit."

"Think about the fact that individuals with disparate backgrounds tend not to congregate together? I was already familiar, Inspector, with last year's little treatise, penned by Dr. Snuffles' erstwhile protégé Mr. Pug, on the tendency of societies to stratify themselves."

"No!" Chase burst out. "I thought that being here might have made you think you're too good for me. Although why you shouldn't have thought it before, I don't know." His ears drooped with dejection.

"I have been acquainted with you for the better part of a decade," Edgar said blankly. "Surely, I have had ample opportunities to notice your social position and educational background."

"Well, I thought," Chase said, his voice suddenly very quiet, "that you might have been fond enough of me not to mind all that too much. But I suppose now that you've been here, and you've seen me with my family, and you've heard the way that everybody talks to me—well, I suppose perhaps you aren't fond enough anymore."

"Don't be ridiculous," Edgar said, much more crisply than he had intended to. Unaccountable, really, that curious prickling sensation behind his eyes! Perhaps he was developing an allergy to some specimen of the local flora. And how thoroughly illogical that he should feel the urge to smile, or to reach for Chase's arm, or to let a litany of sentimental nonsense go cascading out of his mouth! He contented himself with clasping his paws behind his back, fixing his eyes on the horizon, and giving a few tight nods. "Do you happen to have any indication as to where Mr. Tenterfield betook himself?"

"Oh, you must be joking." Chase glared at him with some impatience. "*Now*? He went outside somewhere."

"Yes, yes, I had inferred as much. I was merely wondering whether you had gotten any sense of his proposed trajectory."

"I haven't the foggiest," Chase snapped. "Do you know how many back alleys there are in this city?"

"In that case—that is to say, if Mr. Tenterfield may have taken refuge in any one of a vast number of locales—then the probability of us lighting upon the correct one, particularly before he has vacated it, is extraordinarily slim. At a preliminary estimate, I would calculate—"

"Look, if you don't *want* to be my friend, just say so, alright? Don't go spouting mathematics at me as if nothing's happened."

"I shall be your friend for as long as I live: against all reason, in defiance of all bounds of prudence, and certainly without any regard to your relatives' and acquaintances' egregious mistreatment of you. My calculations indicate that, by conducting our own search, we will assuredly give Mr. Tenterfield the chance to flee quite beyond our reach. It is more logical for you to go and give direction to the local constabulary."

Chase was grinning as broadly as Edgar had ever seen him. He must, Edgar surmised, be very excited indeed over the prospect of asserting his authority. "The local constabulary—twice in one afternoon! They'll see the grass doesn't grow under *my* paws. Either that," he added, as an afterthought, "or they'll think I can't make my own arrests."

"I imagine they will have the strongest admiration for your efficiency and commitment to justice—that is, for your vigor and courage," Edgar reassured him.

"Oh, do you really think so? Well, I'll go and find some police dogs to order about. If nothing else, we need them to cart Mongrel out of here; I'll bet he weighs about as much as a whole platoon of Great Danes. Or whatever Great Danes come in. Hogsheads, probably."

"An excellent point. While you are so occupied, I shall return to Miss Chase and Mr. Herder; I imagine that Mr. Mongrel is proving very trying company for them, and perhaps I might be of some assistance."

"Well, go on then," Chase said. He hesitated for a moment, blinking very hard. "And—Mr. Beagle?"

"Yes?"

"Nothing. Only, I really am awfully s—no, never mind. Nothing."

Edgar turned, maintaining a brisk, confident stride for Chase's benefit, and climbed back up the staircase. There was a strange elation bubbling up inside him, which he supposed must be a delayed reaction to having successfully untangled the mystery surrounding Mr. Herder. At the same time, he was suddenly, achingly aware that he had not slept through the night. He checked that he was out of sight, then permitted his ears and tail to gently droop. After all, even if Chase successfully mobilized the police rather than haring off on his own, what hopes did anyone really have of locating one terrier in a city of so many thousands? The thing could be done, Edgar told himself firmly, shaking his ears as if he could rid himself of despair. There was always a way for justice to prevail. Someone could wire the Australian police. Back when Mr. Tenterfield had been arrested, perhaps someone had thought to record his paw prints; it was unlikely, but it was not impossible. Besides, it was not as if he had an infinite range of options. He was surely not so imprudent as to book passage on a ship out of Liverpool, where all the docks were run by Mr. Chase's colleagues; to get out of England, he would need to first travel east or south, overland. The police would have ample opportunities to intercept him. Even if he did manage to flee the country, the situation was not hopeless. In light of his recent journey from Australia, he would hardly be eager to immediately undertake another lengthy sea voyage; perhaps he would elect to travel the shortest possible distance, to France—where the Sûreté could easily send out any number of Malinois squads to capture him upon his arrival. Of course, Edgar mentally conceded, Mr. Tenterfield could simply head north to Scotland, instead of getting onto a ship at all—or, for that matter, he could hide away in England indefinitely—or he could smuggle himself onto the Continent undetected—and he had no particular distinguishing features—and he was certainly clever enough to feign an English accent—and he was far too charming to ever be suspected—and it was not spectacularly plausible that the police in multiple countries would meekly accede to devoting substantial time and resources to searching for him. But surely—*surely*!—the principle of justice was more powerful than a slew of inconvenient facts! Certainly, Edgar was currently experiencing the emotional reactions associated with despair, but it was not as if he was prepared to give any credence to such fleeting and fallible data. After all, he reminded himself firmly, pausing halfway down the hallway and straightening his cravat, he was not Chase. He must hold fast to what he already knew to be true, not be swayed by every momentary whim. But on the other paw, he thought grimly, taking a few more steps and then pausing again, one could not be permitted to willfully shut one's eyes to verifiable data. It was puppyish and absurd to cling to fairytales, once they had been proven untrue. Sometimes—and here, he shuddered all over—justice did *not* prevail. Because he was diligent and methodical in his proceedings, he had thus far succeeded in apprehending every criminal who had come his way. But he had read the newspaper every morning of his adult life, and many mornings during his puppyhood as well, even when Lavinia was attempting to fold it into paper boats and sail it in the duckpond. He knew perfectly well that there existed such things as cases that were never solved and criminals who walked free. He had always supposed that it was simply because the police were careless, though; after all, by and large, they were probably nothing but a rabble of pettifogging martinets like Assistant Commissioner Jowls, or reckless would-be adventurers like Chase. Naturally, justice did not magically triumph, if it had been entrusted to such disastrous paws. If it did, then there would be no need for Edgar. But here was a case he had taken on—and he had observed and analyzed the situation in his usual fashion—and he had solved it; *he had solved it*! And then, he had been careless. The door, hanging open after Emily had burst in—how could he have forgotten to close and bolt and barricade the door? Any fool could have seen that Tenterfield would try to escape! Yet there he had stood gawking, like a spectator at a play, just as if a pair of lovers' paltry little drama was more important than the pursuit of justice. And then, downstairs in the lobby just now—well, it did not bear thinking of. He had behaved shamefully, senselessly barking his heart out like any common puppy, letting sentimental ties drown out the clear voice of reason. It was perfectly obvious that he ought to have left Chase lying there, and gone after Mr. Tenterfield at once; even Chase had been able to see that. Well, his fondness for Chase had always been a liability. Perhaps he ought to sever ties with Chase. Perhaps it was his duty. Perhaps, when

Chase came back, Edgar ought to tell him that their friendship was irrevocably over after all. His chest suddenly clenched as if with panic, and a sense of all-consuming doom began to steal over him. No doubt it was distress at the idea of criminals running unchecked through London, once he was unable to advise the police. A terrible prospect, really; an intolerable prospect. He would have to retain his connection to Chase after all—not for sentimental reasons, of course, but for the sake of justice. Really, it was his duty; there was no way around it. He drew a deep breath, and color surged back into the world in a dizzying rush. Apparently he was prone to emotions of all sorts today.

And now, in all likelihood, Mr. Tenterfield would be at large forever—but that was *not* because of the fallibility of justice. It was all because of his own mistakes. One moment of illogic—one moment of relaxing his vigilance—one moment of letting sentiment sweep aside reason—and he had become one of the careless, unworthy executors of justice he had always despised.

"I have failed," he thought dismally, as he approached Mr. Herder's suite. "I have scented wrongdoing, and I have let it slip away between my paws." As he passed through the door, his steps sounded unnaturally heavy in his ears. Mr. Mongrel was making noises like a faulty locomotive through the bedroom door. Outside, the wind was picking up; the insistent, delicate scratch of a branch could be heard against the windowpane at irregular intervals.

But none of this seemed to matter to Emily and Mr. Herder. They were entwined in the armchair, and—as Edgar discovered before he turned swiftly away for propriety's sake—they were locked tightly in each other's embrace.

Epilogue

The wedding breakfast on Monday was a lavish affair. Edgar was sitting in a magnificent and wholly uninviting chair in the corridor just outside the Adelphi's private dining room. His shoulders were very stiff, his paws were folded neatly in his lap, and he stared straight ahead. Every few moments, a passing servant, laden with a tray of kippers or biscuits, eyed him quizzically, before shaking a bewhiskered head and hurrying onward. It was probably, Edgar thought with a touch of resentment, because he was attired so unsuitably; he was wearing a borrowed tailcoat of Mr. Herder's, which was a full size too large, and a garish heliotrope cravat of Chase's, too stiff to be comfortable and too shiny to pass for real taffeta. Unexpected wedding invitations, he reflected, were really very trying.

Across the corridor, the dining room was ornately festooned and extravagantly lit. Edgar regarded it expressionlessly through the open door. He had a clear view of the table, around which Constable Barks was bounding in jubilant laps with the remains of a boutonnière dangling from his mouth. Emily sat at the center, with her back to the door, all flounced and bustled up in cheap white voile. Blossoming around her ears, there was a little coronet of honeysuckle and pale pink roses—purchased early that morning by Chase, but selected by Edgar, who, after listening to Chase rhapsodize on the fascinations of the Venus flytrap over supper the night before, had undertaken to chaperone the flower-shopping expedition. Her whole body was angled towards her new husband, and her front paws, Edgar reflected with a little wince, were clutching his arm so tightly that his sleeve must be hopelessly wrinkled by now. Mr. Herder, for his part, had turned his head all the way towards her. It was evident from his profile that he was staring directly and fixedly at her face, as if the rest of the room did not exist. On his other side, his new crutches were propped precariously against the table. Chase, across the table, was making eyes at one of the bridesmaids; Edgar made a mental note to alert him to the plethora of crumbs scattered all down his shirtfront. At the head of the table, Chase's father appeared to be heartily accepting various congratulations upon something—possibly the splendid venue and decor, all of which Mr. Herder had paid for—and at the foot, Mrs. Chase was loudly and earnestly chattering to Mrs. Mouser. Peering at her mouth as it moved, Edgar thought he could just make out the words "my eldest," "still a bachelor," and "disgraceful." Joseph stood by the sideboard, steadily eating his way through a platter of expensive imported biscuits, and ignoring Wilhelmina's emphatic beckoning. His mouth was open, and his tail wagged like a metronome.

Scraps of countless overlapping conversations overflowed the room and swarmed implacably into the hallway, weaving around each other until they coalesced into an unintelligible, inescapable mass of noise. Edgar's head ached dismally, and he found himself longing for his bed in London, with its comfortingly characterless white sheets and heavy coverlet. He was probably, he reflected with some bitterness, developing kennel cough.

A few servants had congregated at the far end of the corridor, where they were, Edgar gradually noticed, shooting him covert glances and talking rather too loudly behind their paws. "'Tisn't *natural* to sit still and stare at one spot for fifteen minutes," he could hear a little whippet in a cap and apron insisting in a high, tremulous whine. "Perhaps he's heard a mouse in the wall," a tabby in footman's livery suggested. "Someone's got to send for a physician," the whippet pressed, her whole body quivering in dismay. "He looks the howling type; he might have a fit and let loose, and then there'll be no stopping him for *hours*."

Edgar cleared his throat and hastily stood up. He slipped back into the dining room, uncomfortably aware that several heads were turning in his direction, and reclaimed his seat beside Chase.

"Got your telegram alright, then?" Chase inquired, turning towards him at once.

"I beg your pardon?"

"When you walked away before, while my father was trying to tell you all about his rugby club. I heard you. You said that you had arranged for a very important telegram from London to be delivered to you here at eleven, and that you had better go wait for it in the hallway to make sure it didn't fall into the wrong paws, because it contained confidential information about one of your investigations."

"It did not arrive," Edgar said, with great dignity.

"You could have just told him he was being a bore," Chase said, matter-of-factly. "I often do." He took a long sip of champagne. "I can't think what's got you looking so dejected,

Mr. Beagle, but it makes you look just like a basset hound. I say, you didn't get fleas from our spare room, did you?"

"Certainly not," Edgar said. "I am marking the solemnity of the occasion without undue frivolity."

"That's a lot of words to say you don't like parties."

"This room," Edgar said apologetically, "is really *very* festive indeed."

"I know—exciting, isn't it?" Chase bounced ecstatically in his seat, which had the happy effect of dislodging some of the crumbs. "Something different everywhere you look or sniff! Cheer up; you're meant to be celebrating, and anyway, you've solved your case—though I'm sure I don't know how."

"Inefficiently."

"Nonsense; you were wonderful. Aren't you even going to explain how you figured it out? You *love* explaining how you figured it out."

"If you mean that I experience some measure of satisfaction upon publicly exercising the art of logical thinking, in the modest hope that my hearers may, by my example, learn to cultivate it during the course of their own cerebral peregrinations—"

"Yes, fine. Whatever you like to call it. Go on—you know you want to tell me how you did it. I bet I'll be awfully impressed," he offered coaxingly.

Edgar raised an eyebrow. "I should hardly think my tale of failure impressive," he said. "I reached my conclusions slowly and laboriously; had I taken any longer, Mr. Herder might have fled the city and vanished."

"Oh, is *that* what's made you so glum? You did not take longer, and he did not vanish; he is sitting right there, probably about to knock his crutches over for the seventh time, so who cares what might have been? Everything has turned out beautifully. It was our best case yet. You did loads of clever things, as usual. And Emily listened to me, for once in her life, and dashed over to the Adelphi in time to hear everything and send Tenterfield packing—never say we border collies do things by halves!—and now, thanks to you and me, she has married her cattle dog, such as he is—you needn't elbow me; it's too loud for him to overhear—and I hope she'll be very happy with him. It will be splendid having her in Mayfair."

"But…justice," Edgar said, rather feebly.

"What about justice?"

"It has not been served! Mr. Tenterfield has fled beyond our reach."

"Don't you worry about that," Chase said, in his most authoritative voice. "I'll set the whole Metropolitan Police on his track, if I have to."

"You will forgive me, I trust," Edgar said, "if my concerns are not wholly allayed. I seem to recall several other occasions upon which you undertook to organize large police operations; if memory serves, you devolved rather quickly into giving the junior constables advice on tracking squirrels."

"Well, some of these upstarts nowadays can barely tell a chipmunk from a vole. It isn't *my* fault they need so much training. Anyway, Tenterfield won't dare to put another paw out of line, even if we never do catch him. We'll have his picture and description all over England *and* Australia."

"To be sure," Edgar rejoined gravely, "that is a great comfort. After all, it is not as if there were any other countries in the world."

"Don't be tiresome. You are at a wedding. Have some cake or something, if you won't touch the champagne."

"I am not hungry, thank you."

"Yes you are; you just don't know it. Go on." Chase shoved his half-eaten plate of cake in Edgar's direction. "You've had nothing but toast and tea all morning."

"Not all of us," Edgar said, pushing the plate back, "feel the need to start every day with a pile of biscuits."

"Well, let your ears down, for once. There's loads of food, and Mr. Herder is paying. He ought to do *something* nice for us, after everything he put us through," he added mutinously.

"How remarkably gracious of you, Inspector, to accept atonement in the form of fruitcake. For my part, I should have thought Mr. Herder had undergone enough already."

"Serves him right for being so spineless."

"I imagine that plenty of dogs would have displayed apprehension in his situation."

"You wouldn't have," Chase said loyally, and baselessly. "And I wouldn't have either."

"So we may tell ourselves, never having had his experiences. No doubt the gentleman did his best to persevere."

"I didn't know you were such an admirer of his."

"It is not a question of admiration. Blackmail is common because it is effective; it can generally be relied on to produce a certain emotional response in its victim."

"Not *that* response. He made everything worse for himself." Chase drained his champagne, balled up his napkin, and tossed it lightly at Edgar. "I can't think why you didn't suspect *him*. He behaved as if he *wanted* everybody to suspect him."

There was a sudden thud. Mr. Herder sheepishly leaned down to retrieve his crutches. Edgar uncrumpled Chase's napkin and began smoothing it out against the table with careful, meditative strokes of his paw. "I did suspect him," he said, "and it is not to my credit. I ought to have stopped

270

suspecting him much sooner. I was looking at the thing the wrong way round altogether. Patterns repeat themselves, you know; types frequently recur. It is merely a matter of figuring out which version is in front of you. This one was common enough: the glib-tongued scoundrel who maintains an air of perfect innocence, and lays all his crimes upon some slower-brained companion's head. Shall we call them 'Dog A' and 'Dog B'?"

"Must we?"

"My mistake," Edgar continued, disregarding this, "was not that I failed to recognize the pattern, but that I mislabeled its constituent components. I had permitted myself to be influenced, however unwillingly, by your insistence that Mr. Herder was, in your colorful idiom, evil. I naturally auditioned him in my mind as Dog A, the villain; I was so busy trying to figure out the details of his iniquity that it did not occur to me to try slotting him into any other rôle. In this scenario, Mr. Mongrel would, of course, have been Dog B. There was, to be sure, a certain lack of evidence, or even of circumstantial indications, in that direction—but there were enough suspicious circumstances that I did not think my assumptions wholly unreasonable. The never-explained association between Mr. Herder and Mr. Mongrel! The withdrawals, so suggestive of payments, that Mr. Herder had started removing from his bank account upon Mr. Mongrel's arrival in the city!"

"I *told* you the withdrawals were a clue," Chase said, sulkily.

"No, you told me the withdrawals were proof of either a gambling addiction or a coining ring. If you want to hear the rest of my explanation, kindly do not interrupt—"

"I thought you were finished."

"And yet," Edgar said, a little more loudly, "I could not wholly persuade myself to believe in my own hypothesis. It was a little too convenient; a little too neatly packaged up; a little too hollow. Besides, Miss Chase seemed so very certain of Mr. Herder's rectitude. By her account of him, he was a gentle-natured, unimpulsive, unimaginative dog. Not adept at thinking on his paws—as we could immediately see by his clichéd little strategy of making her acquaintance by pretending to need directions. Noticeably wary of risks. Possessed, in short, of none of the qualities that typify a Dog A. And, from that observation, I found myself looking back and forth between two alternative scenarios. Perhaps Miss Chase was utterly deceived in him—in which case, his deliberate concealment of his true nature was a serious mark against him. Or, perhaps, she was describing him perfectly accurately— describing him, in short, as having all of the qualities that one would expect to see in a Dog *B*! And, on the whole, I could not overcome my impression that she was a reliable judge of character."

"Oh, so you trust *her* intuition?" Chase demanded, firing up.

"I should not call it intuition, *per se*, but—"

"But nothing. You trust her intuition, but not mine."

"But if I recast Mr. Herder as Dog B," Edgar persisted, pointedly raising his voice a little, "then who was his Dog A?"

"Which one is Dog A again?"

"In other words," Edgar said patiently, "if I imagined Mr. Herder to be not a Mr. Tommy Muddypaws but a Mr. *Ollie*—the overlooked and underestimated stooge, forever bearing the blame for a cleverer dog's misdeeds—then I needed to find Mr. Tommy's counterpart. Someone who was close to Mr. Herder; someone who was generally better-liked and more sociable; someone who—"

"Tenterfield, you mean. Because he's a blackmailer, like Tommy."

"Rather a reductive précis, but not essentially inaccurate, although—"

"I say—I'm the one who put you onto the idea of blackmail in the first place, aren't I? Because I figured out what Tommy was up to?"

"I might not otherwise have been primed to theorize in that direction," Edgar said cautiously. "On the other paw, perhaps that situation caused me to subconsciously assume, however irrationally, that I had, as it were, already encountered my quota of blackmailers for the weekend; perhaps, if not for Mr. Muddypaws, the idea of blackmail would have occurred to me sooner in connexion with Mr. Tenterfield."

"What, an hour earlier? That wouldn't have made any difference."

"Or perhaps my eyes were dazzled by the sinister and very silly glamor of your stories about evil; perhaps my brain was held prisoner to lethargy—"

"Perhaps being here tires you out, and besides, you can't concentrate when you've been up in the night—"

"—and I could not see what was really under my nose. When all is said and done, blackmail is really quite a sordid, common, unglamorous sort of crime. I am sure Mr. Tenterfield thought himself terribly clever—blackmailers always do!—but his little stratagem was nothing very special. I ought to have seen through him straightaway." He gave a deep and rather melancholy sigh, and then hurriedly blocked the tabletop with his paw as Chase moved to push the cake toward him again.

"Tenterfield took us all in," Chase said. "You mustn't fault yourself. Anyway, you worked it out in plenty of time. You've been brilliant."

Edgar shook his head, making his ears flap gloomily. "I have bungled this investigation at every step," he said. "First, I have no defense for having suffered my brain to become infected with your wild imaginings. I should, for a start, have taken it as fact that you had experienced *something*; rather than wholly dismissing your original report out of paw for its irrationality, while still permitting it to take root in the unguarded reaches of my mind, I should have calmly and logically examined—"

"So, really, what you are saying," Chase interrupted, suddenly gleeful, "is that you ought to have listened to me in the first place."

"Not precisely, Inspector; although you did, in an undeniable flash of what you are evidently determined to term intuition, find yourself unsettled by something in Mr. Tenterfield or Mr. Mongrel's demeanor, or perhaps by some covert interplay between them and Mr. Herder, you must admit that you entirely misattributed your reaction. I should not have rested until I had satisfied myself of the actual circumstances—"

"What you are saying is that I was right all along—"

"No."

"And that the next time I tell you my ideas, instead of planting yourself in the middle of the pavement and rattling on about *psychological effects*, you will do as I say straightaway—"

"*No*. I am saying that, due to various failings on my part, a dangerous criminal has walked free."

"It is not as if Tenterfield's escape were your fault, you know."

"Of course it is my fault."

"Nonsense," Chase said robustly.

"It is not nonsense. I should have closed the door after Miss Chase came in."

"If it comes to that, Mr. Beagle, *I* should have closed the door! It is not your job to attend to everything in the whole world yourself. Anyway, I expect Tenterfield would just have knocked us both down and then opened the door back up again."

"We might have found an opportunity to detain him."

"We might have, yes. But you may as well say that we might have grabbed hold of him as soon as we had put Mongrel in the bedroom, or that we might have brought Barks with us in the first place. Or that you might have studied martial arts instead of microscopes and things, and also been born a cat, and then you could have climbed up the wall when he wasn't looking and dropped onto his head with an earsplitting yowl. For that matter, I might have stopped him from getting away in the lobby. Why bother with what we might have done?"

"He laid violent paws upon you in the lobby. You were not to blame for that. I ought to have pursued him at once."

"Well, you were worried about me."

"No, I made the mistaken calculation that the likelihood that I could apprehend him—given various factors including the topography of the surrounding area, my inability to actually arrest him, and my lack of expertise regarding physical combat—was significantly lower than the likelihood that you would require urgent medical attention—"

"Which you, not being a physician, could not have given me anyway. You were worried about me; why bother trying to dress it up?"

275

"I would not wish you to think," Edgar said stiffly, "that I imagined you to be in any way incapable or in particular need of my assistance."

"Oh, stop that. I'm not going to quarrel with you and give you an excuse to leave early." Chase leaned back in his chair and absentmindedly ate another forkful of cake. "This may be expensive," he informed Edgar, rather loudly, "but it is not very good. When we get back to London tomorrow morning, we go straight to the first pastry shop we see."

"If you are so anxious to return home, then we could take the 6:04 this evening, or even the 3:41, if we wished to dine in London. We would, of course, have to absent ourselves from these festivities presently, to leave you time to pack up your valise—"

"Tomorrow morning will do nicely," Chase said, with a sharp, sideways glance at Edgar. "Do you think you are being subtle?"

"At any rate," Edgar said hastily, "All that is quite immaterial. The point is that I came here with the intent to serve justice—an intent which has guided me all of my life—and then failed to do so."

The two dogs sat in silence for a moment. Edgar continued to look straight ahead. In his peripheral vision, he could see Chase fidgeting irritatingly with his boutonniere.

"But Mr. Beagle," Chase said at length, "that is *not* why you came here."

"I beg your pardon, Inspector?"

"I know perfectly well that you never believed in the least that there was any wrong to be righted, or whatever you like to say. You were not operating in your role as private investigator; this whole episode has been part of your personal life—or it would be, if only you had one."

"Crime never sleeps, Inspector, and neither should justice. I am afraid I cannot delineate between my job and my personal life in the manner you rather crudely suggest; it is not as if I pursued justice for the sake of money and solely during business hours, as one might sell biscuits, but rather—"

"Oh, come off it, Mr. Beagle!" Chase cried, loudly enough that several nearby guests glanced over at him with varying degrees of curiosity and alarm. "You may see—or pretend to see!—a justice-seeking machine when you look in the mirror—but when I look at you, I see my dearest friend. You know as well I do that you did not come here for the sake of justice. You came here at my entreaty and for my sake, to save my peace of mind and my sister's wedding—and you have succeeded brilliantly. Cannot that satisfy you?"

"I was sentimental and careless—"

"You were *not* careless; you simply cared more for Emily's happiness and my safety than for your dreary obsession with justice. Do you know, Mr. Beagle, I think you are finally growing a heart."

"There is really no need to insult me, Inspector."

"Oh, sit back down, Mr. Beagle. You needn't raise your hackles. You know perfectly well what I mean. You and I both made a mistake; it was my job more than yours to stop Tenterfield scarpering. I know you are the obsessive one—"

"The *diligent* one—"

"—but I am the one who is actually a police dog. But both of us were paying attention to the more interesting things in the room instead. And there is probably no harm done anyway. I bet Tenterfield will just slink off and lay low; he doesn't seem the sort of fellow who would risk going back to prison again."

"That is not at all the point. He deserves to be condemned in a court of law, and it is through my negligence that justice has been perverted."

Chase expelled a long, gusty sigh. "Do you care for *nothing* but justice and the law? Just look around you for a moment. Think of something other than your ideals and things."

Edgar surveyed the room. He tried to see it as Chase would. He supposed the lack of squirrels must be very disappointing, but there his imagination gave out.

"Look at Mr. Herder, since you think him so sympathetic," Chase prompted.

Edgar looked. "He is markedly ill at ease in a morning coat," he said.

"Yes, yes," Chase broke in impatiently, "he looks a fool in his wedding clothes, and that flower is going to fall right out of his lapel, and he hasn't had the sense to put the crutches somewhere else, so I expect he'll knock them over again at any moment. That's not what I meant. Look at his *face*."

"He is certainly very attentive to your sister. And he does not appear to be in any distress from his injury; I have every hope that, as the surgeon predicted, he will sustain no lasting harm aside from some scarring."

"*No*, the point is—oh, never mind; I suppose he always does look a little like he has just been hit in the head. Try looking at Emily instead."

Edgar dutifully shifted his gaze to Emily. She glanced over at him questioningly, and her mouth quirked into a slight smile. There was, he realized, as she turned back to Mr. Herder, a sort of transcendent, unbelieving rapture in her limpid eyes; she looked as if she had been given unexpected access to some glorious fairyland.

"See?" Chase prompted, nudging Edgar with his paw. "She is happy! And Mr. Herder is happy—if a fellow like that can be happy with something that does not involve cows. Do you know, he had an actual conversation with me today?"

"But the *justice* of the thing, Inspector—"

"And I am happy," Chase interrupted firmly. "It would have broken my heart to see my sister's life in ruins, you know. Cannot that be enough? If you really do hold me in esteem, or whatever funny words you use for saying you like me, then of course your interest in my family's affairs has leaned towards the personal. It would have been cold and unfeeling in you if you had allowed this to mean nothing more to you than one of your everyday cases full of strangers Anyway, didn't you *notice* what date it was on Saturday?"

"The ninth of June, 1877," Edgar said blankly.

"And what was the ninth of June, 1876?" Chase prompted.

"Friday."

"No! I mean, yes, it was, but that isn't at all the point." He drew in a deep, dramatic breath. "On the ninth of June, 1876, you and I—well, mainly you—defeated Camille La Chatte."

"Indeed we did, but what of that?"

"Well, for one thing, I expect she'll break out of prison any day now. She always has before."

"I fail to see how Mademoiselle La Chatte's future criminal activities are relevant to this conversation, Inspector—"

"And, for another thing—well, you remember what happened, don't you? How you came out of hiding to rescue me?"

"Vividly."

"And?"

"And…?"

"And you've had a whole year to think it over, haven't you?

"If you mean that my processes of ratiocination are gradually deliquescing in your company—"

"What's 'deliquescing'? No, never mind, I don't want to know. I'm sure it *isn't* what I meant. I only meant—well, don't go getting cross again, but didn't you learn *anything*?"

"I learned that you cannot be trusted to maintain your composure in important situations."

"Well, you already knew *that*," Chase said impatiently. "Look, do you regret it? Do you wish you had let me die?"

"Certainly not. This weekend has not been nearly *that* unpleasant."

"Very funny. My point is, if you didn't regret that, then you can't regret *this*."

"I am afraid I do not follow your reasoning."

"Well, you just did the same thing again, didn't you?"

"Indeed, I have displayed the same weakness and committed the same resultant error twice in a row. It is not altogether kind of you, Inspector, to recall it so forcibly to my attention. I had rather imagined you were trying to console me."

"I *am*. It isn't my fault you keep missing the point. Look, it wasn't a weakness or an error, alright? Loyalty is just as good a thing to prize as logic—indeed it is, Mr. Beagle! You did the right thing both times."

"No, I behaved very foolishly," Edgar said. "Even if we accept what I take to be your implicit assertion—that is, that one dog's physical safety may be fairly bartered for the wellbeing of a criminal's future victims, let alone for the upholding of justice—"

"That you should care more about your best friend than about dogs and cats who might not even exist or about ideas that no one can see?"

"However it pleases you to phrase it. Even if we accept *that*, I still have not acted logically. I was never actually in a position to make that trade; your safety never lay in my paws at all. Last year, I stood no chance against your assailant. Had his pistol been loaded, he could easily have shot us both; I would have had no power to save you. And, two days ago, it is exactly as you said: I am not a physician. Any of the dogs or cats in the lobby could have helped you just as effectively as I could have, if not better."

"Alright, fine; you made a mistake. What of it? Every dog and cat is bound to make a mistake sooner or later. You are the cleverest fellow in the world, but you are not magic. Anyway, if you've made your biggest mistakes out of wanting to protect me, then I think that makes you even more splendid than before."

"You *would*."

"Just think it over for a minute, will you?"

Edgar sat up very straight, and turned his head away, and thought it over. He looked down at the tablecloth, and traced an embroidered flourish with his paw. He thought of the Inns at Court, and of the iniquitous terrier—now miles away, no doubt!—who would never be called to account there. He thought of the Yard, and of his avenged father; he thought of the dead Baron von Mousehunt, and of the imprisoned Camille la Chatte. He could still hear her revolver ringing out in the shadowy church. He thought of Chase, forever galloping about with mud on his shoes and his cravat coming loose and keys and coins and half-eaten biscuits tumbling out of his pockets; he thought of himself always folding his handkerchief just so, always checking that his door was locked, always straightening cushions and alphabetizing

281

books, always steering himself inexorably onwards, ears cocked and eyes fixed on the horizon.

He raised his head blindly, and stared past Chase. Images flashed into his mind with dizzying rapidity. The open door; Emily's face as she turned on Mr. Tenterfield; Chase gasping for air on the polished parquet floor.

Justice, perhaps, was not the *only* virtue in the world.

And besides, said a voice in the very back of his head, the rules, for better or for worse, always seemed to be different when it came to Chase.

Edgar had put his head to one side and was panting very slightly. Chase leaned forward and stared at him with big, liquid eyes. "Just this once, Mr. Beagle," he pleaded, almost in a whisper. "Just this once—cannot my happiness be enough? Cannot *I* be enough?"

Edgar shook off his thoughts. He turned, and held Chase's gaze, and placed a paw on Chase's arm, and smiled.

"Alright, Gabriel," he said. "Just this once."

Made in United States
North Haven, CT
21 January 2025

64706663R00171